DON'T LET ME FALL

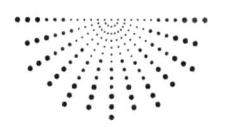

KELSIE RAE

Don't Let Me Fall
Cover Art by Cover My Wagon Dragon Art
Editing by Wickedcoolflight Editing Services
Proofreading by Stephanie Taylor & Marjorie Lord
Published by Twisty Pines Publishing, LLC
May 2022 Edition
Published in the United States of America

Copyright © 2022 by Kelsie Rae

All rights reserved.

No part of this book may be reproduced in any form or by any electronic or mechanical means, including information storage and retrieval systems, without written permission from the author, except for the use of brief quotations in a book review.

*To my TikTok followers
This one's for you. :)*

PROLOGUE

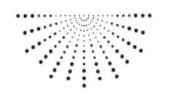

ASHLYN

My head bobs up and down to the music on the radio while I wait for the red light to turn green and fiddle with my car's heater. Even though it's late in the afternoon, the temperature is dropping, and I know as soon as the sun slips beneath the horizon, it'll get cold again. It doesn't help that my last class is with Professor Williams, who likes to keep her classroom colder than Antarctica. A chill races down my spine as I turn the heat to full blast. At least it's my last class for the week. I'm ready for a nice, hot bubble bath with a side of ice cream. After the week I've had, I need it—big time.

As I make a mental checklist of my upcoming assignments in my classes while tapping my finger against the steering wheel, a massive truck pulls up beside me.

From the corner of my eye, I peek over and catch a glimpse of a corded forearm resting against the steering wheel and a chiseled chin.

Um...hello.

I crane my neck a little further while attempting to be inconspicuous.

Hot damn.

Clearing my throat, I look back at the stoplight. Because, ya know, it's rude to stare.

The light's still red.

I click my tongue against the roof of my mouth for a few seconds and go back to my checklist, but the stranger tugs at my curiosity despite my best efforts to ignore him. Unable to help myself, I glance at the guy again. My mouth practically waters as I take in his silhouette.

He has dark sunglasses propped on his nose, and his full lips are mouthing the lyrics to whatever song he's listening to. His dark hair is somewhat wavy and is pushed away from his face, showcasing his tan skin and stubbled jaw as he stares at the stoplight in front of us. Thankfully, he appears to be oblivious to the fact I'm most definitely checking him out when I most definitely shouldn't be.

I gulp.

Who is this guy? He doesn't look familiar.

It's not surprising, though. LAU's campus isn't exactly small, but when your boyfriend's on the hockey team and is LAU's golden boy, you get to know people. A lot of people. Especially the good-looking ones. I swear they group themselves together.

But this guy?

I tilt my head, continuing my perusal.

No, I for sure don't know him.

If I'd seen him walking around campus or around the Taylor House for one of Theo's parties, I would've noticed. I *know* I would have.

The guy's good-looking. *Very* good-looking.

His mouth quirks into a smile as if he can read my mind as he looks down at his lap. I glance back at the stoplight--which is still red--then steal another peek at the stranger.

Is he texting someone?

My phone dings with a notification, and I flinch at the obtrusive sound, my heart kicking up a notch as if I was caught doing something I shouldn't be, which, I guess, isn't exactly off-base. Digging the phone out of my purse, I scan the notification. My cheeks heat, and a gasp slips out of me.

Holy crap on a cracker. It's an airdrop notification. From someone I most definitely don't know.

Colt Thorne would like to share a note.

Colt Thorne?

Is *he* Colt Thorne?

My teeth dig into my bottom lip as I glance up at the truck again, but the space is empty, and the light is green.

Shit.

A loud honk blares from behind me, feeding my embarrassment until I'm pretty sure I'll never live it down as I press the gas. As I drive through the intersection while staring at a certain truck a few yards in front of me, indecision gnaws in my lower gut.

Because if my intuition is right, and Colt Thorne is the tall, dark, and handsome stranger in the truck--*and* he decided to airdrop me something--should I be stupid enough to accept it? What if it's a dick pic? Or a list of names from his latest killing spree, since I don't exactly know the guy, and Ted Bundy was attractive, too, or--

I shake my head.

Calm the hell down, Ash, I chide myself.

But time isn't exactly on my side if I want to download this message. After all, it only works if you're within a certain distance from the sender. I stare at the truck's brake lights as he flips on his blinker, slowing down so he can make a right-hand turn. My thumb hovers over the "accept" button for a solid three seconds. My curiosity gets the best of me, and I tap it.

The notes app opens, and the message sent from the stranger pops up.

This message is for the cute girl in the beater who was staring at me at the light. Hope this is you.

You should text me.

547-555-4119

My jaw drops, and my gaze snaps back onto the road, but the truck's gone. He must've turned while I was reading his note.

The guy's ballsy. I'll give him that much. I glance at the phone again, scanning the message another time, when my phone dings with an incoming text message. It's from Logan, my boyfriend.

I toss my phone onto the passenger seat as if it's burned me and turn off the music, too, feeling like I'm on sensory overload. I drive the rest of the way home in silence, parking in the driveway while attempting to erase the last ten minutes from my life like it's a dirty bathroom in need of bleach.

Unfortunately, it's a waste of time.

Because even though I'm in a relationship, I can't erase the fact that it's nice. Being wanted. Appreciated.

I haven't been given a guy's number in years. Probably because most of them know I'm in a relationship with Logan, so it would be a waste of their time. But still.

A guy just gave me his number.

A good-looking guy.

A *really* good-looking guy.

My lips pull into a nervous smile at the memory, but I shake my head and shove the feeling aside.

Get a grip, Ash.

It doesn't matter how good-looking the guy is or how flattered I am he reached out. I'm in a relationship. And I'm not going to jeopardize it for a stranger, no matter how attractive he is.

I reach for my phone and pull up the message my boyfriend sent, anxious to move on with my day and push the stranger as far away from my thoughts as possible.

Logan: Hey! You coming tonight?

With a frown, I close my eyes, my enthusiasm for this conversation draining before it even had a chance to begin. I don't need to ask where Logan's referring. I already know.

Me: Next time, all right? I had a long day and just want to chill at home tonight.

Logan: Come on, babe. Live a little. It'll be fun.

Me: You know Theo's parties aren't exactly my thing, Logan.

Logan: But what about us? I want to see you.

Me: This week was rough. The girl I was helping for Buchanan's class dropped out, so now I need to find a new student to tutor. Not to mention Mia's already freaking out about her portion of the rent. Seriously. It's a mess, and I have a headache. You're welcome to come over and watch Netflix or something, but I kind of want to take it easy tonight.

Logan: I already told the guys I'd hang out, and I don't want to bail on them. Come on. You should come over.

I roll my eyes and lean my head against the headrest, nearly choking on the groan in my throat.

Theo's parties are…a lot.

A lot of booze.

A lot of dry humping.

A lot of loud music.

And a lot of headaches the day after.

But I've also been avoiding them for way too long, and it isn't exactly fair to Logan. He keeps inviting me, and I always keep saying no.

After all, relationships are all about give and take, right?

Puffing out my cheeks, I unlock my phone again and type a quick response.

Me: Next time, I promise. Have fun with the guys. We'll do something tomorrow. Love you.

Logan: Love you, babe.

With a sigh, I pull up the note from the mysterious Colt Thorne and delete it, despite how flattering the sentiment is.

I'm in a relationship.

And that's that.

1
COLT

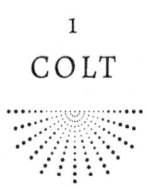

"Do you know how good it is to have you back?" Theo asks. "It'll be like high school all over again. Parties. Girls. Booze. Hockey––"

I glare at him, and he raises his hands in defense. "All right. Just the parties, girls, and booze. Happy now?"

Satisfied, I return, "Thanks for letting me stay."

We spent the day unloading my shit into the spare bedroom on the second floor of Theo's house. Once we finished, the main floor was already thumping with a party. One Theo's anxious to join.

"Come on, man." He slaps his hand against my back and guides me toward the stairs leading to the main floor. "You don't need to thank me. What's mine is yours. Always has been."

And he's right. It *has* always been this way between us. Or at least, it was before the accident. Theo, Logan, and I received hockey scholarships to LAU right out of high school. They both took their opportunity here, and I decided to get as far away from this place as I could.

Until I got kicked out of Dixie Tech, and my mom made a

few calls to her friend in LAU's dean's office. Apparently, if you tell my sob story to the right people, they'll sweep almost anything under the rug. Including a sex scandal with your professor's wife.

But LAU? It's a real university. With an actual campus, school pride, and an athletic department capable of winning. Not here for sports, though. Nothing is going to get me back on the ice. Including a thinly veiled promise or two between my mom and Coach Sanderson.

I look around the crowded, makeshift dance floor in the center of Theo's place as we walk down the stairs. I guess I shouldn't have expected anything less. Theo's family owns the house, and the hockey god is a sucker for parties. Theodore Taylor runs off booze, tits, and hockey like a toddler does with sippy cups, Disney+, and naptime.

Take one away, and he's a fucking baby over it. This is why the bass is thumping, and a pair of blondes are eye-screwing him from the corner. Bodies are sandwiched into the house like sardines in a can. And almost every one of them is holding red Solo cups and sloppy grins.

The place might not be a frat house, but it's about as close to one as the team could get. Again, I have Theo to thank for it. Being one of the best players on the ice and one of the youngest team captains, he invited half of the starting line to room at his place. The coaches agreed, saying the bonding time would be great for team building, which means I'm even more of a black sheep here than I ever was at my old school.

A few of Theo's teammates are watching me from across the room. Their voices are too low to hear over the thumping rap music, but I don't need to hear them to know they've already jumped to the same conclusions everyone else does.

They think I'm washed-up.

A coward.

That I had a mental breakdown or some shit.

That I was selfish for wasting my talent.

That I was a fool for turning down the scholarship of a lifetime only to throw my future down the drain.

It's a bunch of bullshit.

Even after years of staying under the radar, I'm not an idiot. I know they know who I am. I know I *can't* fly under the radar, no matter how much time has passed. I know the only reason my mom was able to convince LAU to accept my shitty transcripts was because they're hoping I'll play again.

Too bad she only set them up for disappointment.

I would've been great, though. Would've had it all. Would've gone pro if my dad hadn't convinced me to play for a university first. It's a shame he isn't here to make me follow through. I was a legend on the ice. It's not arrogance. It's fact. But I threw it all away.

"Sorry I didn't have a chance to introduce you to the rest of the guys before the party started," Theo continues, adjusting his worn black baseball hat on his head and drinking from his red Solo cup. He'd slipped out of my room as I was screwing together my bed frame and returned with one in hand, finally helping me put the mattress in place. "Lemme give you a quick rundown. Depp, Shorty, and Graves are over there," he points across the room to a leather couch surrounded by gyrating bodies. "Depp's the guy dry humping on the couch, Shorty's the giant sitting on the arm of it in the LAU jersey, and Graves is the angry asshole fighting with his girlfriend, Sally." He scans the open family room before turning toward the kitchen, then the staircase. "Logan's around here somewhere too. I dunno where, though."

"The guy's been busy," I note.

"You know how he is. Always up to something."

"Guess he hasn't changed much since high school?"

Theo shrugs. "Not really. His room is next to yours, and you guys will also share a bathroom," he adds as an afterthought.

"He still shit at cleaning?" I ask.

With his cup pressed to his lips, Theo chuckles. "Same old Logan." Then he swallows more of whatever's in his cup. His expression pinches, hinting it must be something strong, but he goes in for another drink anyway.

"Any questions so far?"

"So, there's six of us?" I confirm.

"Seven, including Burrows, but he's recovering at home from knee surgery. I'm sure he'll pop up later. His room is in the basement with Depp and Shorty. You, me, Graves, and Logan share the second floor. Fridge is always stocked with food. Everything's fair game unless there's a name on it. The dipshits usually break the rule, though, so you might wanna get a mini-fridge for your room if you're worried about your leftovers. We all split chores around the place. My mom made a chore chart. It's on the fridge, and I already added you to it. Things like vacuuming, dishes, that kind of thing."

"Chore chart?" My mouth quirks up. Sounds right up Mama Taylor's alley.

In high school, we used to always skip school at Theo's house. When she'd catch us in the basement, she'd refuse to make us chocolate chip cookies until after school officially let out. But as soon as three o'clock rolled around, she'd whip out the apron and scold us for missing school while the scent of homemade cookies wafted from the kitchen. Our consequence was homemade cookies and an empty threat to smack us with her spatula if she found out we were skipping school again.

I smile at the memory.

She's the biggest pushover with the biggest heart I've ever met, and I'm surprised how much I miss her.

Theo rolls his eyes. "You know how she is."

He's right. I do.

"How's she doing, anyway?" I ask.

"You know Mama Taylor," he mutters, mentioning the nickname Logan and I gave her when we were in middle school. "She told me to tell you hi, though."

"Tell her I said hi back, and I'll be sure to keep up with the chore chart."

He chuckles. "Good. 'Cause I'm pretty sure you'll be the only one. Also, I feel like I shouldn't even have to say this, but I don't care if you have sleepovers, I don't care if you smoke weed in your room, and I don't care if you use the hot tub in the back. My only rule is to keep your stuff out of the main area, 'cause I don't feel like being anyone's daddy. Except theirs," he jokes, giving the blondes who've been staring at him across the room a smirk as he slaps my shoulder. "Glad to have you here, Colt. We're gonna have fun."

"Thanks, man. I really appreciate it."

"Like I said. What's mine is yours. Any other questions?"

I shake my head, squeezing the back of my neck as I take in the new place. There are people everywhere, jam-packed into every nook and cranny of the first floor. And even though there aren't any walls separating the kitchen from the family room, the lights are dimmed, and the furniture is pushed aside but kept bunched together in small groups, creating intimate areas around the edge of the room. And when I say intimate, I mean they're perfect for people who are done dry humping on the dance floor and have decided grinding on the couch is more appealing for the night.

Gotta love college.

With a low chuckle, I scan the kitchen on the opposite side of the house.

There's a pretty little redhead pushing aside a bunch of mixers and bottles on the white granite island in the kitchen, making space on the opposite side. Once she's satisfied she has enough room, she climbs on top and lays down. She's lifting her shirt when a familiar face appears next to her.

"Aaaand there's the man of the hour," Theo mutters, motioning to Logan.

Logan pours tequila into the redhead's belly button and laps it up, pinning the girl's hips against the counter as she giggles beneath him.

"Seems like not much has changed since high school," I joke, turning around and dipping my chin toward the group of girls grinding against each other in the middle of the main room. "Is it like this every night?"

"Usually only on the weekends or after a game. Speaking of which--"

"Not gonna happen," I interrupt.

"You know, I gotta ask, Colt."

"Not gonna happen," I repeat.

"Just train with us. See how you feel. Coach Sanderson--"

"Theo," I warn through gritted teeth.

He sighs. "All right. We'll talk later."

"I think I'm good," I mutter.

"Get yourself a drink. You need one after moving all day." With another slap against my shoulder, Theo lets go of the lecture he's probably been preparing since the moment I asked if I could stay with him. He leaves me alone, weaves between the crowd, and hooks his arms around the two blondes, guiding them upstairs.

Same old Logan.

Same old Theo.

I chuckle under my breath as I watch them go, then head to the kitchen and grab a beer from the fridge. Theo's right. I need one. But not from moving. From being back here. Surrounded by memories and the reminder of everything I gave up.

DON'T LET ME FALL

"Why hello, stranger," a feminine voice says from behind me. The stainless steel refrigerator closes with a soft thud, and I turn around, finding the voice's owner. Dark skin, thick, curly hair, red lips matching her short dress. She's stunning.

"Hey," I answer.

"Hi." She offers her dainty little hand to me while her confidence and perfume hit me at the same time. "I'm Gwyn."

Her skin is like velvet beneath my touch as I shake her hand. "Colt."

"Nice to meet you."

"You too."

Her tongue darts out between those red-painted lips as she shamelessly looks me up and down. "Are you new?"

"How could you tell?"

"I have a feeling I would've remembered a face like this." She runs her hand across my cheek and grins. "What are you studying?"

I open my mouth to reply when Logan stumbles into the room and tosses his arm around her shoulder. "Gwyndolen, Gwyndolen, Gwyndolen," he tsks. "Why are you bothering my buddy over here?"

"Buddy?" She looks me up and down again, surprised. "You two know each other?"

"We go way back. Right, Colt?" He offers his hand and pulls me into a quick hug, slapping his hand against my back.

"Good to see you, man," I reply.

"Likewise. Glad to have you back. You're not taking my spot on the team, though, right?"

I laugh and shake my head. "We both know I don't play anymore."

Tilting her head to one side, Gwyn studies me more closely. "Wait. Are you Colt…Colt Thorne?"

"The one and only," Logan answers for me. "We'll have to

catch up later, all right? But I gotta steal Gwyn for a bit. She and I have a"--he smirks--"prior engagement."

"You think I'm still gonna suck your dick when you bailed on me last time?" She scoffs and flips her dark, thick hair over her shoulder. "Not gonna happen, Logan. You, however..." She drags her fingers down my chest and steps closer. "You have potential."

"Nah, he's not interested in puck bunnies," Logan answers for me.

She licks her lips. "Seemed interested before you interrupted."

"Nah, he isn't," Logan argues and looks at me again. "Ain't that right, brother?"

Biting back my laugh, I scratch my jaw and scan Gwyn up and down. "Are you a puck bunny, Gwyn?"

"I like hockey, and I like hockey players."

"And there's nothing wrong with that," Logan interrupts, putting his hand on Gwyn's back as he sidles up next to her.

"Nothing at all," I agree. "But I think I'm gonna leave you to your hockey player. It was nice to meet you, Gwyn. I'll see you around."

The bodies gyrating in the main room are a bitch to get through, but when I finally reach the stairs, I find Gwyn in the crowd, grinding on Logan as he grabs her hip and pulls her closer.

Apparently, they didn't waste much time.

And yeah. She's a definite puck bunny. I'll be sure to thank Logan for the heads-up the next time I see him. There's nothing wrong with a girl who likes the game almost as much as she likes screwing all the teammates. But I'm not about that life anymore. And the more distance I put between myself and hockey, the better.

Theo's right.

Same old Logan.

2
COLT

The Bean Scene is one of my favorite areas on campus. Well, here and SeaBird. But the bar isn't exactly on campus, so I'm not sure it counts. Regardless, the coffee shop serves great coffee, doesn't cost an arm and a leg, and is right next to the gym, making it the perfect pitstop after having my ass kicked by Theo.

He collapses into the metal chair across from me and kicks his legs out. "You're getting better."

"Glad I can be your guinea pig for training."

"Not gonna lie. It's nice being able to kick your ass again. We'll have you bulked up and ready to play on the team again in no time."

I snort and take a sip of my coffee. "Yeah, 'cause that's what I want."

"Hey, the ladies like it."

"You think I need hockey to get laid?" I challenge.

Chuckling, he takes a sip of his iced mocha with whipped cream. I swear, the guy's sweet tooth is about as insatiable as his dick.

"No, but it doesn't hurt. Those puck bunnies, man." He

hums low in his throat and covers his smirk with his hand as one of them wiggles her fingers at him from behind the counter.

"I've noticed," I grunt, ignoring her. "It's been what, a month since I moved in?"

He tears his attention from the puck bunny slash barista and nods at me.

"And I've yet to have a full night of sleep without hearing Logan screw a girl in his room. I wouldn't care if it was at least the girls making the noise, but Logan sounds like a dying moose." I shiver, and Theo laughs.

"Yeah. Why do you think the room was open before you moved in?"

I take another drink of my black coffee with Stevia and shake my head. "Thanks for the heads-up."

"My bad. I think he's taking full advantage since his girlfriend's been busy lately."

I pause and set my mug down on the table. "Logan has a girlfriend?"

"Logan always has a girlfriend," he reminds me. "You know how he is."

"Good point," I concede. "I guess I assumed he'd grown out of it."

"Not even close. Doesn't help that his girl is a damn saint, either. Speak of the devil," Theo mutters under his breath, tilting his head toward the door. Logan appears with his hand pressed to a pretty blonde's back. Screw that. Pretty is an understatement.

Shit. She's the girl from the street.

She's like a doll. With big blue eyes and pouty lips. She's fucking precious.

Innocent.

Untouchable.

Ignoring the way my heart ratchets in my chest, I ask, "Is that her?"

He nods. "Yeah, that's Ashlyn."

Head cocked, I drag my gaze from her long, lean legs to the sliver of skin between her shirt and jeans as she tugs at the sides of her dark jacket and covers herself. "Why haven't I seen her at the house?"

"'Cause she hates parties. Whenever they're together, it's usually at her place, SeaBird, or around campus, which all the puck bunnies have learned are off-limits."

"Very convenient." I scoff and settle back in my chair, hooking my arm over the back of it as I study the wet dream in front of me. She tucks her hair behind her ear and smiles up at Logan as he slides his card toward the barista––who I'm pretty sure I saw sneaking out of Logan's room the other night––to pay for their drinks.

"You really think she doesn't know he's screwing random girls every night of the week?" I ask.

"You know he's the golden boy."

"Still," I argue. "Is she really that naive?"

"Logan knows how to cover his tracks. He shows people what he wants them to see and nothing else."

"So, she really is naive," I mutter, surprised by how disappointed I am.

Theo grimaces. "Maybe not naive. More like too trusting."

I bite back my scoff and take another sip of coffee while Theo defends, "It's not her fault. The girls know not to say anything, or they'll never touch a hockey player again. And the guys know to keep their shit out of his business, or he'll be a dick on the ice. Besides, it isn't any of our business, no matter how sweet she is," he clarifies. "Ashlyn's a different breed. She's happy giving Logan his space. She isn't clingy, and she has her shit together. Except where he's concerned.

And she isn't some puck bunny, either. She doesn't even come to any of Logan's games."

"Again. Convenient," I point out.

Theo nods, swirling the straw in his drink, mixing the whipped cream with the rest of his coffee. "Again…different," he repeats, taking another sip. "She isn't with him because of his talent on the ice."

"Then why's she with him?" I joke. "Thought it was the only thing he had to offer."

With a dry laugh, Theo shakes his head. "You'll have to ask her yourself. But be careful. Like I said. She's different."

"Different, how?"

"Gorgeous, though she has no idea. Smart. She takes the time to tutor other students without making them feel stupid for it. And loyal as shit. Logan might not care if you talk to her 'cause he knows you'd never do anything, and you like to be an ass. But, Ash? She'll let you know you're barking up the wrong tree if she doesn't like your attention."

"Who wouldn't like my attention?" I argue with a grin.

"Not saying she wouldn't. Just saying she's loyal, and she's already planned out her entire future with our buddy over there. He practically pissed on her like a dog, claiming his territory during freshman year."

My eyes widen in surprise. "They've been together that long?"

"Yeah. But he didn't start messing with other girls until a couple of months ago. Hasn't been as reckless to do it openly at a party until recently, either. Doesn't matter. None of the guys are stupid enough to approach her. Not only because they know they'd get their ass kicked by Logan, but also because they know it would be a waste of time. Like I said. She's head over heels for him."

I scratch at the scruff on my jaw and take one more look at the girl. "Challenge accepted."

"Don't be an ass," he warns.

"You know I'm just messing around."

He grunts and stretches out his legs. "Yeah. That's the problem. Logan's gonna kick your ass."

"Nah, he'll get over it."

"Ass," he mutters into his coffee.

And I laugh with him. "If Logan's reckless enough to openly cheat on her at a party, he deserves me messing with her."

"You're still an ass," he counters.

My mouth quirks up on one side as I finish the rest of my coffee.

He's not wrong.

3
ASHLYN

I shouldn't have come.
This is a bad idea.
"This is a bad idea," Mia mutters beside me, reading my mind.

We stare up at the infamous Taylor House, but neither of us moves. It's red brick with painted shutters looking straight out of the *Home Alone* movie and screams regular suburban house. This is ironic because it's more of a bachelor pad than any of the houses on fraternity row.

Where are all the good parties?
Taylor House.
Where is all the good alcohol?
Taylor House.
Where are all the sexy hockey players?
Taylor House.

My nose scrunches with distaste. And yet, Logan's been living here for almost six months. He insists it's because his coaches like the bonding time sharing the same roof with your teammates creates, and it has nothing to do with the puck bunnies who like to slip in and out of this place at every freaking hour of every freaking day. But what do I know?

It's not his fault. He's a hockey player. Puck bunnies come with the territory. Doesn't mean I have to like it, though.

Trust, I remind myself. *Every good relationship has trust.*

And I do trust Logan. He's always been an amazing boyfriend. Showing up on my doorstep with flowers. Bringing me chocolate and ice cream whenever I'm on my period. Always planning special dates for our anniversary and my birthday.

He's basically LAU's golden boy.

Who also happens to live in a whorehouse.

With a deep breath, I grab Mia's arm, and we head inside.

"Seriously. We should leave," Mia mutters, but she follows along anyway.

"He's been asking me to come for like a month," I tell her over my shoulder. "It's the least I can do since he's been skipping so many of these to come hang out at our house." The bass from the speakers nearly drowns out my voice as we step over the threshold. "Besides, it'll be fine."

"No, it won't be fine because he might ask you to come to these things, but it's not like he's actually expecting you to show up."

"He says he misses me."

"If he missed you, he'd come hang out at our place instead of the Taylor Whorehouse during a rager."

"One. He always comes to our place to hang out."

"Not lately," she mutters.

"And two," I continue, ignoring her. "He's part of the team."

"Which means he has to be an accomplice for all their shenanigans?" she challenges, propping her hand on her hip.

"It means there's nothing wrong with Logan wanting to

hang out with his friends on the weekend instead of hiding away at our place all of the time. You know that."

"I know you're gonna end up sleeping over tonight, and I'll have to get an Uber home," she argues. "I know *that*."

I toss her my keys. "You can take my car. I'm sure Logan won't mind giving me a ride home in the morning. If I stay," I clarify, turning sideways as a pair of blondes nearly runs me over in the entryway.

"*If*." Mia snorts. "Yeah, sure. *If* you stay. Not gonna lie, Ash. I have no idea how you convinced me to come to this thing when we could be binging literally *any* TV show on Netflix with Kate."

My nostrils flare as she describes exactly what I wish we were doing tonight with our other roommate, Kate. I pull Mia to a darkened corner and drop my voice low. "Look. You're an amazing friend, and I love the crap out of you. But can we please not do a lecture tonight? Especially when we both know you're exactly one to talk."

She frowns, her gaze shifting to the crowded family room, searching for her ex, who she's been avoiding like the plague ever since she ended things with him.

She met Shorty--aka Bradley Ackerman--through Logan. And it was fun double-dating while it lasted. But to say their breakup was messy would be a massive understatement. The fact she even bothered to come with me tonight proves how amazing of a friend she really is. I squeeze her hand, grateful for her presence, and help search the premises for Shorty so we can keep a wide berth between us. After all, it's the least I can do.

All of the furniture has been pushed to the edges of the room, leaving an open space for people to dance. Or dry hump. Poe-tae-toe, poe-tah-toe.

Thankfully, Shorty isn't in sight.

I hate Theo's parties. Logan does, too, but since it's where his friends like to hang out, it's not like he's always able to avoid them.

"Man, I'm a good friend who loves you," she mutters under her breath.

"And I'll never forget it," I promise. "Come on. Let's find Logan."

Fingers entwined, I lead us through the throng of people as a familiar voice yells, "Logan! Your girlfriend's here to see you!"

Shorty's sitting on the couch with his arm wrapped around a gorgeous girl from my chemistry class. When he sees Mia beside me, he forces a smile, gets to his feet, and lifts his finger to Mia. "I'm gonna go find Logan. Then you and I are gonna have a chat."

She shakes her head. "I don't want to have a chat."

"Mia," he starts, but I cut Shorty off.

"Hey, Shorty." I tilt my head up, my neck craning as I look him in the eye and step between them. "I promised Mia she could have a night off from the drama. It's been months, and it's clear you've moved on"––I motion to the floozy on the couch––"so, if you could please allow Mia to do the same, that'd be great."

He glares at me, his usual laid-back façade slipping to reveal the asshole who broke my best friend's heart as he moves past me and heads upstairs.

"Thanks." Mia's shoulders relax, and she points to the kitchen. "I'm gonna get a drink."

The white granite island is littered with cups, bottles of liquor, and soda cans. Mia reaches for the Sprite and adds a generous splash of gin with shaky hands.

I frown, hating how much Shorty's presence has affected her.

"You okay?" I ask.

"You said he wouldn't be here."

"I didn't know he would be. Logan said——"

"Logan's an asshole."

I sigh and pinch the bridge of my nose. "He isn't an asshole."

Or at least, he *usually* isn't. I'm not naive enough to wonder whether or not he lied about Shorty attending the party just to get me here, though. And if that's the case? I kind of want to smack him.

It's annoying. And frustrating. And makes my hands clench at my sides. I take the gin and Sprite from Mia's hand, swallow a mouthful, and sputter as the liquid burns my throat.

"Damn, Mia," I choke out, handing the cup back to her.

She laughs and takes a sip. "Sorry."

"I'm going to the bathroom. I'll meet you in a few."

She nods, and I head toward the dark hall where the bathroom on the main floor is located.

I screech to a halt.

There's a girl with her back pressed to the closed bathroom door, and her head is angled up toward the ceiling. She's blocking my way. Her eyes are closed, and her sleek ponytail is a mess as she whimpers, tangling her fingers in a dark mop of hair belonging to the guy nibbling on her neck. He tilts his head further to the side, slipping his hand beneath her black crop top. He's feeling her up. In public. Okay, maybe not entirely, since we're in the only dim hall on the main floor. But he's most definitely massaging her breast, and I'm most definitely staring.

My breath hitches, and I take a small step back, too surprised to actually turn around even when I know I should. I'm used to seeing people getting busy in the Taylor House. It's one of the reasons I rarely come to these parties. But this? This is different. More heated. More lustful. Like the rest of the world doesn't exist. They're too caught up in each other to notice anything else.

And it's weird, but I miss it.

The need that should accompany sex. But I guess when you've only been with one person, it shouldn't be surprising when the *need* dissipates into a comfortable routine.

With another soft moan and her eyes still pressed closed, the girl pushes at his chest and twists the guy around until his back is to the door and he's facing me in the dark hallway.

Shit.

It's the guy from the truck. The one who'd airdropped me his number.

His smirk shoots straight to my core as his gaze flicks up and down my body while his partner--who's oblivious I'm here--pushes his shirt up and palms his killer abs. Seriously. The guy's ripped. He must be on the team or something. Other than the lack of missing teeth, he screams confidence and arrogance like every other hockey player I've ever met. It doesn't stop my curiosity from taking in every inch of him, though. If anything, it fans it.

Who is this guy?

Her hands look so pale against his tan skin and the fine dusting of hair leading to his--

"Wanna join?" he asks. His invitation is nothing but an amused growl as he watches me.

I blink and clear my throat before shaking my head. "I was just..." I lick my lips, avoiding his gaze.

Oh my hell.

Did he catch me staring at his crotch?

I need to get the hell out of here.

"You were just, what?" he challenges while the girl continues sucking on his neck, either too drunk to realize

I'm standing here and her boy toy is talking to someone else or too turned on to care.

My guess is the latter.

With a guy like that? His hands on her waist. His arrogant smirk. I can see the appeal.

When I realize he's still waiting for me to answer him, I snap back to reality.

What did he ask me again?

Oh. Right.

"I was just needing the bathroom," I finish, forcing myself to look him in the eye and instantly regretting it.

Dark eyes. Strong, stubbled jaw. And the same arrogant smirk setting off tiny warning bells in my head.

He chuckles, and the sound makes my stomach clench. He grabs the girl's waist and tugs her a few inches to the right, leaving me a little room to slip by them and into the bathroom.

"M'lady," he says, his tone laced with sarcasm.

I look down at his hand still hidden beneath the girl's crop top. My lips pucker like I've tasted something sour. "Such a gentleman."

But as I try to slip past him, he grabs my bicep with his free hand and keeps me in place, his hot gaze holding mine and wreaking havoc on my insides. He leans closer and whispers, "You have no idea."

Then he lets me go, and I disappear into the bathroom like a scared little mouse. My face feels flushed, and my blood is hot as I press my hands to my cheeks, leaning against the door with weak knees.

What the hell *was that?*

4
ASHLYN

After using the restroom, I splash some cold water on my face, torn by my own curiosity as to whether or not he's still out there. Still waiting. Still feeling up a girl in the middle of the hallway. The sexy stranger from the stoplight. The one who airdropped his number to me.

Apparently, he isn't too bummed I never reached out.

It doesn't matter.

This is why I don't come to the Taylor House. Why I don't like the infamous Taylor parties. The late nights. The random orgies apparently *not* happening behind closed doors.

And your boyfriend lives here, a tiny voice reminds me.

I shove my hair away from my face and wrench the door open, ready to take on whatever's on the opposite side. Except the hallway is empty.

Shaking off the realization, I head back to the kitchen, desperate for a drink while praying it'll erase whatever happened in the hallway from my memory because I do *not* need to relive it ever again.

I should leave.

But I promised Logan I'd come tonight.

And I always keep my promises.

"Hey, baby. You all right?" a familiar voice asks when he sees me staring at the smorgasbord of alcohol set in front of me.

I look up at Logan and smile. "Hey."

His hair is a disheveled mess of blonde, sparking an image of the stranger in the hall and how his hookup ran her hands through it. When he catches me noticing, Logan runs his fingers through it and pats it down before grabbing my hips and pulling me into him. "Missed you, baby."

"You, too." I peck his lips. "Where were you?"

"Playing a game of pool in the rec room."

"You hate pool."

"The guys convinced me to play a round. Can I get you a drink?"

With a quick scan of the copious options laid across the island, I say, "Be my guest."

As Logan starts pouring a concoction I have no doubt is going to leave me with a headache in the morning, an awareness settles over me, causing tingles to race down my spine. I glance around the crowded main floor, searching for the catalyst. The same dark, hypnotic eyes from the hall greet me. Same strong jaw. The girl's gone, though. My expression sours, causing his lips to turn up on one side as if he can read my mind.

Which only fans my annoyance.

The guy's sex on a stick in nothing but a dark T-shirt and jeans. And he's staring at me. Shamelessly. And even though he knows he's been caught, he isn't deterred. If anything, my quick glances are only spurring him on. A knot of anticipation forms in my lower gut. I'm drenched in proverbial guilt as Logan hands me a drink, breaking whatever connection was building between the stranger and me.

"You okay?" Logan asks. "You look flushed."

"I'm fine." I take the cup from him and drink half its contents, tilting my head toward the new guy while refusing to look at him again. "Who's that?"

Logan looks around the room. "Who?"

"The new guy."

He scans the room again. "Who? Colt?"

Colt.

Yup.

He's definitely the guy who airdropped his number.

I peek at the stranger from above the rim of my cup and catch him still looking at me with the same cocky smirk.

Logan follows my gaze, chuckles, and tosses his arm around my shoulders, pressing a kiss to my cheek and not-so-subtly claiming me in front of the stranger. "Yeah. That's Colt. He was buddies with me and Theo in high school. Just transferred."

"Oh." I peek over at him again.

He's still watching me. Curious. Confident. Undeterred.

With a thick swallow, I turn in Logan's grasp until my back is to Colt, though I can still feel his stare. "And the reason he's staring?"

"He must like what he sees."

I laugh. "And it doesn't bother you?"

"You're beautiful, babe." He kisses my temple. "I'm not the only one who can appreciate it. And Colt is *Colt*."

"What do you mean?"

"I mean, he likes getting under people's skin. Come on." Logan grabs my wrist and tugs me toward the stairs. "Let's go to my room."

"What about the party?" I ask.

"I'd rather finish it in my bedroom with you. Come on," he repeats.

But as I follow him to the second floor, the same swell of anticipation floods my system as I peek over my shoulder and find Colt watching my every step.

And I hate how I notice.

5
ASHLYN

With a light yawn, I cover my mouth and roll toward the alarm clock on Logan's nightstand. The red digital numbers make me squint in the otherwise pitch-black room as I register what time it is. Three in the morning. Despite what I'd told Mia, I'd wanted to spend the night in my own bed. But after making love with Logan, she'd already bolted, and he was too tired to drive me home. He's been so busy with practice and classes, I couldn't blame him.

It's still weird sometimes. Being here. Picturing what our future would look like. How we'd promised each other forever our freshman year and are actually bringing it to fruition, despite his hockey star status and my less-than-popular one.

Sometimes it still blows me away that he picked me. *Me.* Out of everyone. All the girls at LAU. All the puck bunnies who attend his games. It's surreal. Unbelievable. But sometimes, it makes me feel like I'm paralyzed, waiting for the other shoe to drop. The moment when Logan decides he's done dating the girl next door and wants to trade her in for the Victoria's Secret model.

And he can.

He's destined for greatness.

The problem is...he knows it.

He's changed since we first met. I'm not naive enough to deny it. Not necessarily for the worse, but...different. More confident, I guess. Still Prince Charming whenever I'm around. Busier, though. Especially lately. I feel like we've hardly seen each other. Hopefully, things will calm down when the hockey season's over, but I'm not holding my breath. Between practice, games, school, and his job, his life has been crazy. And so has mine.

Which is why it's good I stayed over.

If only I could get some sleep.

With a sigh, I slip from beneath Logan's covers and climb out of bed.

I need sleep.

But I can't make my brain turn off.

Rubbing at my not-so-tired eyes, I grab a T-shirt from the pile of clean laundry at the foot of his bed, slip it on, and pad downstairs into the kitchen.

The house is finally quiet. Everyone either passed out in their rooms or on the couches, or they finally stumbled home after a long night of partying.

I chew on my lower lip, scanning the cluttered kitchen like it's another planet.

I don't know why I still feel like a stranger in the Taylor House. It doesn't matter if Logan's lived here for six months. It doesn't matter that I've been here a handful of times. Right now? In the middle of the night? When it's quiet and almost peaceful? It feels different. Like I'm trespassing. Like I don't belong here.

Puffing out my cheeks, I open the stainless steel fridge and search for a drink of some kind when a soft creak from the hall makes me jump in surprise.

My spine is a steel rod, but I turn toward the entrance to the kitchen and find a very shirtless, very handsome guy staring at me in nothing but a pair of gray sweatpants.

It's *him*.

The new roommate.

Colt.

The light from the still open fridge bounces off his features, casting shadows along his strong jaw and quirked brow as he watches me. He looks like he's as amused as earlier tonight, though I can't put my finger on why.

I gulp and offer him a tight smile. "Hi. Sorry. I didn't think anyone would be awake. The guys are usually pretty deep sleepers, so…I, uh,"--I hook my thumb over my shoulder toward the still open fridge--"I was, uh, thirsty, and…"

He stays quiet and crosses his arms, making his biceps bulge while clearly enjoying watching me squirm.

And boy, am I squirming.

I've never had this response to a person before. Especially not a physical one. Like every inch of me is hyper-aware of the man a few feet away from me. Like I can feel him. His gaze. What his skin would feel like beneath my fingers if I dared to touch him. He could let out a breath, and I'd somehow feel it too.

It's unnerving.

And *so* not appropriate.

Blindly, I reach into the fridge and grab the first handle my fingers touch, pulling out a jug of orange juice.

"I'll, uh…" Again, my voice trails off as I try to calm the freaking swarm of butterflies assaulting my stomach. I turn around and open the dark cabinets, blindly searching for a glass while the jug of juice hangs limply from my other hand.

A cup. A cup. Where's a freaking cup?

I shouldn't be unnerved. I've been around half-naked guys before. Okay. I've been around a fully naked Logan, but that's about it. Men and I? We've never really been super chummy.

Which is why I'm so glad I found Logan. He was the hockey star. The sexy guy who was going places, and he offered to take his goody-two-shoes-slash-bookworm-girlfriend with him.

This is why I most definitely should *not* be drooling over his roommate--I peek over my shoulder--who is still watching me.

Great.

"Cups?" I ask, fed up with my search. "Do you have any more cups?"

"Oh, 'cause you're *thirsty*?" he returns, his tone thick with sarcasm.

I toss a quick glare his way but continue my search. The wood cabinets sound like clashing cymbals in the otherwise silent kitchen as I open and close the doors nearest to the sink. The entire lower shelf is empty, and since I'm barely over 5'3", having a glimpse of the upper ones is bleak at best. Standing on my tiptoes, I blindly reach up, desperate to get the hell out of here, when warmth spreads along my spine.

"You never texted me," he murmurs, the sound low and raspy.

He's standing behind me. Not touching me. But I can still feel him—his heat. Hell, I can smell him. His scent taints the air. Like musk and man and--I hold my breath, keeping myself from going into full-blown Bloodhound mode as his corded forearm reaches above me and grabs a cup from the upper shelf.

With a soft clink of glass on granite, he sets it next to my hip on the counter and trails his hand along my bare arm. His fingers tickle against my sensitive flesh, making my knees weak as he takes the orange juice from my hand, twists the dark green cap, and removes it. Then, he splashes some of it into the cup while I hold my breath.

Goosebumps pebble along my skin, but I keep my attention on his strong hands as they lift the glass and offer it to me, all too aware of the gorgeous man behind me who's practically pinning me against the counter. My hands shake slightly as I take the offered drink and bring it to my lips. It's sweet and tart with low pulp, but I barely taste a thing. My senses are too busy zeroing in on the stranger whose heat is branding my back. The way his breath tickles the top of my head, his subtle scent teasing my nostrils.

As if he can tell I'm close to breaking, he steps back, giving me another foot of space. I turn around and face him again. I should be frustrated right now. Or annoyed with his presence.

What I *shouldn't* be is curious. But I am. I can't help it. I've never been curious about anyone. Even Logan had to pursue me, begging me to let him take me on a date before I agreed.

But the man in front of me?

He's distracting.

That much I know.

Maybe it's because he's the opposite of Logan in every way. Where Logan screams Prince Charming, Colt screams bad idea. Logan has blonde hair, and Colt has dark. Logan's shorter, stockier. Colt is long and lean-ish. Still built for hockey, though. Logan also screams gentleman while his buddy screams...

I gulp and wet my lips.

His attention slides to them, and his mouth flickers with amusement.

He's toying with me, leaving my mouth dry and my palms sweaty with a look alone. And he knows it.

I need to get out of here.

"Thanks," I whisper, wiggling the glass back and forth to showcase what I'm talking about.

He stays quiet.

Unable to hold his dark, flinty gaze, I look down and follow the light trail of hair beneath his belly button instead.

Nope. Bad idea, Ashlyn.

I take another sip to wet my dry throat, giving the guy a tight smile.

"Still *thirsty*?" he asks.

I shake my head, my breath shallow and unsteady.

What is this guy doing to me?

Amused, he captures the drink from my hand--his fingers warm but calloused as they brush against mine--and takes a long pull from my glass. I watch his Adam's apple bob up and down as he swallows the last bit of juice, ignoring how it makes my stomach tighten with anticipation.

Because it's ridiculous.

There's nothing to anticipate.

With a soft shake of my head, I blurt out, "I have a boyfriend."

I don't know why I say it. It just comes out. And honestly? I'm not quite sure who I'm trying to remind. It doesn't even matter who I'm reminding because it's true. I *do* have a boyfriend. And I'm currently wearing his shirt. And he's currently sleeping in his room on the floor above us. Which means I shouldn't be standing here in front of a stranger. I should be upstairs. With Logan.

"I know. Logan," Colt tells me. "He's a good guy."

I peek up at him, surprised by his admission. Not because Logan isn't a good guy, but because I'm not used to his teammates voicing it out loud.

"He is," I agree.

"Yeah. Kind of an asshole sometimes, but hey. Aren't we all?"

"I thought you said you were a gentleman," I counter, referring to our little run-in in the hallway earlier tonight before almost slamming my hand against my mouth to keep me from blurting out anything else.

He chuckles and steps closer. "I *am* a gentleman. Especially to the ladies in my bedroom."

"Or the hall," I point out.

"Or the kitchen," he adds, surprising me.

I open my mouth to say something else, but he stops me. "You should run along now, Sunshine."

Sunshine.

Either he doesn't know my name or hasn't bothered to ask. Although, he does know I'm dating Logan, so he isn't completely oblivious... I stick a pin in my thoughts, asking, "Why?"

I hate how curious I am about the man in front of me. But I can't help it. There's something about him. Something I can't quite put my finger on. I noticed it the first time at the stoplight, but now, I'm in his presence, and it's even more potent. Because he's cocky, sure, but I feel like it's almost a protective mechanism, and I can't figure out why.

"Because joking with my friend's girlfriend is one thing but screwing her in the kitchen is probably against the roommate agreement, don't you think?"

I gulp, folding my arms and ignoring how Logan's shirt rides up on my thighs, and argue, "Who says I would let you screw me?"

"See, that's what makes it more fun." He steps closer, pinning my hips against the counter, picks up the jug of juice, and steps away again. "'Night, Sunshine." He sets the juice back into the fridge and walks away, the stupid dimples along his lower back above his gray sweatpants distracting me as he leaves.

What the hell is wrong with me?

6

COLT

After setting the last dirty mug into the dishwasher, I turn it on and rinse my hands in the sink. I swear, Logan's the laziest asshole I've ever met. He'll wait until every single utensil, cup, plate, and bowl is used before bothering to wash any of them, knowing it'll drive me crazy, and I'll do it for him if he waits long enough. Which is exactly what he did yesterday, even though it was his turn to do the dishes.

Asshole.

I shake off my annoyance and fill the last clean mug with coffee when the garage door opens behind me.

"Hey, man," I greet Theo. "How was the gym?"

The door to the garage closes behind him with a soft thud as he heads to the fridge and grabs a protein drink. "Good. You should've come."

I nod as he chugs the thick chocolate liquid in one go.

I should've. But I slept like shit. After my little encounter with Ashlyn in the kitchen, I couldn't stop thinking about her. Her silky skin. The breathiness in her voice. The way she looked in nothing but my T-shirt. I'm still not sure how the hell she wound up in it, but I'm not about to complain. It almost makes up for the shitty orgasm I had to give myself while imagining it was her after I went back to my room.

Almost.

I should've invited Sophie to my room last night. It would've prevented a lot of issues after I turned her away in the hall. But I didn't. I told her I wasn't in the mood. The truth was, I wasn't in the mood for *her*, which I still don't fully understand.

"How's your little sister doing?" Theo asks, bringing me back to the present.

I blink slowly, whiplashed. "Blakely?"

"Do you have another sister?"

I laugh and shake my head. "She's fine. Why?"

"Just wondering." He leans against the counter, trying to act casual, which only sends the warning bells in my head into full-blown beast mode.

My gaze narrows, but I continue anyway. "She's coming to LAU soon."

"Yeah?"

I nod. "Yeah. She asked if I could help her find a place. She was offered an internship with the sports program, and the school wants her here before fall semester, so it makes things a little tricky with roommate contracts and shit."

"We have an extra room," he offers, his mouth curving up on one side.

"You think I'm gonna let my little sister move into *this* house?"

He bursts out laughing. "There's the overprotective brother I'm used to."

"Do you blame me?"

"She's a pain in the ass," he reminds me.

I laugh and take another swig of coffee. He's not wrong.

Blakely has the mouth of a sailor and the right hook of a boxer, but I wouldn't expect anything less after being raised with three older brothers. My mom always said they kept having kids in hopes of one of them being a baby girl she could treat like a princess. Instead, she got Blake, who's basically one of the boys.

When we were little, she even begged to sign up for football, but my mom enrolled her in soccer instead. She would've gone pro, too, if she hadn't exploded her kneecap during her sophomore year in high school. Now, she's studying to become a physical therapist in sports medicine, and since LAU has one of the best programs in the US, and she's finishing her associates from the community college near our mom's house, it made sense for her to apply here.

"Yeah, she is," I agree. "A pain in the ass who will be at LAU soon, so I expect you to help me fend off all the guys who'll be drooling over her. Think you can do it?"

"We'll see. Speaking of pains in the ass, the girl I brought home. Did she already leave? I told her we could shower together after the gym."

"Nah, I haven't seen anyone yet this morning," I reply, surprised by my disappointment. "Only in the middle of the night."

He frowns. "Huh. I didn't know she'd woken up."

"I meant Ashlyn."

His eyes widen. "No shit?"

"Yeah." I bite back my laugh and add, "She was wearing my shirt."

"What?"

I nod.

"How the hell did you manage that?"

With my hands raised in defense, I say, "Must've been karma or some shit, 'cause it wasn't me. You think Logan noticed?"

"Doubt it. He was probably too busy setting up his hookup for tonight."

My amusement morphs into annoyance, and I mutter, "Probably."

"Be careful, though. I know you're only messing around, but you know Logan. You don't want to get on his bad side."

"One. You're right. I'm only messing around. And two. Yeah, I know Logan, but he knows me too. And *he* knows I wouldn't cross the line."

"All right," Theo concedes, tossing the empty protein drink container into the recycle bin beneath the sink. "It's been a while, man. And with how things played out our senior year…"

"I know."

"I'm just saying––"

"I know," I repeat, biting back the swell of emotions thrumming through me as I set my coffee onto the counter and fold my arms.

"You know we're here for you, right? Me. Logan."

I stare blankly at the wall behind us, grateful everyone who'd passed out on the couches has already left for the day. I dip my chin. "Yeah. I know."

"Good. And if you ever wanna talk––"

"I don't."

"All right," he repeats, sensing how close I am to snapping. "I'll drop it, okay?"

He pauses until I look at him and nod.

Satisfied my feelings aren't hurt or some shit, he adds, "Good. I'm gonna go find Angela."

"Ah, so the hookup has a name?" I ask, grateful for the subject change.

"Maybe."

"You two exclusive?" I don't know why I bother to ask. While I've only had one solid girlfriend, and it was in high school, Theo's never cared to have a relationship. Ever. He insists it's because there's only one Theo to go around, and it would hurt too many women's feelings if he was off the market.

I insist he's a dipshit.

He shakes his head. "Nah. You know me. One and done. Well, except after a workout."

He winks.

I snort. "Nice. As long as she knows she's sleeping with a slut--"

"Trust me," he interrupts with a smirk. "She knew exactly what she was getting out of the deal, and I even paid it forward. Twice." He stretches his arms over his head, walks toward the hall, and stops to look back at me. "We should do something, though. You. Me. Logan. Like old times."

"All right. I'm in."

"Good." He taps his knuckles on the hallway wall. "See you in a few."

7
ASHLYN

The light from Logan's window filters in through the blinds, casting streaks of dark and light lines across his sleeping face. He's changed so much over the years. But when he's like this, I can almost transport back in time to when we first met. When things weren't so complicated. When he wasn't so busy. When we went out on actual dates instead of scheduling quickies between classes.

I miss those days.

As if he can feel my stare, his eyelids open, and he gives me a sleepy smile.

"Morning," he croaks.

"Hey."

"What time is it?"

"A little after eight."

Tossing his forearm over his eyes, he lets out a long yawn and rolls onto his back.

"How'd you sleep?" I ask, sitting up and stretching my arms over my head.

"Good." He grabs my neck and pulls me down, stealing a

DON'T LET ME FALL

kiss and trailing kisses down my neck as his hand slips under his T-shirt and cups my bare breast. His eyes are half-closed, proving how much he had to drink last night and how tired he still is, even with the morning light filtering through the window.

With a soft moan, I flip my hair over one shoulder and straddle him as his phone dings with a text. He pauses his exploration and reaches for his iPhone on the nightstand. As he reads the message, his mouth quirks up with a smile. His attention darts to me, and he sets his phone face down on his bare chest, puts his hands on my hips, and gently pushes me off him.

"Hey, babe," he says, kissing me softly again, but his lips pull into a frown. "Give me one sec."

"Oh." I tug at the hem of his T-shirt I'd thrown on in the middle of the night and smile tightly, surprised he's putting our morning sexy time on hold. "Okay."

Distracted, he unlocks his phone, scans the message, glances back at me, and clears his throat. "It's work. Why don't you go down to the kitchen and make us some coffee? I'll be down in a few."

"Okay." I start to climb out of bed, but he grabs my hand and pulls me toward him, planting a slow kiss on my lips.

I smile against his mouth, and he murmurs, "Love you."

"Love you too."

The hardwood floor is cold against my bare feet as he lets me go. I climb out of his bed, head to the door, and pause near the hallway, turning to Logan again. "Cream and sugar like always?"

His gaze stays glued to his phone as he answers, "Just black today. Gotta stay cut for the team."

Okay, then.

I open his bedroom door and close it behind me with a

quiet click. It's still relatively early, at least for college students, so I don't bother to find my clothes. I step down the stairs and head to the kitchen.

It's funny how different the Taylor House feels during the day versus at night. It's nice. Almost homey. With exposed brick walls, dark hardwood floors, sleek chrome accents, and decorated in different shades of gray. The stairs hug the left-hand side near the front door, while the right is a giant entertainment room complete with a big-screen television, gaming console, and a worn leather couch looking like it's seen better days. On the far wall opposite the front door and tucked behind the stairs is the kitchen.

It's quiet. Nothing but the soft creak of the stairs as I head to the main floor. The scent of coffee guides me until I screech to a halt.

Colt's facing the window above the sink. The muscles along his back are etched into his perfect torso and flex as he brings a cup to his lips.

"You again," I blurt out and snap my mouth shut.

Realizing he isn't alone, he turns around and faces me.

"You again," he returns. The same soft gray sweats hang low on his hips as he smirks over the rim of his white coffee mug. Watching me. Peeling away whatever shred of clothing and decency I've shrouded myself in until I'm left bare with a simple look. My pulse quickens, and my palms grow sweaty, but I fist them at my sides.

With a huff, I ask, "Do you always walk around half-naked?"

His gaze slides from my head down to my bare legs, landing on my baby blue toenails. "Says the girl dressed in nothing but a T-shirt." He meets my face again. "I like it. Suits you."

"Thanks." I tug at the hem, grateful Logan's a tall dude, or else my ass would be hanging out while ignoring the blush I have no doubt is spreading across my face.

Get a grip, Ash.

"I'm Ashlyn, by the way," I announce. "I don't think we've formally met."

"Colt Thorne." He lifts his chin. "Nice to meet you, Ashlyn."

"You too." Rocking back on my heels, I fold my arms across my chest, debating whether or not running back to Logan's room is a smart idea. I paste another tight smile onto my face as I step further into the kitchen. "So…mind if I steal some coffee?"

Biting the inside of his cheek to contain his amusement, he challenges, "Still *thirsty?*"

Aaaand, I need to get out of here.

But running back to Logan's room doesn't exactly feel like an option. Not when Colt's looking at me like this. Like he's daring me to come closer. Like he can see how much I want to scurry away. Like I've intrigued him somehow, and I hate to admit it, but I'm not ready to back down. Not yet.

I roll my eyes, frustrated with myself as much as the guy in front of me, marching toward the same cabinet as the night before. The one where the orange juice cup was located. Unfortunately, it also happens to be behind Colt's muscular body, and the bastard doesn't bother to move aside as I approach him.

With his head cocked, he waits. Curious about what I'll do next.

My pulse thrums a little faster as I bump his shoulder with my own, refusing to back down. "Do you mind?"

He moves over a few inches, leaving barely enough room for me to open the cabinet door. I rise onto my tiptoes, blindly searching the second shelf for a mug while ignoring the twisted déjà vu overwhelming my senses.

Same mouthwatering scent. Same cocky smirk. Same gray sweatpants leaving little to the imagination. Or *a lot*, if the bulge is anything to go by.

With a huff, I motion to the second shelf. "Wanna help a girl out?"

The bastard doesn't bother to hide his dark chuckle from whatever innuendo I might've set him up with as he lifts the mug in his hand and offers it to me without a word.

"I think spit swapping with the orange juice earlier is enough sharing for one day," I snap.

"Then it looks like you'll have to wait for your caffeine intake." He tilts his head toward the running dishwasher beside the sink. "Your boyfriend forgot to do the dishes yesterday."

I glare back at him, unable to decide if I'm annoyed because I have no coffee or because he's clearly dissing on Logan even though, yeah, he's kind of got a point. Logan's always been a messy guy who prefers his mom or girlfriend––aka me––to clean up after him instead of doing the work himself. Don't get me wrong. Logan's an amazing guy, but we all have our flaws, and a lack of cleanliness is one of Logan's. The clean laundry spread across the end of his bed being a not-so-blissful reminder from yesterday.

Apparently, some things never change.

Lovely.

I don't realize how close we're standing until he looks down at me. The same arrogant amusement claims his handsome features over the rim of his stupid white mug as he takes another sip.

Clearly, I'm entertaining him.

And clearly, it's pissing me off.

My nostrils flare as a throat clears from the entrance to the kitchen, and my neck snaps in its direction.

Arms folded, Logan's gaze slides down my body, his expression hardening. "Why are you wearing my roommate's T-shirt?"

8

ASHLYN

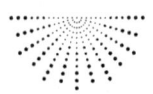

My face is on fire as I look down at the white T-shirt with LAU's black and red logo on the front of it. You know, the one covering my naked body. I turn to the roommate in question.

The bastard hides his smirk behind his mug, waving his opposite hand around the room as if to say, "Floor's all yours."

With a glare, I spin back toward Logan. "I didn't--"

"You know what?" Logan cuts me off. "I don't wanna get angry at you. We'll talk later." He turns on his heel, heading toward the front door.

I march after him, anxious to explain myself while frustration boils in my veins. Why didn't Colt tell me? Why is Logan refusing to let me explain myself? Why didn't I piece together I've never seen Logan wearing this shirt? I'd assumed it was his because I found it in his room. I'm not crazy for jumping to such a conclusion, am I? I didn't think so but based on the way Logan's ignoring me, I apparently have some explaining to do.

"Logan, wait!"

He shakes his head and grabs a jacket hanging on the coat rack next to the front door.

"Seriously, stop." I reach for his arm, but he tugs it away from me. "Where are you going?"

I know Logan. I know he's annoyed. Jealous. Angry. And when he gets this way, he doesn't listen. He needs space to cool down, or he'll never register a single word I say. But it doesn't stop me from grabbing his arm again.

"Seriously, Logan. I didn't know it was his shirt!"

With a glare, he spits, "So, what? It magically slid onto your naked body? What the hell, Ash? You serious?" His nostrils flare, and he takes a slow breath. "Shit. I'm sorry. I can't talk right now. I'm not in the right headspace."

I glance over my shoulder toward the kitchen and drop my voice low. "Can we please talk about this in private? Maybe in your room or something?"

He shakes his head again. "I gotta get to work."

"I thought you didn't work today?"

"Yeah? Well, now, I do. I'm covering the morning shift for Kendall. I was gonna drive you home, but now I'm frustrated, and I don't wanna say something I'll regret. I need to cool down. Can you call an Uber?"

"Logan," I grit out, desperate to explain myself. "It was in your room. I grabbed it from the pile of laundry on your bed."

"Babe--"

"It must've gotten mixed in with your stuff by mistake or something, but whatever you're insinuating is bullshit."

His nostrils flare, but he tries to keep his voice calm as he argues, "I'm not insinuating--"

"Then, you're not allowed to be mad at me."

"You're in my roommate's shirt," he snaps. "What else am I supposed to think, Ashlyn?"

"You know me, remember?" I plead. "What? You think I'm

going to fall into someone's bed when I've been nothing but faithful to you since freshman year? Are you seriously going to believe––"

His phone dings with another incoming text message, cutting me off.

Jaw tight, he shrugs out of my hold and pulls out his phone, scanning the message. He tucks it back into his pocket and mutters, "We'll talk later. I gotta get to work. Your clothes are still in my room, in case you feel like changing."

"Logan," I try again, but he opens the front door and says, "I'll call you later."

Then, he closes it in my face.

What. The. Hell?

Fuming, I march back into the kitchen where a still amused Colt is leaning against the stupid counter, continuing to sip his morning cup of coffee like everything's fan-freaking-tastic. It only pisses me off more.

I storm closer and shove him in the chest, but he barely budges an inch.

"What the hell is your problem?" I seethe.

He scans me up and down, making me somehow feel naked, when I know I'm still fully covered in his T-shirt.

His. Freaking. T-shirt.

I grit my teeth and fold my arms, two seconds from smacking the smirk off his face.

Once he's finished examining the way I look in his clothes, he returns, "I don't have a problem."

"Why didn't you tell me I was wearing your T-shirt? You could've told me last night or hell, maybe this morning," I spit.

His amusement dissipates as he sets the cup of coffee on the counter behind him. "It wasn't my job to tell you you're wearing my shirt. It was your boyfriend's."

I laugh, though there isn't any humor in it. "He *did* notice I was wearing your shirt. Why do you think I'm in the doghouse right now? You and I don't even know each other. Why would you--"

"I meant earlier," he growls, pushing himself away from the counter. He leans over me, his breath fanning across my cheeks as his upper lip curls in disgust. "He should've noticed before you walked out of his room. Before you came down the stairs. Before he recognized another guy was noticing you, and he didn't like it. So tell me this, Sunshine. Why didn't he notice you were wearing my shirt *before* you left his room?"

My response catches in my throat. I don't know what to say. Because even though I don't want to admit it, I know why he didn't say anything. He was distracted. He was texting someone from work. He was too busy to notice.

I don't have a chance to admit the truth out loud as Colt leans closer, keeping me hostage in his already familiar gaze.

"Want to know a secret, Sunshine?" His tongue darts out between his lips, and his gaze drops to my mouth, then flicks back to my eyes. "I would've noticed."

He walks away but pauses near the stairs. "And you're right. You and I don't know each other. But I'll let you keep the shirt. It looks good on you."

The corner cuts off my view as he disappears up the stairs.

9
COLT

"Come on, man. One more. You got it," I say, spotting Logan in the weight section at the gym. He's lying on the bench, and his chest heaves as he bends his arms one more time, making the 300 pounds his bitch.

Sweat beads across his forehead, but he extends his arms, puffs out his cheeks, and sets the bar back into its holding place with a metallic clang.

"Shit, I hate arm day," he groans.

I offer my hand and help him sit up.

With his elbows on his knees, he catches his breath, and I say, "You're doing good. You're benching about a hundred pounds more than you could in high school."

He laughs and puts his hands on top of his head, his breathing still staggered. "Yeah, 'cause I was a scrawny ass in high school."

"Not anymore, man. You're gonna show me up if I'm not careful."

"You should see me on the ice," he jokes. "You gonna come to any games?"

I shake my head and adjust the weights, adding a few more pounds specifically to watch Logan's shoulders deflate, and I answer, "Nah. Probably not."

"You should," he argues as we switch spots. I lay down on the bench, and he moves into position by my head to spot me.

Gripping the bar, I bend my elbows and shove the weight into the air as I grit out, "Not my thing anymore."

"At least come hang out on the ice with us. Just for fun," he clarifies. "You should be out there with me and Theo."

I do a few more reps and set the bar back into its position, sitting up and resting my elbows on my knees. "You mean I should be out there beating your ass?"

He laughs. "I think I can hold my own now."

"Oh, really?"

"Yeah. You should come practice with us. We'll see if you still got it."

I stand up and stretch my arms, shaking my head. "Yeah, I don't think so."

With a frown, he prods, "How are you doing? Other than the hockey part."

I know why he's asking. I know it's coming from a good place. I know I disconnected after the accident and pushed everyone away. But it doesn't make his question any easier.

"I'm all right," I lie.

"Yeah?"

"Yeah."

"You been home to see your family?"

I lift one shoulder. "Here and there."

"That's good, at least," he concedes, rubbing his hand along his sweaty hair.

We each do a few more reps, adjusting the weight when needed. Finally, I ask, "Are we gonna talk about your girlfriend in my shirt yet?"

Logan glares back at me but rolls his eyes. "Damn, man. Why'd you do it?"

I laugh dryly and raise my hands in defense. "I didn't do anything. Some of my laundry must've gotten mixed in yours when I changed your clothes from the washer to the dryer the other day. If you want to blame anyone for the mix-up, you can blame yourself."

The same familiar glare stays firmly in place as he exhales and grumbles, "You could've told her she was wearing your shirt."

"*You* could've told her she was wearing my shirt," I argue.

"I was…distracted."

"By what?"

"Other things," he deflects, though I have a feeling I already know.

"No offense, but I can't think of any other girls who would look better than your girlfriend in nothing but a T-shirt." I bite my lower lip and shake my head. "Damn, Logan. You're a lucky bastard."

"Watch it," he growls, but I know he isn't serious.

I take a step back, not bothering to hide my grin, as I surrender. "Just saying."

"She should've noticed it wasn't my shirt."

"*You* should've noticed it wasn't your shirt," I reiterate. "And you shouldn't have lost your shit like you did, either. It was a dick move."

His head hangs between his shoulders, and he pinches the bridge of his nose. "Yeah, man. I know. I was an ass."

"You were," I agree. "But I'm sure you'll find a way to make it up to her."

"I still think she's the one who should make it up to me." His mouth quirks up on one side.

"And I think you should get your head out of your ass and worship the girl, 'cause we both know you can't do better."

Offended, he shoves my shoulder. "Hey!"
"Just sayin'."
But he doesn't argue.
Because he knows I'm right.

10
ASHLYN

"Thanks again, Professor," I tell Professor Buchanan after class as I hoist the nylon strap of my backpack onto my shoulder and head toward the exit.

"Give me one minute, Ashlyn," he calls back to me.

I stop and step aside, leaving plenty of room between me and the door as the rest of the class files out of the room. Professor Buchanan is, hands down, one of the most attractive guys on campus. Obviously, he's off-limits to the students, but he's also one of the most eligible bachelors in the US, thanks to his off-campus job as the CEO of one of the most lucrative companies in the world. To prevent burnout, he decided to teach a couple classes on the side of his main career at his software company. When registration opened, the class filled up within thirty minutes, and almost every single one of the students was female.

I, however, needed the class for my degree.

Doesn't mean I don't enjoy the view, though.

But I also don't ogle him, which is why I think he favors me over most of the other students. Not tooting my own horn or anything.

As the rest of the class files out of the room, he rests his butt against his desk, propping himself up with his arms on either side. His white sleeves are rolled up to his elbows, showcasing his drool-worthy forearms, but I only take a quick peek before focusing on the last student as she leaves the room.

Once we're the only people left, I ask, "Is there a problem, Professor?"

"Not at all. I wanted to tell you I have a student who could use some tutoring. I thought you might be interested in helping him out. The hours you put into helping him will count toward your teaching program, and you'll be paid for your time."

"Oh?"

"He's a transfer student but needs some help in a few of his classes. His mother asked if I knew anyone patient enough to help him out. You came to mind. I thought it would be a good opportunity for you to brush up on your teaching skills."

"His mother?" I ask, surprised.

"She's friends with the dean. Look, I shouldn't be telling you this, but I think it's important you understand the situation." He glances toward the door and makes sure we're alone.

Stepping closer to his desk, I prod, "Go on."

"He had some trouble at his other school, and she called in a favor. Unfortunately, he's continued to struggle since the transfer."

"And he apparently needs a babysitter?" I can't help the sarcasm as it slips into my question, but seriously. This is college. If you don't have what it takes, you should find a different way to spend your time. And LAU? It isn't cheap. I have the student loans to attest to it. So, why is his mom sticking her nose in her son's business? And why is her son still here if he isn't interested in actually applying himself? It doesn't make any sense.

"He needs someone to help him focus," Professor Buchanan continues. "His mother thinks a tutor might be the thing to point him in the right direction, and since you're one of the most patient people I've ever met, I think you could be a good fit. You interested?"

I mean, no. But also, yes. I chew on the inside of my cheek and hike my backpack further onto my shoulder. "I can use the hours for the teaching program?"

He nods.

"And I'll get paid?" I clarify.

"Yes."

Ignoring the nagging voice in the back of my head telling me I'll regret this, I announce, "Fine. I'll do it."

"Perfect." He pushes himself up from the front of his desk and rounds the side of it, wiggling the mouse connected to his computer. Once the screen lights up, Professor Buchanan adds, "His name is Colt Thorne. I have his information right..." His long fingers click against his keyboard as he scans the computer screen. "Yes. Right here."

A buzzing in my ears drowns out the numbers as I register the name. Colt Thorne. Logan's new roommate and friend from high school.

And he needs a tutor?

And I already agreed to tutor him?

This can't be happening. For so many reasons. But most importantly, because Logan will throw a fit when he finds out. Especially after yesterday morning's incident.

This is bad.

This is very bad.

I've had four encounters with the guy, and each one has left me more confused and on edge than the previous one.

But I could use the money.

And the hours for my degree.

And we're both adults. It's not like I haven't tutored guys in the past.

It'll be fine.

Totally. Absolutely. Fine.

"There a problem, Ashlyn?" Professor Buchanan prods.

I blink slowly and clear my throat. "Nope. No problem."

"You sure? You look a little flushed."

I tuck my hair behind my ear and force a smile. "I'm fine. Can you give me Colt's number one more time, please?"

11
ASHLYN

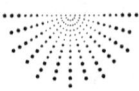

As Professor Buchanan rattles off Colt's phone number, I type it into my cell phone, promise to give Colt a call, and head to The Bean Scene. I'm desperate for coffee despite the fact it's almost two in the afternoon. But with the bomb Professor Buchanan threw at me, I could use something to clear my head. And nothing clears it more than coffee.

"Iced vanilla latte, please," I order, handing my credit card to the barista. "For Ashlyn."

She rings me up and gives my card back. "Coming right up."

I adjust my backpack on my shoulder, then pull out my phone, sending Colt a text while ignoring the way my heart rate picks up at the mere thought of him.

Keep it together, girl.

Me: Hey. This is Ashlyn. Professor Buchanan gave me your number and mentioned you could use a tutor?

"Ashlyn?" the barista calls.

I take the iced coffee from her and pull up my mom's number as I wait for Colt to text me back. I haven't spoken with my mom in weeks.

It rings a few times, and my call is sent to voicemail. I sigh, dragging my thumb along the screen as my contact history shines a blinding light on all the outgoing calls from me to my parents, along with how few they ever return. I guess it's not their fault they rarely keep their phones close by. Honestly, my dad doesn't even own one. They prefer to be one with the Earth and spend most of their time barefoot while polishing their crystals.

It would be fine...*if* they remembered they still have a daughter every once in a while.

I shove aside my disappointment and am about to tuck my phone back into my pocket when it rings. I jump in surprise, registering Colt's name flashing across the screen.

Crap.

A text is one thing. Another conversation when he's still on my shit list from yesterday? It's an entirely different and much more anxiety-inducing scenario. I suck down a quarter of my coffee and slide my thumb across the phone screen, releasing a slow breath.

"H-hello?" I answer.

"Hey, sorry. I hate texting unless it's for a hookup, and since we aren't hooking up, I figured a call would suffice."

Annoyed, I shift my cell from one ear to the other. "Alrighty, then. I'll be sure to keep it in mind in case I ever get a text from you."

He chuckles. "Depends on how good the first tutoring session is."

I roll my eyes. "I'm not sure if you remember, but I have a boyfriend, so I think we'll simply focus on the books. But thanks."

Another low chuckle. "I'll keep that in mind."

I take a sip of my coffee and clear my throat. "So, what classes do you need help with?"

"Depends on who you ask," he jokes.

"All right. Let's say we're asking your mother. Which classes does she think you need help with?"

"Ah, so you know about my mom, huh?" He doesn't sound mad, but I shouldn't have let it slip anyway.

Shit.

I dig my teeth into the inside of my cheek, regret pooling in the bottom of my stomach. "I assume you're in Buchanan's statistics class?"

"Yeah." His tone is sharper but almost detached, too, leaving me on edge and *so* ready to end this conversation as soon as possible.

"Okay," I murmur. "What if we start there?"

"Whatever you want, Sunshine."

There's the nickname again.

"When's a good time to meet?" I ask.

"I'm free tonight."

"All right."

"Want me to come by your place?"

The idea of Colt at my house sends a shiver racing down my spine, but I shove the feeling aside. Besides, if we're at Logan's place, it'll prove I have nothing to hide from him, and I'm already feeling guilty enough, thank you very much.

"Let's meet at your place instead," I counter.

There's a slight pause before Colt's gritty voice echoes through my phone. "See you then."

The call ends, and I stare at my call history once more, then press my mom's number. Again. It rings for another few seconds and goes to voicemail.

Of course, it does.

When the beep sounds, my voice is clipped as I say, "Hey,

Mom. It's me. Just wanted to see how you and Dad are doing. Call me back. Love you."

I tuck my phone back into my purse and head outside. The grass is still a dull yellow from winter, but the air is surprisingly warm as I walk down the path toward the parking lot.

I could've walked, and I probably will from now on. But with how temperamental the weather's been lately, I decided to play it safe. There's a dark path surrounded by grass, tall maple trees, and a few benches along the edge of it leading to the student parking area.

I pause on the path and lift my head toward the warm sun. I let it soak into my cheeks, praying it'll give me the strength to figure out what the hell I'm going to do with Logan. And Colt. And my screw-up from yesterday morning I've been avoiding. Oh, and let's not forget my parents and their lack of communication. It's nothing out of the ordinary, but still.

The questions swirl around my brain, refusing to go anywhere as I take another sip of my drink. When I open my eyes, I find a familiar face from yesterday morning.

My annoyance spikes.

"See you found your caffeine," Colt notes, motioning toward my iced latte.

"No thanks to you," I return.

He clutches at his heart. "Ouch. Seems someone's still prickly from yesterday."

"Seems someone's still unapologetic," I counter.

Head cocked, he tucks his hands into his front pockets. "And what would I have to apologize for?"

"For dragging me into a fight with my boyfriend."

He pulls out his phone and unlocks it, muttering, "We've already covered this."

Even more annoyed, I watch him type something into his cell, effectively avoiding me.

"You know, it's rude to use your phone when you're in the middle of a conversation," I huff.

With a quick glance up at me, he smiles, and my phone rings in my purse.

I dig it out and see his name on the screen. "Seriously?"

"You're a lot nicer on the phone," he returns as he lifts his phone to his ear.

"And yet you're just as annoying." I ignore his call, tuck the phone back into my purse, and slip off my backpack, digging into the pouch. "Which reminds me…"

I can feel him watching me as I rummage through my bag, but I ignore him. Like how I'm ignoring the dryness in my mouth and my fluttering pulse. It's like he knows how to shock my senses with nothing but a simple look or a cocky smirk.

It's…unnerving.

And irritating.

I don't like it.

"You know, it's rude to dig in your backpack when you're in the middle of a conversation," he points out, his tone laced with amusement, but I ignore that, too, collecting my defenses around me like a woman preparing for war.

"I have something for you," I mutter, pulling out his freshly washed T-shirt and offering it to him. "Here you go."

He stares at the piece of clothing for a beat too long and leans away from it. "Said you could keep it."

"I think I'm good. Thanks, though."

His gaze slides down my body, and his mouth ticks up on one side. "You sure? Don't get me wrong. I like the jeans and sweater look, but--"

"If I change my mind, I'll be sure to let you know."

He opens his mouth to say more when his attention

catches on something behind me. His mouth closes, and he takes the T-shirt from my hand, albeit grudgingly.

"See you tonight, Sunshine."

He walks past me, and I turn on my heel, watching him leave as another familiar face grabs my attention.

Logan's on the path, standing next to a girl, though his focus is on his roommate. They stare at each other as Colt approaches. And I watch, holding my breath. I don't know what I'm waiting for. What I'm expecting. But I can't help it.

Unfortunately, when Colt reaches Logan, they're too far away for me to hear what they're saying. Logan laughs, though, and shakes his head as Colt continues walking down the path with his hands in his front pockets like he's taking a stroll through the park instead of heading to his next class.

I take another sip of my coffee, more curious than I'd like to admit. Logan looks at me, says something to the girl beside him, and strides toward me.

"Hey," I greet him, trying to lighten the mood while still unsure where we stand after he left.

He avoids my gaze and stares at the guys throwing a frisbee on the grass off to his left. "Hey."

"You still mad at me?" I ask.

"Why were you talking to Colt?"

"We ran into each other."

He shakes his head as if he doesn't believe me. As if he's still hurting when he has no right to be.

"Why were you talking to another girl a second ago?" I counter, pointing to where he'd come from.

He tosses a quick glance over his shoulder to where he'd been standing, chatting with a random girl. And he knows I have a point.

With a sigh, he turns back to me. "You're right. If I can have an innocent conversation, so can you."

"Thank you."

"You're welcome," he grunts, but he's still avoiding my gaze. He's still sensitive. Still unsure. I can see it. Feel it. It's tainting the air around us, causing every exchange to be stilted and forced.

It sucks.

"Listen, I'm sorry." I let out a slow breath and touch his arm, dragging my hand along his tan skin and tangling our fingers together. He's wearing a red T-shirt, and I'm grateful for it. For the opportunity to touch him. Skin to skin. Because he needs the innocent intimacy almost as much as I do.

His muscles soften beneath my fingertips, but he stays quiet, waiting for my explanation.

"I know it sounds ridiculous," I start, "but I promise I found his shirt in your room and assumed it was yours."

He sighs and finally graces me with his attention, looking almost sheepish, closing a bit of the distance between us. "I believe you, baby."

"Finally," I quip, the tension slowly releasing from my shoulders as I take another sip of my coffee. "I want to make you dinner, though. I feel like the last few weeks have been crazy. I want to reconnect. When are you free?"

Lifting his hand, Logan cups my cheek and drags his thumb across my jaw. "You really are beautiful."

I roll my eyes. "That isn't an answer."

"Let's have dinner tonight."

"Tonight?" I cringe.

"What? You already have plans?"

"Buchanan got me a tutoring gig. It's with Colt, actually. I'm meeting him tonight."

"Colt?" he chokes out, wavering between being frustrated and butt hurt all over again. Like he can't believe it. Like he doesn't *want* to believe it.

"Look, it's not a thing, okay? So please don't make it one."

"First, I find you in my roommate's shirt, then I see you talking to him on the quad, and now you're tutoring him?"

"Logan--"

He shakes his head, pinching the bridge of his nose. "You can't be serious, Ash."

"You have no right to be jealous."

"No right?" He scoffs. "Do I need to list off the shit again?"

"No. You don't." Defeated, my shoulders hunch, and I rub my hand over my face. "But I'm not going to turn down a tutoring opportunity simply because you don't trust me."

He flinches away from me, surprised. "You think I don't trust you?"

"I think you should use this opportunity to prove you trust me. It's only a tutoring gig, Logan." Gently, I tug at the collar of his T-shirt, fisting the material in my hand in hopes he'll look at me. When he does, I smile. "Let me make it up to you, though. For the shirt debacle *and* the tutoring gig. How 'bout tomorrow night? I'll make spaghetti. Your favorite."

He frowns. "Can't. I'm going out with the guys."

"How about the night after?" I offer. "You can come to my place, maybe bring a bottle of wine? I'll ask my roommates to make themselves scarce. It could be fun."

"No roommates, huh?" He grabs my hip and pulls me closer to him. "So we'd have some privacy?"

"Yes." I bat my lashes and peek up at him. "A lack of privacy has never stopped you before, but...."--he laughs--"Let me make it up to you."

"And how, exactly, do you plan to make it up to me?" he asks, his eyes sparking with interest.

I bite my bottom lip and shrug. "I think we both know how creative I can be when the occasion calls for it."

With another dark chuckle, he leans down and kisses me. It's hot and hungry and *so* not appropriate for the middle of campus, but I tilt my head up and let him. Because he needs this. This confirmation we're okay.

And so do I.

I need us to be okay.

His phone vibrates in his pocket, bringing him back to reality. He softens the kiss and mutters against my lips, "See you later. I gotta get to class."

I smile back at him. "Sure."

12
COLT

The house is empty. Not sure if it's a good thing or not. Ash should be here any minute. And despite my own rules about not touching something not belonging to me, I have to admit, she *is* tempting.

There's a soft knock against the front door, and I know it's Ash without even looking. I'd know it was her even if we didn't have plans tonight. It's a quiet knock. Unobtrusive. Almost shy, if knocks can sound that way.

My mouth quirks up on one side, and I open the door, bracing myself for another night of banter I can't help but crave. She's the most interesting thing I've encountered since my life went to shit, and I'm starting to look forward to our conversations more than I'd like to admit.

"Um, hi," Ashlyn greets me as I open the door. Her thumb is hooked beneath her backpack's dark nylon strap on her shoulder, and her hair is pulled into a high, messy ponytail. So effortlessly sexy.

The fact she has no idea still blows my mind.

I scratch at my jaw and step aside. "Hey. Come on in."

"Thanks."

The scent of vanilla tickles my nostrils and makes my mouth water when she slips past me, and I close the door behind her.

She's less salty than she was in the quad earlier. More shy, like her knock. Her blue gaze flitters around the room, refusing to land on me or anything else for more than a second before darting to the next object. I shouldn't like watching her squirm--but I do.

"It's quiet in here," she notes, looking around the empty family room and kitchen.

I nod. "Yeah. Most of the guys are at the rink, getting in another practice."

"Got it." She nods and peeks at me. "Do you skate? Or play, or...?"

"No."

"Really?" She looks me up and down, surprised.

"That a problem?"

"I guess I assumed..." Her voice trails off, and she bites her lower lip.

"Assumed what? I play hockey?"

"You have the vibe, I guess."

"What kind of vibe?"

"You know, the cocky, hot, competitive, alpha hockey player kind of vibe. All you guys have it."

"Hot, huh?"

Her lips pull into a thin line. "You're right. I don't know what I was thinking. So, where do you want me to set up?"

I almost suggest my bedroom to see her reaction, but I motion to the kitchen on the opposite side of the house. "What about the kitchen table?"

"Sounds good." Her tennis shoes squeak softly against the hardwood floor as she walks to the kitchen, slips off her backpack, and pulls out a laptop, binder, and a couple of textbooks, spreading them across the table. "So...statistics, right?"

"Sure."

"Sure?" She looks up at me, confused. "Should we be studying something else? I thought you said––"

"Stats is fine." I sit down in the chair next to her and wait. She's got the whole sexy librarian thing going for her, and I'm here for it.

"Ooookay." She opens her stats textbook, slams it closed, and turns to me like she can't help herself. "Can I ask you something?"

"Sure."

"What are you going to school for?"

Hooking my hands behind my head, I lean back in my chair and reply, "Undeclared."

Her eyes dim with disappointment, and it hits a little too close to home, though I refuse to acknowledge why. Leaning forward, I rest my elbows against the table––ready to deflect the attention away from me––and rub my hands together, asking, "You?"

A bit of the brightness returns to her blue eyes. "Elementary education, actually."

"Which is why you're a tutor," I surmise.

"Exactly. You'd be surprised how many college students like to act like kindergarteners."

I laugh, surprising both of us. "I bet the similarities are uncanny."

"You have no idea." She picks up her pen and clicks the top of it with her thumb. "So, what brought you to LAU? Especially when it's clear you don't want to be here."

"You think I don't want to be here?"

She opens her mouth but closes it and bites her lower lip while shifting in her chair like she's stepped in dog shit, and I think I know why.

"Oh, you mean because I said I'm undeclared, and you know my mom called up her buddy, the dean, and enrolled me at LAU after I got kicked out of my other school? Is that what you're talking about?"

"I didn't mean––"

"I know what you meant."

She pauses, clicking the top of her pen a few more times. "I guess I'm surprised. You seem like someone who wouldn't be afraid to go after what they want, yet here you are. Undeclared and clearly with no interest in school."

Leaning back in my chair again, I fold my arms and say, "You're right."

She blinks. Surprised by my admission. "Did you just admit I'm right?"

"Are you not usually right?" I counter.

"No, I'm almost always right, but you don't seem like someone who concedes easily."

"I'm not afraid to call it like it is."

"Well, if that's the case, and you're fully aware you have no interest in school, what are you doing here?"

It's a good question. One I've been asking myself for weeks. Years, actually. Not since I got kicked out of Dixie Tech, but before. Before everything went to shit.

When I had my entire life laid out for me. When I knew what I wanted to do and who I wanted to be.

If only the answer was simple. But it isn't. It's messed up. Like my head. Like my past.

"You really don't know who I am?" I ask, my tone sharper than I intend.

She shakes her head. "Why would I?"

"You're dating Logan."

"So?"

"I figured he would've told you."

"Told me what?" she whispers.

I sit up again and rest my elbows on the table, unable to get comfortable in this stupid chair. Then again, maybe it's the conversation making me on edge.

I shove the thought aside and clarify, "About my dad and why I don't play hockey anymore."

"So you *did* play?"

"Cocky, hot, and competitive. Your words, not mine," I remind her with a smirk. "I was good too."

"I believe it," she admits with the same shy smile taunting me like a carrot to a horse. "Why'd you stop?"

"Guess I learned it's not all it's cracked up to be."

"And your parents? They were okay with it?"

It's an innocent question, but the answer isn't quite as simple.

"My dad died my senior year of high school," I tell her numbly.

Her lips part, releasing a tiny gasp as the pen slips from her fingers and clatters onto the table. She recovers quickly and looks down at her closed laptop, probably trying to think of the right thing to say.

It's funny, though. There is no right thing to say. If there was, I would've heard it by now. But no *I'm sorry*, or *my condolences*, or *he's in a better place*, or *give it time, you'll feel better soon*––none of it has ever done shit to make me feel better.

"I'm sorry," she murmurs a few seconds later.

Ah, so she went with the classic choice. Interesting. I would've expected something a little more unique, but I guess I can't blame her since I caught her off guard and all.

The same familiar numbness spreads through my chest as I answer, "Not your fault."

"Doesn't mean I can't be sorry it happened."

I nod but stay quiet.

She wipes beneath her nose with her index finger and sniffs softly. "Seriously. It sucks donkey balls."

I laugh, surprised. There's the unique answer I'd been expecting. "Yeah, Ash. It does suck donkey balls."

"What about your mom? How's she?"

"She's good, I guess. It would probably help if I got my head out of my ass, but the rest of my siblings are doing all right, so at least that's something."

She smiles and puts her hand on mine, squeezing softly. Her touch surprises me, but I try not to show it as she murmurs, "I don't think you're doing too bad, Colt."

I look down at where she's touching me. There are so many things I could do with her touch. So many places I could take her if she weren't dating Logan. So many things I could do right now, if only...

I shake off the thought and pull my hand away from hers.

With the same shy smile, she tucks a few strands of hair that've fallen out of her ponytail behind her ear. "So...where are your siblings?"

"My oldest brother's going to school to become a doctor, and my other brother's in the military."

"A bunch of boys, then? Must've been fun for your mom."

"I have a little sister too. Blakely," I clarify. "She's going to school for sports medicine at LAU this fall."

Her smile brightens. She's probably grateful for the subject change. Then again, so am I. Who wants to talk about a dead parent during a study session?

"Exciting," she replies.

"Yeah."

"You guys sound like you're all pretty close."

"I guess so. I could probably hit up a few more Sunday brunches since I'm closer now, but we'll see. How about you? Do you have any siblings?" I ask.

"Nope." She shrugs. "Just me."

"Ah, an only child, huh?"

"Yup. It's like I'm the golden child and the black sheep all rolled into one. Very exciting stuff."

I laugh. "Sounds like it. Are you close with your parents?"

Her smile falls for a second, but she pastes another one on her face. This one is less real. More forced.

"You don't have to--"

"They're free spirits, you know?" she interrupts. "Like... we're good. And they love me, and I love them. But they didn't exactly sign up for parenting if you know what I mean. I think they were pretty happy when I finally graduated, and they didn't have to be on the parenting train twenty-four-seven."

Shit. It sucks. But I can't tell her that.

I want to touch her hand. To comfort her for having shitty parents even though it isn't my job. But the tiny flicker of disappointment when I mentioned them? It fucking stung.

"Are you from around here?" I ask, shifting in my chair to be closer to her.

She shakes her head. "No, actually. My parents live in Maine."

"You grew up there?"

"Yup. Did you know it's legal to grow your own marijuana there?" My eyes widen, and I choke back my laugh as she continues. "Yup. When I say they're free spirits, I mean they're *free spirits*."

I laugh, surprised by her openness. "Why'd you choose to go to LAU, then?"

"My favorite teacher in elementary school, Mrs. Mock, graduated from LAU and was all about school spirit. Her classroom was littered with black, red, and white LAU memorabilia hanging on every single wall. She would even grade our papers with an LAU marker and would pass out stickers with the mascot on them. I guess it kind of stuck."

"So, you moved across the country and away from everyone you knew because you looked up to your teacher?"

"Damn straight, I did," she replies. "And it was the best decision I could've made. I seriously love LAU."

"Really?"

"Uh, yeah." She nudges her shoulder against mine. "It's the greatest school ever. Don't get me wrong. Moving was rough, but I'd felt alone for so long, I think I was ready for a new start. A chance to do something on my own," she adds, lost in the memory. She shrugs one shoulder. "Then, I met my roommates, who are awesome, and I met Logan during one of my classes. He asked me out and swept me off my feet. And the rest, as they say, is history."

"Logan swept you off your feet?"

Doodling a flower on the edge of her notebook, she avoids my gaze and mumbles, "Why are you surprised?"

"Didn't know he had it in him. Is he still mad at you? For the whole T-shirt thing?"

She peeks up at me, a slight blush kissing her cheeks as she looks back at the dark blue pen in her hand. "Not anymore. I promised I'd make it up to him, so…"

"So, I need to buy some noise-canceling headphones. Got it," I joke, ignoring the swell of jealousy hitting out of nowhere.

"Colt!" She smacks my shoulder, her face brightening with embarrassment.

"I meant because of Logan," I argue. "The guy sounds like a dying moose when he's having sex. Please tell me it's not a turn-on."

Her jaw drops, her eyes crinkle in the corners, and she drops her head to her hands, laughing harder than I've ever seen. And I like it. That I could make her smile. That I could turn her frown upside down. I like it a lot. Her face turns redder and redder as she peeks at me between her fingers,

DON'T LET ME FALL

too shocked to even catch her breath. "I. Cannot. Believe you said that!"

"But am I wrong?" I challenge.

Again, she shakes her head, refusing to look at me. A muttered, "no comment," sneaks its way between her palms. Then, she wipes at the tears beneath her eyes from laughing so hard and looks up at me.

I like her laugh. It's sweet. Light. And somehow manages to ease the ache in my chest from our earlier conversation. I wanna grab hold of it with both hands. Maybe record it and save it for a rainy day. For when it's the anniversary of my dad's death or something.

"So. How long have you known Logan?" she asks, calming down.

"Forever. We were next-door neighbors growing up. Played on the same hockey team. Did everything together."

"How come I hadn't heard of you?"

"Some shit went down right before graduation, and I kind of fell off the face of the earth, I guess."

"Oh. I'm sorry."

"It's all good," I lie. "But yeah. Logan's a good guy most of the time."

"He is," she agrees. "Most of the time."

And for some reason, it bugs me. Because he *isn't* a good guy when it comes to her. Not that I've seen, anyway. He's sneaking around behind her back, and she has no idea. She's not like other girls. She's too sweet. Too innocent to understand the kind of guy she's getting with Logan. Maybe it's because of her shitty parents and her need to cling to anyone who gives her the time of day. Regardless, it pisses me off.

"Sometimes, I have to knock him down a peg or two," I add as I fend off my frustration. "And since we went to different colleges initially, it seems Theo forgot to do it while I was away."

"What do you mean? You're going to knock Logan down a few pegs now that you're back?"

"Maybe."

She smiles, pressing the edge of her pen against her bottom lip as she eyes me curiously. "And how will you do it?"

My attention drops to her mouth. "Depends on my mood."

"And right now?" she whispers, nibbling on the back of her pen. "What's your mood telling you?"

Fuck.

I lean away from her, putting some distance between us as I open my laptop. "It's telling me we should probably get started on the assignment."

Sucking her lips between her teeth, she nods and sets the pen on her notebook, reaching for her own laptop like it's a lifeline. "You're right. Once practice ends and the guys get home, I'm sure paying attention to li'l ol' me will be a bit more difficult."

Doubt it, I think to myself, but I don't reply.

"Which assignment do you need help with? If you're not sure, I can always help you look up your grade. Buchanan's pretty good about posting assignment grades through the student portal. I can show you if you'd like."

"Yeah, I have no idea how to sign in to the portal."

"Seriously?"

I shrug.

Lips pursed, she leans closer. "Let me show you."

Her breast brushes against my bicep as she takes the lead and guides me through the online portal on my laptop.

Stealing another glance her way, I watch her straight, white teeth dig into her lower lip. She rolls her eyes and looks at me. "Dude. A zero? Seriously? You didn't even turn the assignment in?"

I shrug again but don't deny it.

I'm not here because I want to be.

Scratch that. I'm at this table, sitting next to a hot girl because I want to be, but I'm not going to *college* because I want to. I'm doing it because my mom begged me to, and I don't want to see the look of disappointment in her eyes again. Not after my dad's accident. Not after the part I played in it.

But attending college and graduating from college are two different things. The latter of which I'm not sure I have the willpower to achieve. Not when I know I don't deserve it.

"All right, mister," Ash says, settling back into her chair, picking up her blue pen, and clicking its back with a bit more zealousness. "Let's see if we can catch you up on expected values. Let's turn to page 103."

And even though I already know this shit, I listen, mesmerized by the lilt in her voice and the way her eyes light up as she explains everything in the chapter, making my cock harder than ever beneath the kitchen table in her boyfriend's house.

I'm screwed.

13
COLT

SeaBird's the only bar close to campus. Normally, I'd bitch about it, but the place is actually pretty sick. There's a stage at the back for live music, a bar lined with every alcohol choice a guy could ask for, and it's packed with students from school.

Who needs Tinder when there's a place like this? And after a long-ass, tortuous tutoring session with a girl who's off the market, I need to get laid now more than ever.

Logan drags out a barstool from under the counter and collapses onto it while Theo flanks his opposite side. I take the last seat available as a pretty bartender in her thirties takes our orders.

Once we've been served, Logan says, "All right, man, I gotta know. Since when do you need a tutor? You graduated at the top of our class."

"Guess I lost my touch," I mutter.

"You sure?"

I turn on my chair and tilt my head. "What else would it be?"

"Just wanna make sure you're okay," he lies, his attention

darting from me to a pair of girls in short skirts grinding against each other on the dance floor.

I scoff into my glass and give them my back. "Or maybe you're asking because your girlfriend's my tutor? I didn't exactly plan it, man," I clarify with a dry laugh. "But it's been amusing to watch you squirm."

Annoyed, Logan turns back to me, asks, "Were you always this much of a dick?" and presses his beer bottle to his lips.

Personally, I prefer tap, but who am I to judge?

Theo laughs beside Logan. "Colt's always been a dick, and you know it. He hits on anything with boobs."

I bark out my laughter and shake my head. "Come on. Not *anything*. I do have *some* standards."

"Guess I wondered if the last few years would've changed anything," Logan mutters into his drink. "Apparently not."

"You know me," I return, my tone dripping with sarcasm as I gulp down some of my beverage.

"Give him a break, Logan," Theo interrupts. "Buchanan set Ash up with Colt for tutoring. Colt didn't have anything to do with it. And even if he did, Colt's messing with you. You know he wouldn't cross the line."

Logan's gaze shifts from Theo to me. Anxious. Frustrated. On edge.

Theo's right. I wouldn't. I might like messing with Logan, but I'm not *that* much of an ass.

"But Ashlyn?" Logan argues, unconvinced. "Come on, man. She's special."

"No offense, but I heard you screwing a different girl every night before Ashlyn showed up at the party last week."

His knuckles turn white as he throttles the beer bottle in his hand. "That's between Ash and me."

"And every other girl you've been with," I remind him.

"Stay away from her, all right?" he orders.

I laugh, biting back my frustration no matter how satisfying it is seeing me getting under his skin. "And why should I?"

"Because she's a good girl who wants a relationship and shit, and since you haven't had a real one since high school, you're not exactly her type. She deserves some respect."

"And you think cheating on her shows respect?" I challenge. "Tell me...does she know?"

"It's between me and her."

Theo's hand slams against the bar, cutting us off. "All right, guys. Enough. I'm here to get buzzed, not listen to pointless drama when we both know it doesn't matter. Colt wouldn't stab you in the back, and Ash is head over heels for you. End of story." He turns to Logan and narrows his gaze. "But listen carefully. You don't need to worry, but you do need to start treating her better. Ash is one of the nicest girls on campus, and despite you and your bigass head, you *are* replaceable to her. She could have any guy she wants, including Colt, and I don't care what the bro code says. If you screw up, she's free game. Me. Graves. Depp. Colt," he adds. "She can have anyone she picks. And it'll be on you. Now, let's order another round and end this pissing contest." He taps his knuckles on the dark, polished bar top and waves the bartender over, ordering another round for everyone.

We shoot the shit for another thirty minutes or so, reminiscing about old times and upcoming games, when one of the waitresses starts arguing with a customer. The guy's back is to me, but he's big and is towering over a pretty blonde who looks like she's seconds from crying.

"Shit," Theo mutters when he sees what's going on.

"What's the problem?" I ask. The tall guy shifts slightly, and I recognize him.

Shorty.

One of my roommates who plays on the hockey team with Theo and Logan.

Watching the shitshow with wary eyes, Theo mutters, "Shorty and his ex are going at it again."

"She caught Shorty cheating on her, so she ended things," Logan explains to me, his gaze still glued to the drama unfolding.

"Which is why we don't cheat," Theo reminds Logan, adding, "But Shorty's a possessive motherfucker and doesn't want to let her go."

Shorty grabs his ex's arm and tugs her closer to him like she's nothing but a rag doll, and she winces in pain.

"Shit," Theo mutters under his breath and sets his drink down, ready to get up.

"Stay here," I growl. "I'll be right back."

"Colt‑‑"

"I'll be fine." Pushing myself up, I walk toward them and call out, "Hey, Shorty. Is there a problem?"

Shorty lets the girl go and rubs his hand against his jeans as if he's been caught red-handed.

Meanwhile, the girl's eyes widen in surprise, and she wipes at her tear-stained cheeks. "There's no problem‑‑"

"Hey, man." Shorty slaps his big sausage hand against mine, cutting the waitress off. We haven't talked much. But I've seen him around the house. He's even come to the gym with Theo and me a time or two. But he's more of the strong, silent type, and right now isn't any different.

"How you been?" I ask.

His attention shifts to the waitress, and his jaw tightens. "Kinda busy right now."

"I can see. Thought you might wanna cool down and get a drink with the guys and me." I tilt my head toward the bar where Logan and Theo are watching. Waiting. And despite the shit going on with Logan and me, I know they'll both have my back if I need it.

I wait for Shorty to take the bait, but he only shakes his

head. "Maybe later. Unfortunately, you're kind of interrupting me and my girl here."

"I'm not your girl," she seethes, hugging the black tray to her chest while looking...scared. It only pisses me off more.

Stepping closer, I place myself between them and tilt my head up. The guy has at least fifty extra pounds on me and a few inches too. But if anything, it's to my advantage. Because he's underestimating me. What I can do. How I was raised. He thinks he can get away with pushing a girl around, but he doesn't know me, and he doesn't know I'm *this* close to slamming my glass against his skull if he dares to touch her again.

"She's right, you know," I tell him. "She's not your girl. And she doesn't want your hands on her. I suggest you give her some space, and if, for some reason, she changes her mind and decides you're worth her time, she'll reach out. All right, man?"

His nostrils flare, the vein in his forehead throbbing as he glares down at me. Someone flanks my right side.

"Hey, Shorty," Theo says. "Logan and I are heading home. Let me give you a ride, yeah?"

Shorty's attention shifts from me, to his ex, to Theo, then to Logan, who's closing out our tabs at the counter as he weighs his options. When he realizes he has none, he points one of his sausage fingers at the waitress and growls, "We'll talk later."

"It won't be necessary," she spits back at Shorty, her features so sharp they could cut glass.

Gotta hand it to her. She's ballsy.

But he ignores her and turns around, his steroid-induced muscles bulging as he walks outside.

There's an awkward silence combating the music filtering through the speakers. It leaves the waitress and me in some weird standoff, so I take a step away from her, ready to get the hell out of here.

"Have a good night," I mutter.

"Wait," she calls before I can take another step.

I pause.

She peeks up at me and smiles tightly. "Sorry about that."

"What? No thank you?" I joke.

She rolls her watery eyes and continues to hug the tray to her chest. "Thank you."

"You're welcome."

She's cute in a sex kitten kind of way. With dark makeup and multiple piercings along the shell of her ear. A few tattoos are scattered on her exposed arms too. Big ones. The girl screams broken wet dream with a side of daddy issues louder than a siren.

And I don't have time for that shit.

"Have a good night," I offer, turning back to the bar lining the wall.

"Wait," she repeats.

I face her again.

"Can I...I dunno? Maybe take you out or something? As friends," she clarifies. "My treat."

My grip is tight as I squeeze the back of my neck, unsure what the hell I'm supposed to say. I don't want to go out with her. Which is messed up because I *should* want to go out with her. I should want to push her up against the nearest wall and fuck her. I should want to see how many tattoos are hiding beneath her black tank top and jean shorts. I should want a lot of things, but I don't. Not with her. And it has nothing to do with being her ex's roommate and everything to do with a certain blonde tutor who doesn't belong to me.

"What's your number?" she asks. "I'll text you."

With a sigh, I rattle off my phone number. She types it into her cell and slips it into the front pocket of her black apron wrapped around her waist.

"Thanks," she repeats with a smile.

I nod and head back to the bar, surprised when I find Theo sitting on the same barstool.

"You know you just put a target on our backs," he mutters as I collapse onto the one next to him.

"He was grabbing her."

"You can't be everyone's hero," he reminds me.

I gulp down the rest of my beer and set it on the counter, hating how I can feel his words as if they're a solid blow to my stomach. He's right. I know he is. But when you're the villain in your own story, it's hard to stop yourself from fighting for the opposite in someone else's. Even if it's only for a minute.

Swallowing back the bile in my throat, I drag my finger along the rim of the now-empty glass and mutter, "Yeah. I know."

14
ASHLYN

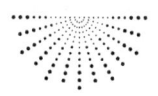

"You gonna wake up before noon?" I ask the lump on Mia's bed.

She groans and rolls over, shoving her sleeping mask onto her forehead, though she doesn't bother to open her eyes. "What time is it?"

"11:45."

"I didn't get home until after two."

"I know." Her second-hand mattress feels like lumpy mashed potatoes as I sit on the edge of it.

How does she even sleep on this thing?

I smooth down a bit of her black and pink comforter with my hand and add, "But you told me to wake you up before noon, and since it's before noon, I'm doing my best friend duties."

"Always a peach," she mutters, peeking one eye open to look at me. "Where's Kate?"

"At her class already. How was work?"

"Fine, I guess," she croaks, rubbing beneath her black-smudged eyes.

A dark ring wraps around her wrist, and I reach for it. "Dude. What's this?"

Confused, she blinks slowly and looks at her bruised forearm.

"Who grabbed you?" I demand. "And did Chuck or Ashton see it?"

Chuck and Ashton are two of the guys who work at SeaBird. They pour drinks, handle the books, and toss out the trash, both the inanimate and scummy ones with penises who like to manhandle women. Apparently, they missed some yesterday.

"They didn't see," Mia mutters, dropping her hand back to the bed. It lands with a soft thump. "Shorty stopped by SeaBird again."

"Mia, I told you to tell Chuck--"

"I know! I know I need to tell my boss about my shitty ex, but I don't want to rock the boat."

"I don't care if you don't want to rock the boat. You need to be safe, Mia."

"I know. And I was," she argues.

I scoff and motion to her bruised arm. "Do I look stupid to you?"

"A guy intervened, all right?"

"A guy?" I ask.

"Yeah. He stood up for me and told Shorty to leave."

"Who is he?"

"I didn't get his name, but I did get his number. He was super cute too. Dark eyes. Kind of edgy. Totally my type but still a gentleman."

"So, not your type then," I point out.

"Ash," she whines, pushing herself to a seated position.

But she knows I have a point. The girl attracts bad boys like a flower does bumble bees. Except hers aren't as sweet, and they do a lot more than sting when they're bothered.

I take in a deep breath through my nose and blow it out through my mouth. "Sorry. I'll be nice. But I hate how Shorty hurts you like this."

"I know." She bites her lip and looks down at the black and pink comforter, picking at a few non-existent pieces of lint. "I guess you can blame the daddy issues, right? You know, for my shitty taste in men."

"Mia," I breathe out.

But I don't know what to say. Anytime Mia mentions her dad, things get…awkward. Not only for her but also for me. I mean, what am I supposed to say? Her dad was murdered a few years ago. It was before we met during our freshman year at LAU, but it's easy to see time hasn't exactly made up for her loss. The girl's broken when it comes to men. Her perspective is…skewed, I guess. Like she feels unlovable. Like she isn't enough. Like she knows whoever she ends up with will always choose someone or some*thing* over her. Like her dad did with drugs and wound up in a ditch somewhere after he took money from a shady loan shark and couldn't pay it back.

I still remember when it hit the news.

It was so messed up.

I never expected to become friends with the guy's daughter.

"Sorry," she mutters, resting her back against the headboard and looking at the ceiling.

"Don't be." I grab her hand and squeeze softly as I fully join her on the bed. Matching her stance, I rest my back against the headboard and stretch my legs out in front of us. "You're allowed to bring him up, Mia."

"Not without receiving looks of pity," she mumbles under her breath, shaking her head. "Anywho, I'm gonna hit the gym. Want to come?"

"Sure. But first, I wanted to talk to you about tonight."

Her brows pinch, and her head rolls toward me. "What about it?"

"I invited Logan over…"

"So, you want me to make myself scarce?" she assumes.

With a grimace, I nod. "I already talked to Kate. She's gonna stay at her parents' house. But I'm sorry--"

"Don't be. Maybe I can convince *Mystery Man* to let me take him out for a drink tonight. You know, for standing up to Shorty yesterday."

My gaze narrows. "And he's a good guy?"

"Yes. He's a good guy. My radar isn't *that* broken, thank you very much."

"Debatable," I mutter. She laughs and shoves my shoulder. "Gee, thanks for the vote of confidence, Ash. Now get outta here. I'm going to text Mystery Man and change into some workout clothes so we can hit up the gym."

"All right. And, Mia?"

"Yeah?"

"Thanks."

"For what?" she asks.

"For supporting me and Logan even when I know you aren't his biggest fan."

Her lips purse, then she mutters, "You're welcome."

"As for Shorty--"

With her hand in the air, she says, "I don't want another lecture, Ash."

"I'm not going to give you one. I'm just saying…maybe if he sees you with someone else, he'll finally take the hint and leave you alone. And if you say Mystery Man seems like a good guy, I'm rooting for you."

She chews on the pad of her thumb, considering my comment. Her mouth stretches into a smile. A real one reaching her eyes. And I soak it in. Because the sight's rare. Ever since she met Shorty, things have been…hard. Like he'd been sucking all the light out of her, leaving nothing but a shell of my best friend behind. And the girl in front of me with the smile? I could use some more of her. And I know Mia could too.

"Thanks," she replies a few seconds later. "I think I might be rooting for us too. Now get out of here." She grabs her pillow and tosses it at me. "I gotta work up the nerve to send him a text."

"I'll meet you in the kitchen."

"Okay."

I glance over my shoulder one more time as I leave and catch Mia pulling out her phone, letting out a slow breath.

You got this, Mia.

Speaking of relationships. I pull out my phone from my back pocket and dial my mom's number. It rings a few times, then goes to voicemail.

Surprise, surprise.

Frustrated, I open the messaging app and type a text to my mom.

Me: Hey. Long time no talk. How are you guys doing?

Mom: Hey, honey! Sorry I didn't answer. Dad and I are at the crystal shop. Then we're gonna go on a little journey tonight. We'll call you later. Love you!

Shoving aside my disappointment, I reply.

Me: Have fun.

15

ASHLYN

Rubbing my lips together in the mirror, I run my fingers through my long, wavy hair one more time and smooth out the white dress wrapped around my body. I went for innocent today. Not sure if Logan will like it or not, but he's always been a sucker for the girl-next-door look, and I need this. A reminder of why we're good together. A solid night without fighting or feeling like I'm alone in the room with him. A night to shove aside the memory of my tutoring session with Colt and the ease I felt when I was around him.

I need it now more than ever.

The scent of garlic and tomatoes wafts from the kitchen, making our entire townhouse smell like an Italian restaurant. Maybe it was a bad idea to wear white when I plan on eating spaghetti, but I'm hoping it's worth the risk.

My stomach grumbles when a loud knock echoes from the front door and Mia yells, "Shit! I'm not ready!"

"It might be Logan," I call back, giving myself one more look in the mirror, heading out of the bathroom to answer the door.

"If it's my date, will you tell him I'll be there in a few?" she asks as I pass her bedroom door.

I give her a thumbs-up, push my hair over one shoulder, and answer the door.

"Hey, sorry––" My voice catches in my throat when I see him.

Colt.

He's in a dark brown leather jacket, dark jeans, and a white T-shirt, looking like every girl's fantasy as his gaze connects with mine.

"What are you doing here?" I ask.

But before he has a chance to respond, it hits me.

"A-are you here to pick up Mia?" Surprised by the jealousy churning in my lower stomach, I shake my head and add, "Nope. Nevermind. It's none of my business," I remind myself. "Let me, um…" I hook my thumb over my shoulder, motioning to the hallway behind me leading to our bedrooms, and turn around, ready to get the hell out of here.

I don't even have the chance to take a step when Colt grabs my arm and pulls me against him. My breath hitches as the warmth from his chest kisses my spine, sending heat and goosebumps along every inch of my skin. He hasn't touched me like this. Not ever. And I hate how close I am to melting into him. How weak my knees feel. How alert the butterflies are in my stomach.

It's… I shake my head and try to think straight. But I can't. Not when he's this close. Not when he's touching me. Not when Mia could walk out of her room any second and see me in the arms of someone who isn't Logan.

With my back still pressed to his front, Colt leans down, and his breath brushes the shell of my ear. "I like your dress, Sunshine."

My dress?

I look down at the white fabric stretched across my chest

and down my stomach. Hell, it barely reaches mid-thigh. But with the way he's towering over me, Colt can probably see the same sliver of cleavage I can from this angle. He can probably feel the way my breathing is staggered from his simple touch. The way I feel exposed. Like when he airdropped his phone number before he even knew my name. Like when we spoke with the orange juice. Like the time he saw me in his T-shirt and refused to tell me. Like our tutoring session when we talked, and I got to see a side of Colt Thorne I'm not sure he's ever really shown anyone else.

And yet, here he is.

In my entryway.

About to take my best friend on a date.

Screw. Him.

My frustration finally boils over, and I turn on my heel to face him, but he doesn't let me go. He simply looks at me, his expression unreadable. However, I have no doubt he can see the jealousy and hurt twisting my insides into knots as it flashes across my face.

"You're not allowed to like my dress," I spit through clenched teeth.

His voice drops low and husky as he checks the hallway behind me, stepping closer. So close, I have to tilt my head up to hold his gaze.

"Then, you're not allowed to be jealous," he growls.

"I'm not jealous."

"Could've fooled me."

I jerk my arm away from him again, and this time, he lets me. But as I march toward Mia's room, trying to get a handle on my emotions, I still feel his gaze branding my ass.

And I hate him for making me oh so aware of every tiny look. Every tiny movement. Every simple syllable and touch and smirk and...*everything* when it comes to Colt Thorne.

And I shouldn't. I shouldn't be aware of him. I shouldn't

be thinking of him. I shouldn't be wondering what's going through his head or if he looks at Mia the same way he looks at me.

"Mia," I call without bothering to knock when I reach her bedroom door.

She looks absolutely gorgeous in a pair of skinny jeans, a fitted white crop top, and a black leather jacket with her hair pulled high on top of her head and tiny tendrils framing her face.

She freaking matches him.

Hot, thick jealousy surges through my veins.

"Yeah?" Mia answers, putting in her earring as she glances at me through the mirror's reflection on her vanity.

I clear my throat. "He's, uh, he's here."

She grins and lifts her hands from her side, doing a quick turn. "How do I look?"

The slight tang of blood explodes across my taste buds as I dig my teeth into the inside of my cheek, pasting on the fakest smile I've ever felt in my entire life. "Gorgeous, as always. Have a good time."

"Thanks. Don't forget protection with Logan."

My face scrunches. "Ew."

"Just sayin'." Her hips sway as she walks toward me, wiggling her fingers. "See ya later, Ash."

"See ya."

My heartbeat is loud in my ears, blocking out whatever Mia says as she greets Colt at the door, and I hate that I'm watching, torturing myself like this. But I can't help it.

Colt smiles back at her and tilts his head toward the driveway. With a light laugh, she hooks her arm through his. His gaze meets mine one more time through the cracked door as Mia closes it behind her, cutting off whatever connection we'd shared.

And what I hate most? How it hurts to watch them go,

especially when I have no right to let it.

16

ASHLYN

"You're quiet," Logan mentions, settling further into the dining room chair as he tosses a withered napkin onto his empty plate.

I shrug one shoulder, unsure what to say.

I *am* quiet.

Logan arrived at my apartment right on time with a bottle of wine in one hand and a bouquet of roses in the other. But he didn't mention my dress. And I hate how I noticed. We eat dinner, an awkwardness tainting every look and every comment until I'm pretty sure ants are crawling over my skin. But I don't know how to fix it. How to make my insecurities--my jealousy--disappear. Especially when they're so damn unwarranted. I'm not an idiot. I know I shouldn't be thinking about a certain roommate when my boyfriend is sitting across the table from me, but I can't help it.

"You okay?" Logan prods.

I set my fork down and force a smile. "Fine."

"Babe, I know you."

"Just stressed. How was your psych class? I heard the test was brutal."

"You know me. Aced it, as always. Didn't even need to study."

Of course, he did.

I roll my eyes, pushing a few strands of spaghetti around my plate, and mutter, "And the genius is humble too."

"Ouch." His hand goes to his chest, but his smirk stays in place. "Someone's feisty tonight. You sure you're all right?"

"Fine."

"How was tutoring the other day?"

I gulp. "Fine."

"That's good," he offers.

"Yeah."

He leans forward and puts his hand on mine, rubbing his thumb back and forth along my skin. I stare at his touch for a few seconds. Finally, he says, "I'm sorry I overreacted about Colt. You were right. I should've trusted you more. I know you wouldn't do anything with him. And I know he wouldn't cross the line with you, either."

"Thanks."

"And thanks for the food," he adds, patting his stomach. "You know how to treat a guy right."

I scoff. "Glad I could indulge you."

"What's wrong?" he demands, surprised by my outburst.

I know he's trying. I know he wants to make things better. I know I'm overreacting about nothing. I know I'm the one with a stick up my ass tonight. But I can't help it.

Why hasn't he commented on my dress? Why do I feel like he's here, and he's present, yet my mind can't seem to focus on anything other than a certain someone who's on a date with my best friend.

What is wrong with me?

"Babe," Logan prods.

I sniff and shake my head. "Nothing's wrong."

"You're lying."

"I'm not lying."

"Then talk to me, Ashlyn. You're acting pissed at me--"

"I'm not pissed."

"You're lying," he repeats. "Did something happen at the tutoring session?"

"What? No. Nothing happened!"

"Don't give me that."

"I'm not giving you anything, Logan," I argue. "I had a long day. And then--" His phone dings with a notification. It's at least the tenth one since he walked into the room. My annoyance spikes.

"You wanna get it?" I ask, waving my hand toward his stupid cell.

He shakes his head and keeps the phone face down in front of him on the kitchen table.

"Want *me* to?" I press.

With a quiet scoff, he tucks the phone into his front pocket without bothering to see who the message is from. "It's work."

"Oh, really?"

"Yeah."

"And why would work be texting you?" I demand.

"Because Kendall missed her shift tonight, and they wanted me to cover for her, but I told them I couldn't. I told them I had a date with my girlfriend tonight, and I couldn't miss it because I love her, and I care about her, and I wanted to spend my night with her. All right, Ash? Is that a good enough answer for you?" he spits.

I flinch at the harshness in his words. Because he's right. I'm overreacting. I'm being a bitch. I wanted a night where we could reconnect, but I'm the one keeping us from doing it.

Me.

"I'm sorry," I whisper, twirling a stray noodle around the prongs of my fork while avoiding his gaze.

"Is it your parents? They avoiding you again?"

"They don't avoid me," I mutter. "They…get busy. And, no. I'm not pissy about my parents, but thanks for the reminder."

"So what is it?" he pushes.

"Things have felt…off with us. And it sucks."

"Look at me, babe."

I bite the inside of my cheek and peek up at him.

His expression softens as he stands, rounding the second-hand oak table and grabbing my hand, helping me up.

With his arms wrapped around me, he rocks us back and forth slowly, resting his forehead against mine. "I love you, Ash. I've loved you since I first saw you freshman year."

"Love you too," I murmur, closing my eyes and resting my head against his chest. The words hit differently this time, though. And I'm not sure if he can hear the indecision in my voice––the years of doubt building until I feel like I might suffocate from them––or if it's all in my head.

"I think I'm just tired," I whisper. "That's all."

"Wanna go to your bedroom?" His hands slip down my body, cupping my ass as he rubs his semi-hard shaft against my stomach.

I smile tightly up at him. "Not tonight."

His brows furrow. "You sure? I want us to reconnect."

"And we will," I rush out. "But…not tonight. I think I'm going to change into some pajamas and go to sleep. I'll call you tomorrow."

He sighs and cups my cheeks, tilting my head up and leaning down to brush a kiss against my mouth. It's soft and sweet, causing whatever butterflies still belonging to him to bat their little wings, but they barely put a dent in the swarm I feel anytime Colt enters the room.

And I hate how I notice the difference.

I pull away and rest my forehead against his chin, hating how torn apart I feel.

"Sleep," I whisper. "Sleep will fix everything."

"You sure?"

I nod. "Yeah. Let me walk you to the door. I'll clean all of this up tomorrow." I motion to the dirty plates and empty wine glasses on the table. Thankfully, I'd done the majority of work before Logan got here. Everything else will only take a few minutes. And all of it can wait until I find a semblance of sanity.

I need it now more than ever.

"All right." He pulls out his phone and smiles when he reads the text message from a few minutes ago. I stand there, chewing on the pad of my thumb as he replies to whoever is on the other end.

"Work?" I ask.

He nods. "Yeah. I might pick up the extra shift since you want to go to bed early."

"Got it," I mutter. "I'll walk you to the door."

He grunts his response and ambles toward the front door, distracted by his phone.

The air is cool as I open it, jerking back, surprised. Mia's head is tucked against Colt's chest, and his arms are wrapped around her. Like a knife is lodged between a couple of my ribs, I breathe in a slow, unsteady breath, convinced I'm hallucinating.

This can't be happening.

17
ASHLYN

I shouldn't have to see this. Colt and Mia hugging each other. But so what? Why does it matter if I do? I've walked in on Mia and Shorty full-blown having sex on our couch, and it never bothered me.

So why does this?

I tear my attention away from Colt's arms resting on Mia's lower back and force a smile when their heads snap in my direction. I have no idea whether or not my fake amusement conceals my hurt from peeking through as Colt's gaze connects with mine. But he doesn't move away from her. He simply looks at me, his words from earlier tonight like razors.

You're not allowed to be jealous.

But I am.

I'm so fucking jealous I might puke. And I know I have no right. I know I made dinner for Logan tonight. I know I shouldn't be thinking of someone else, let alone letting that someone ruin a night with my boyfriend. But he did. He still is. And I can't shake him, no matter how much I've tried to.

So where does it leave me, exactly?

Logan's laughter is like a bucket of ice water as he tucks his phone back into his pocket and steps onto the front porch. "Hey, maybe you guys should get a room."

Mia pulls away and looks up at Colt, her cheeks a little red. "Actually," she pauses. "Do you *want* to come inside?"

Colt's attention keeps me pinned in place, and he never breaks our connection as he mutters, "Not tonight."

An unoffended Mia rises onto her tiptoes and kisses his cheek. "No worries. Why don't you call me tomorrow?"

He gives her a non-committal shrug, still refusing to tear his attention away from me while I stand there, dumbfounded and most definitely interrupting their...whatever this is. And while I should feel guilt, all I feel is hurt and confusion. Like I deserve an explanation when I know I don't. I don't deserve a damn thing from Colt *or* Mia. If anything, they deserve an apology from me. And so does Logan.

"Thanks again for tonight," Mia adds, heading inside and leaving me alone with Colt and Logan. My attention darts between them as Logan puts his hand on my waist and kisses me. In front of his freaking roommate. And because I'm pissed and jealous, I kiss him back, running my tongue along the seam of Logan's lips as I push my breasts against his shirt. And I hate how it leaves me feeling dirty and even more confused. Like it feels wrong, somehow. And how is it even possible? We've kissed a million times. And even when I'm not in the mood, it's never felt wrong. Not until this moment.

Logan pulls away, his eyes bright with lust as the porch light reflects in them. "If you change your mind, call me."

"I thought you had work."

"You come first, babe. Always." He lets me go and turns to Colt. "You comin'?"

"Forgot to tell Mia something," Colt replies with his hands in his front pockets.

"All right." Without a backward glance, Logan takes the steps to the driveway and leaves me alone with Colt.

I should go back inside. I should get the hell out of here. I should slam the door in Colt's face, take a very cold shower, and drown my sorrows in Ben & Jerry's. But instead, I'm standing here like an idiot with my arms folded and a fresh dose of jealousy ripping every single inch of my insides to shreds.

Wake the hell up, Ash, a voice inside of me screams.

I shake my head and turn on my heel when Colt grabs my arm, the memory from earlier tonight hitting me square in the chest.

"Tell me, Sunshine." He pauses, and I hold my breath. "Did he notice?"

I scoff, blown away he even has the audacity to ask me such a stupid question. But I don't pull away.

Why the hell am I not pulling away?

"Notice what?" I seethe, all too aware I know what he's going to say. But I need to hear him say it. I need the reminder of what an asshole Colt Thorne really is. And I need it right now if I have any hope of keeping my sanity when it seems to disappear anytime he comes around.

His chest rumbles as Colt voices exactly what I need to hear. "Your dress."

Yanking my arm out of his grasp, I turn and rise onto my tiptoes, getting right up in his face until less than an inch separates us. "You're not allowed to ask me that question."

"It's a simple question, Sunshine."

My upper lip curls in disgust. "No. It's not. It's not a simple question. Nothing about you is simple. And guess what, Colt? I want simple. And Mia *needs* simple after all the shit she's been through. So, no. You're not allowed to ask me that question. And you're not allowed to notice my dress, especially when we both know Mia would happily let you take hers off tonight, and I wouldn't have a say in shit."

I walk inside with my head held high and close the door behind me. Quietly. Carefully. Like he hasn't gotten under my skin. Like he doesn't matter at all. Because he doesn't.

I have a happy relationship with Logan.

And whatever spell Colt has cast on me needs to end. Now.

Striding toward the window, I slip my fingers between two wooden slats of the blinds and peek at the driveway, anxious for Colt's truck to disappear. Once the coast is clear, I grab my keys from the counter and yell, "I'm going to Logan's, Mia. See you tomorrow."

The night air feels good against my heated skin as I climb into my car like a demon is chasing me.

Scratch that.

It isn't a demon.

It's my freaking doubts.

And they're screaming louder than ever.

18
COLT

Fucking hell.

I can hear her. And she isn't quiet. The bed frame slams against the wall between my room and Logan's, eviscerating any chance of sleep as Ash chants expletives over and over again. Never would've pegged her for having a dirty mouth, but I guess she's up for anything when the occasion calls for it.

I toss my arm over my eyes, shutting out the image of what she must look like right now. Her hair a mess of waves down her back, her skin tinted pink and flushed, her mouth slightly open as she rolls her hips, chasing her orgasm.

Fuck. Me.

I turn onto my side and shove a pillow over my ear, but it doesn't block anything out. It does nothing but feeds my addiction to a girl who doesn't belong to me. I know it's her. Sex can sound like anyone. But this? It's different. It's tainted somehow. Fake. Over the top like a bad porno. Like she knows I'm listening. Like she wants me to hear to prove a point. I doubt she's even getting off. The realization only pisses me off more.

Chucking my pillow against the opposite wall, I head to the bathroom, shut the door behind me, and grip my cock through my black boxers.

I'm hard.

Hell, I'm dripping. For her. To be the guy pulling those sounds from her throat. Even if it sounds fake and over the top, the noises still belong to her. *Sunshine*. And because it's her, I'm still hard as a rock. It's like she's crawled under my skin and refuses to leave me the hell alone.

Her sounds are like a ghost. A premonition. A promise.

It's torture.

Closing my eyes, I rest my back against the door and pull out my dick from my boxers, rubbing my hand over the head of it as I imagine my name on her lips, my hands on her body. I pump my hand faster and faster, picturing my fingers tangled in her hair, her wet heat clenching around me. My breath quickens, and my heart pounds against my ribcage as I come in my hand with her name on my tongue.

I lean my head against the door, realizing exactly what I've done and how messed up it is.

Now, I really do need to buy some noise-canceling headphones or some shit. Because hearing Logan is one thing, but listening to Ash screw someone who isn't me? It's the worst form of torture.

But I guess I deserve this.

This excruciating misery.

After all, I hurt her first. I could see it on Mia's doorstep. When she caught me comforting her best friend.

Like a kick to the balls, she simply stood there. Hurting.

And it's all my fault.

I shake my head and squeeze my eyes shut, desperate to erase the memory, but it doesn't go anywhere. If anything, it's amplified. Like a knife twisting in my chest.

I screwed up. But I didn't know they were roommates. I

didn't realize my attempt to get Ash out of my mind would only solidify her place there.

But I do now.

And she sure as shit isn't going anywhere.

I cock my head to one side and listen for a second as my muscles relax. At least it's quiet now. Logan must've finished. Maybe I'll finally get some sleep. My dick is still unsatisfied as I tuck it back into my boxers, wash my hands, and open the door. Wrapped in a blanket, a shy Ash stands there looking guilty as hell. Like she caught me doing something I shouldn't. Like she heard me jerking off. Like she heard me say her name as I came in my hand like a teenager.

Her skin is flushed as I'd imagined, and she's biting her lower lip, peeking up at me through her dark lashes.

"Uh…sorry if I…" Her voice trails off, the light from the bathroom casting our shadows along the dark hallway.

"Interrupted me jerking off?" I ask, stepping closer to her, too amped up on adrenaline to back off now with her in front of me. She mirrors my movements until her back hits the opposite wall. Still, I continue my pursuit, and she gasps quietly as I move so fucking close to her only the blanket and my boxers separate us. She smells like sex and vanilla. It shouldn't turn me on, but it does.

"Or are you sorry you kept me awake with all the moaning?" I growl.

She gulps.

"What exactly are you sorry for, Ash?"

Again, she peeks up at me, shrugging one bare shoulder. The sheet slips down a few inches and exposes more of her smooth skin. My mouth waters, and I have to force my spine to stay straight when all I want is to dig my teeth into every inch of bare flesh on display in the dark hallway.

I'm not sure how she managed to get so far under my skin in such a short period of time, but she did. And I'm seconds from tugging at the little knot of fabric between her tiny fists at her chest to see if she's as perfect as I imagine.

"I see he noticed the dress," I add, daring her to tell me otherwise.

Her gaze darkens, and her pouty lips press together. "It's none of your business."

"I think you made it my business when you decided to audition for a porn film in the room next to mine."

With a gasp, her jaw drops. "You think I was faking it?"

"I think you were a lot more enthusiastic than the last time you were here."

"Maybe I was more in the mood today," she counters, her shallow breath making her breasts even more mouthwatering as I tower over her.

"And why's that, Sunshine?"

The tip of her tongue slips out between her lips as she peeks up at me. Again. Tempting me. Teasing me, though she has no idea. I cage her in on both sides of her head, pressing my hands against the wall behind her and leaning close. Her air is my air. Her breath is my breath. And her scent? I want to rub it all over me. Commit it to memory. Mix it with mine until we're one, and nothing can take her away from me.

"Tell me this," I rasp. "Did you think of me when he took it off you?"

She gulps again, but I can see the truth in her timid eyes. She did. Meaning her sounds might not have been quite as fake as I'd been hoping. The realization only pisses me off more.

I lean closer, my upper lip curling as I press my forehead to hers, demanding her full attention. "Wanna know something, Sunshine? You can't compare the two—me and him. You can't imagine what it would be like to be with me while his dick is inside you. Wanna know why?"

"Why?" she whispers, the sound soft and breathy and

shooting straight to my already hardening cock. It takes every ounce of willpower inside of me to keep from grinding it against her.

"It's like I said. I'm always a gentleman," I remind her. "And the asshole you've been sleeping with? He doesn't care if you come or not. Does he." It isn't a question, but her cheeks heat nonetheless. "So, tell me," I push. "Did you come?"

"It's none of your business."

"I think you did," I decide. "But only because you were thinking of me. And if your imagination got you there tonight, wait 'til I get my hands on you." I push myself away from the wall and head to my bedroom. The same LAU T-shirt I first caught her wearing is folded on my dresser. I grab it, walk back to the hallway, and toss it at her. She catches it on reflex, exposing a glimpse of her chest before she curls the cloth around her again.

Her big blue eyes stare back at me.

"The sheets are tempting," I rasp. "But I think I still prefer you in my T-shirt."

I close the bedroom door behind me, leaving her in stunned silence, and pull out my dick to rub another one out while replaying our conversation and a dozen other scenarios where we wind up on the same side of the door instead of opposites.

19

COLT

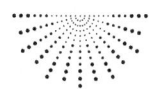

"Have a good night?" Theo jests as Logan practically skips into the room with a shit-eating grin. One my hands are begging to wipe off his fucking face.

He reaches for an apple from the fruit bowl on the island, tosses it in the air, and takes a bite. "You could say that."

"I thought Ash was staying home last night," I say, pretending to scroll TikTok while every sense is acutely aware of Logan's every movement.

Theo and Logan turn to me, confused. "Huh?"

I glance up from my phone. "When I was dropping off Mia, it looked like Ash was staying home. Why'd she end up coming over last night?"

With a shrug, Logan sits on one of the barstools. "Guess she changed her mind."

"Yeah. We heard," Theo jokes. "Guess whatever funk you guys were in was worked out?"

Logan chuckles, and his mouth turns up with an arrogant smirk. "You could say that," he repeats.

"So, you won't be screwing random women anymore?" I

challenge, crossing my arms and leaning my hip against the counter as I stare down at Logan, daring him to lie to me.

He takes another bite of the apple, wiping the back of his mouth with his hand. "There a problem, Colt?"

"You know how he is," Theo answers for me. "Ever since Brooke cheated on him in high school––"

"He's been sensitive about this shit," Logan finishes, continuing our little stare down. "Yeah. I know. Which is rich, coming from you."

"What about me?"

"You'll screw anything with boobs. You even took Shorty's girl out last night. What the hell, man?"

"Shorty's an asshole," I tell him. "And if he comes within ten feet of Mia, I'll beat the shit out of him."

Logan scoffs and tosses the apple core into the trash can across the kitchen. "So, you're gonna piss on Mia too? Claiming her? Sorry to disappoint you, Colt, but I don't think you can have every girl on campus."

"I don't want every girl on campus."

"What do you want?" He gets up and stalks closer to me, but I stand my ground, refusing to retreat.

"I want you to treat Ash right," I tell him.

"That's it?"

The knife in my chest digs a little deeper.

I nod. "Yeah, man. That's it."

"So, you don't want her?" he challenges.

My jaw ticks at the memory of my hand on my dick last night and the way she sounded, torturing me from the other room. The way I found her in the hallway wrapped in nothing but a blanket, left to clean up after herself. The way I promised I'd get my hands on her one day. The way her lips parted as I said it aloud. The way she watched me as I disappeared into my room and tossed my T-shirt at her. The way she's haunted my thoughts ever since.

But she's still his. And it doesn't matter if she thought of me while they slept together last night. It doesn't matter if I want her. She's with Logan, so she's off-limits. And after her little performance, it's clear Logan's more invested in their relationship than ever. I need to remember my place.

"She's your girl, Logan," I return, my jaw ticking. "I might mess around, but we both know I wouldn't cross the line. It's like Theo said. I know what it's like to be on the other end."

He nods and steps away, satisfied. "Thanks. And you're right. I'm gonna treat her better. She's the only girl for me."

My chin dips back at him. "Good."

"So, what's going on between you and Mia?" Theo asks me, his attention shifting from me to Logan and back again. Like he's our very own peacemaker, anxious to sweep the shit with Ash under the rug.

"She took me out to thank me for intervening with Shorty the other night," I reply.

Unconvinced, he cocks his head to one side. "And that's it?"

"Yeah, man."

"She's a nice girl, though. Hot too," Theo adds.

I nod and roll my shoulders, trying to ease the tension, but it doesn't erase the hurt in Ash's eyes when she found me on her porch, waiting to pick up her best friend.

"Yeah, she's pretty," I answer.

"You two should go out," Theo suggests, turning to Logan. "On a double date. Mia and Colt. You and Ash. Hell, maybe I'll come too. It'll help bury the hatchet."

You mean the one lodged in my back? I almost offer but bite my tongue.

"We'll see," I mutter.

But we won't. 'Cause there isn't a chance in hell I'd put myself through it. Not now.

Not ever.

20
ASHLYN

It's been four days. Four days of constant texts from Logan asking when he can see me again, telling me how much he misses me. Four days of stilted conversations with Mia, avoiding anything and everything to do with a certain new friend of hers. Four days of dreading my upcoming tutoring session with a certain someone who refuses to leave my subconscious alone.

Four. Freaking. Days.

And it's driving me insane.

Puffing out my cheeks, I lift my hand and knock on the door as regret pools in my stomach. Like part of me already knows how much of a mistake this is. To be here. But what other choice do I have?

When the door opens, Logan is on the other side.

Shit.

He wraps me in a massive bear hug and sticks his tongue down my throat as he squeezes my butt.

My eyes are wide with surprise as I push at his chest. "Whoa, there. Hi."

"Hey, baby," he returns, going in for another kiss, almost all tongue and no lip.

I kiss him back briefly and pull away, wiping the corner of my mouth with my thumb.

"Hey," I repeat. "I thought you were working tonight?"

"I'm leaving in five. Why didn't you tell me you were coming over?"

"I have a tutoring session."

"How come I haven't seen you?"

I fold my arms, rubbing along my bare arms. "I've been kind of busy. I'm sorry."

"If I didn't know any better, I'd say you've been avoiding me," he jokes, but his cocky smirk doesn't meet his eyes, and there's a hint of vulnerability shining back at me.

It makes me feel like crap.

"I haven't been avoiding you," I lie. "And let's be honest, with how busy both our schedules are, we usually only see each other once or twice a week anyway. It's not like this is anything out of the ordinary."

He steps aside, letting me into the Taylor House as he argues, "I know, but with how awesome our last date was, I figured we could've seen each other a few more times or something."

"I know. And I'm sorry," I add. "But my schedule is still chaos despite good sex, so…"

He frowns, sensing my reservation. "What's wrong?"

"Nothing's wrong. I'm late for my tutoring session with Colt."

His gaze narrows as he closes the front door behind us. "Are you mad at me?"

I sigh and pinch the bridge of my nose. "Why would I be mad at you?"

"Because you've been avoiding me."

Dropping my hand to my side, I shake my head and argue, "Logan, I haven't been avoiding you."

"Then, come upstairs with me. Ten minutes."

"You said you have work in five."

"So, I'll be late." He takes my hand and starts leading me toward the stairs. But the idea of him touching me feels wrong, somehow. And I can't wrap my head around why. I came harder than ever four nights ago. But Colt was right. I wasn't thinking of Logan. I wasn't present with Logan. I was playing out every single fantasy I'd been harboring inside of me since the first time I met Colt. And Logan liked it. Hell, he loved it.

But I used him. I used him, and I wanted Colt to hear me using him.

What kind of sick person does it make me?

"Logan, stop," I order. "It's unprofessional for me to come over here for a tutoring session only to hook up with you instead."

"Colt's my buddy. He'll get over it. Come on."

"Logan, stop." I dig my heels into the ground. "I need some space for a minute."

He pauses and turns around, facing me fully as whatever ounce of want dissipates into thin air, replaced with suspicion. "You need *space*?"

The blood drains from my face. "Not like that."

"Like what?"

"Nothing, okay?" I rush out. "I… You know how much I hate being late for things, and I have an appointment. When do you get off work? We can talk after or something."

Indifference oozes from every pore as he shrugs one shoulder. "Can't tonight."

"Logan…"

He shakes his head and steps away from me. "Sorry."

He isn't sorry. He's pouting because I turned him down.

Reining in my temper, I reach for his hand. "Logan, I've missed you. I promise nothing's wrong," I add, though I'm not sure who I'm trying to convince this time. "I've been busy. But as for us sneaking in a quickie before my tutoring session, it's not that I don't want to, I--"

"You hate being late," he finishes for me. "I get it." He leans forward and presses a weak peck to my cheek. "I'll let you go. We'll talk later."

"Logan--"

"I'm fine, Ash." His tone is cold. Hell, it's frigid.

Liar, I want to spit, but I bite my tongue. He isn't the only liar right now. I am too. And I hate how I'm questioning our relationship all because I have chemistry with a guy who isn't him. A guy who's dating my best friend. A guy who, if I had to guess, doesn't do relationships. He's good for sex and nothing more. And I'd be a fool to throw away my relationship with Logan because of it.

I'm not a fool.

"Logan, talk to me," I beg, my fingers digging into the white cotton of his long sleeve shirt.

"Don't want you to be late." He slips out of my grasp, walks toward the kitchen, and out the garage door without a backward glance. Leaving me alone with my indecision and regret.

"Everything okay?" Colt murmurs from the top of the stairs. Like he might not have witnessed what went down, but he can still feel the aftermath hanging heavy in the air.

I look up and give him a pathetic smile. "Just dandy."

He takes the stairs two at a time, his footsteps light and sure as he reaches the main floor.

We haven't really spoken since I overheard him pleasuring himself in the bathroom. Not since he caught me eavesdropping. Not since he pushed me against the wall, and I was convinced he was going to kiss me.

Which is insane on so many levels.

I'm not a cheater. I refuse to be. And I know Colt isn't, either. Or at least, I thought he wasn't. But considering how much I've been avoiding Mia and her little get-togethers with Colt, maybe I'm wrong. Maybe they're officially a thing. Maybe I'm not the only one playing with fire.

The idea causes a knot in my stomach as I chew on my thumbnail, anxious to get the hell out of here. But I can't. I need the tutoring hours for my teaching program. I need the money for my rent. I need––

"What's wrong?" Colt asks when he reaches me, his eyebrows pinched with concern.

"Nothing."

"You sure?"

"Yup. Let's get started." I head to the kitchen table without bothering to see if Colt follows, ripping open my backpack and slamming a textbook on the hard surface with so much force the table shakes.

But I'm angry.

And I also feel like crying.

I'm confused.

Frustrated.

I shouldn't be here.

But I don't want to go home, either.

Not when Mia's there.

Not when I have to wonder if they've kissed. If they've had sex. If he's touched her the way I imagine he'd touch me.

This is so messed up.

Colt stops me and grabs my arms, forcing me to look at him. "Stop, Ash."

I shake my head and wrench myself away from him, digging through my bag for a stupid pen and a stupid notebook.

"Ash––"

"Stop it," I snap.

He lifts his hands in surrender, but his eyes never leave the side of my face as he sits down on the edge of his seat while I stand there, helpless. And I hate how I'm so aware of him. His every move. The way his breathing is slow and steady. The way he's being patient. The way he hasn't lashed out at me for acting like a crazy person when anyone else I know would've lost it by now.

I sniff once and try to keep my breathing in check as I stare blankly at the table in front of me.

"Ash," Colt murmurs. It's softer than I've ever heard it. More genuine. Gentle, even. And I hate it too. How much I want to give in to him. How much I want to cave, to tell him what's wrong, and why I'm so upset when I know it's the last thing I should do.

Collapsing into the chair beside him, I steel my shoulders and ask, "How was your date?"

I grab the dark blue pen and click the back of it, staring at the blank lined paper in front of me when all I want to do is look at Colt. To watch his face. To see if his eyes soften when I mention Mia's name.

"What?" he rasps beside me.

"With Mia? How was your date? Since I never asked you and all."

He pauses. "It wasn't a date."

"What was it?" I look over at him.

"She bought me dinner because I helped her out with Shorty."

"And last night?" I prod.

The blood drains from his face. "She told you?"

"Why wouldn't she? We're friends. She didn't get home until almost midnight, not that I was paying attention, but…" I bite my lip to keep from rambling. "She's poor as hell, and it's not like she'd go out on her own. Not without me. Unless she had a date or something. So, are you guys…official now? Seems like you've been spending a lot of time together--"

"We aren't dating, Ash."

"Got it." I click the pen again. "Shall we, uh, get started?" I motion to the closed textbook with a wave of my hand.

"Ash."

"What was your last score? Anything we should focus on?"

"I'd like to focus on our conversation."

"It's none of my business, Colt. And I most definitely shouldn't have asked about it in the first place. Let's just"--I scratch the side of my temple with the unclicked pen--"focus on your next assignment, all right?"

"Ash."

"Or I can leave. Whichever you'd prefer."

He holds my stare for a solid thirty seconds, my heartbeat quickening with every passing moment as my fight or flight instinct threatens to consume me. I shouldn't have asked. I know I shouldn't have asked. It's none of my business. But I can't help how my brain wants to play out every sordid scenario. Every possible touch. Kiss. Look. That might've transpired between Colt and my best friend.

But what's worse is I know I should be happy for Mia. Because she was right. Her mystery man is a good guy. So good, in fact, I've been comparing my boyfriend to him since the moment we met, and it's only shed a blinding light on all of the traits Logan doesn't have, and Colt does.

Breaking our staring contest, he sighs and opens the textbook without another word.

The rest of the night is all business.

Which is good.

It's what I asked for.

What I need if I want to keep my sanity.

Isn't it?

21

COLT

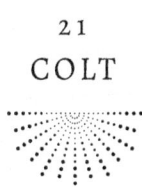

"Hey." Logan's voice echoes across the hall from his room as I wipe my wet hands on the towel in the bathroom and open the door. It sounds like he's on the phone, but when I hear Ash's name, I pause and listen.

"That sucks, Ash," Logan replies.

The floor squeaks slightly beneath my weight as I inch closer.

"Yeah, it's a bitch," he continues.

Silence.

"I can't."

Pause.

"No, I'm not mad at you. I have plans."

Pause.

"I'm working. Don't assume shit," Logan growls.

Pause.

"You know I would drop whatever I needed to help you."

Another pause.

"I can't leave, Ash. I'm already here."

Pause.

"Yes, I know it's raining, and I'm seriously sorry. Did you try Mia?" he asks.

Silence.

"Yeah, it sucks. But like I said, I'm working too." Logan sighs. "Call an Uber, all right? I'll help with your car in the morning."

I shouldn't be eavesdropping. It's a dick thing to do. But he's full of shit. He isn't at work. Ashlyn's right, though. Mia's working tonight. I was heading to SeaBird right now to keep an eye on her. But why would Ash need to call an Uber?

"Yeah. I'll talk to you in the morning," Logan adds.

Stepping into view, I lean my shoulder against the doorjamb and scratch my jaw. Logan's sitting on his bed in a button-up shirt, his ankle resting on his opposite knee as he ends the call and tosses his phone onto his bed.

He hasn't noticed me yet.

"You're not at work," I point out.

He looks up at me, surprised. "Shit, man. You scared me."

"You're not at work," I repeat.

His brows furrow. "Were you eavesdropping?"

Realizing what's going on, I clench my jaw and try to stay calm. "You told me you were gonna cut the shit with Ash."

"And I have."

"Bullshit," I spit.

He stands from the side of the bed and tucks his phone into his pocket. "Why do you even care?"

"Because I have a little sister," I argue. "And if I ever found out she was dating an asshole like you, I'd beat the shit out of him."

"Guess it's a good thing I'm not dating Blakely, isn't it?"

Scratching the scruff of my jaw, I push myself away from the doorway and stalk closer to him, my blood beginning to boil. "Where is she?"

"Who? Ash?" he asks, surprised.

"Yeah. Where is she?"

"None of your business."

"You're making it my business by refusing to pick her up. It's almost ten at night, and it's pouring rain outside, asshole."

"Look, she's not far. She's right by SeaBird, and I told her to hire an Uber. I'm even gonna Venmo her--"

"It's no excuse, Logan," I grit out. "You're leaving your girlfriend to fend for herself so you can wet your dick with someone else."

"I told you, I have work," he argues.

Grabbing the collar of his shirt, I yank him closer to me. "It's bullshit, and you know it. If you had a shift at the restaurant tonight, you'd already be there."

"You don't know--"

"I *do* know. And I know you, too, you lying sack of shit. I'm not going to sit by and watch you lead her on. She deserves better than this, and you know it." I let him go, and he collapses back onto the bed like a sack of worthless potatoes. "You have one week to tell her. If you don't, I will."

My feet feel as if heavy with lead as I storm out of his room without waiting for his response, afraid I'll lose my self-control and beat the shit out of him if he has a chance to open his mouth.

Fucking asshole.

Keys in hand, I head to my truck parked in the driveway. The rain is coming down in torrents as I pull out my phone and send Mia a quick text.

Me: Hey. I might be late tonight, but I'm still planning to pick you up, so don't leave unless we talk.

I toss my phone into the cupholder and shove the truck into reverse while ignoring the fact I'm about to save a girl who most definitely does not belong to me.

22

ASHLYN

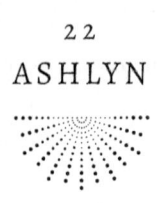

The windshield wipers swish back and forth against the glass as I rest my head on the steering wheel. It's pouring, and thanks to it being past ten o'clock on a Friday night, all the Uber drivers are busy dropping people off at the local bar to have time for a girl like me.

I check the time on the dashboard and look at the little green dot representing my current Uber.

Seven more minutes.

Great.

Stupid car problems. I've had this bad boy since high school. It was my dad's, but I really thought I'd be able to get at least a thousand more miles out of it without the stupid thing breaking down.

Jokes on me, though. Because here I am, stranded on the side of the road, at least a mile and a half away from any real civilization, with no one to rely on except a stranger I ordered through a phone app.

Lovely.

If I'm murdered tonight, it's Logan's fault. I still can't believe he refused to help me out. Ten minutes. Okay, twenty tops. It would've taken him twenty minutes, and I would've felt safe.

I bet if I'd given him a blow job before my tutoring session with Colt, he would've shown up.

Asshole.

Scrubbing my hand over my tired eyes, I take a deep breath when lights glint off my rearview mirror, blinding me. It's too dark to place the vehicle, but it's slowing down as it inches closer.

Great. I really am going to be murdered.

My palms are sweaty as I wait for it to pass me and go on its merry way, but it doesn't. It stops near my driver's side window, lining up next to me. My life flashes before my eyes as the passenger window rolls down, and a very familiar pair of dark eyes that've been haunting me for weeks comes into view.

"Colt?" I breathe out, my heart still pitter-pattering away.

He yells something, though I can't hear what it is over the pouring rain. Waving his hand, he mouths, "window down," and I do as I'm told.

"What are you doing here?" I yell as the rain splatters through the crack in the glass, wetting my dashboard.

"Get in!"

"How did you know——"

"Get in the damn car, Ash!"

Frowning, I roll the window back up and take my keys from the ignition. Once my purse is hooked on my shoulder, I shove the door open and slam it behind me, sliding into Colt's passenger seat. My hair is already soaked, and my shirt clings to my body, leaving me a shivering mess as I buckle the seatbelt, fold my arms, and peek at my savior.

With wrinkles etched into his forehead, and white knuckles throttling the steering wheel, he looks pissed. His eyes are glued to the road, and he doesn't say a word as he pulls back onto the street.

He's ignoring me.

The realization hits like a ton of bricks and leaves me speechless.

Am I supposed to apologize or something? And for what, exactly? I didn't ask him to pick me up. In fact, I've never asked for anything from him. And yet here he is. Furious.

Digging my teeth into my lower lip, I glance at him again, a not-so-deserved apology tumbling out of me. "Look, I'm sorry."

The bastard's jaw tightens, but he stays quiet, leaving me even more uncomfortable. I feel like the walls are closing in on me. Like the cab of his truck might as well be a sardine can. Like all of the oxygen has been sucked out of the space, leaving nothing but annoyance and resentment in its wake.

Which only pisses me off more.

"I didn't ask for your help," I remind him.

He scoffs and shakes his head, continuing to pretend like I don't exist.

Frustrated by his iciness, I finally spit, "You know what? Pull over. I'm just going to walk home."

His hand darts out, and he grabs my upper thigh, branding me with the heat from his palm.

"Stay," he orders.

Twisting in my seat, I look at him and say, "You don't want me here."

The seat belt digs into my shoulder as he pulls the truck over, slams on the brakes, and looks me dead in the eye. "Why the hell are you still with Logan? He's an asshole."

As soon as our gazes connect, I realize I wish they hadn't because the dark look? Those eyes? They're bad news. Promising passion and lust and heat in a way I can't even imagine. Scratch that. I can imagine. Because I *have* imagined how much passion, lust, and heat could transpire if I gave in to him.

But it's a bad idea.

Terrible, actually.

I stay quiet, unsure what to say while squirming under his intensity because, honestly? I've been asking myself the same question for far too long. But I can't help it. When you've been with someone for years, it's easy to write off the little things. To stay loyal because it's what a loyal person does.

And I am loyal.

Despite my feelings for Colt.

Despite my waning feelings for Logan.

I am loyal, dammit!

Swallowing thickly, I look down at his hand still clutching my thigh. His fingers flex, digging into my skin in the most deliciously rough and desperate way possible. Then, he lets me go.

"Answer the question," Colt pushes.

"I can't believe you called him an asshole."

"He is an asshole."

"And here I thought you two were friends," I quip.

"Used to be," he mutters, losing a bit of his sharpness.

"What changed?"

He looks at me but stays quiet.

"Tell me," I push because there's something in his eyes. Something that's been driving me crazy ever since we first met, and I'm about ready to snap from the weight of it.

"You should dump him," he murmurs numbly. The headlights of a car passing us light up his sharp features before blanketing the cab in darkness again as my eyes widen in surprise. Sure, we've danced around whatever is going on between us, but he's never been this bold. This outspoken. I don't know how to handle it.

After another few seconds, my quiet voice breaks the silence. "And why should I dump him?"

"Because you deserve better."

I laugh, blown away by Colt's audacity. "Oh, really?"

"Yeah. Really," he returns, more somber than I've ever seen.

"Like who? You?"

"Maybe."

"Says the guy dating my friend."

"We're not dating."

"Oh, so the late nights, you driving her to and from work, texting and calling at every freaking hour. What would you call it? Huh?"

Only silence greets me, and it pisses me off more. Because I know I've backed him into a corner. I know I have a point. A freaking good one. And he deserves to be backed into a corner. This game? This back and forth we've created? It isn't fair to me. It isn't fair to Mia. And it sure as hell isn't fair to Logan.

"You know what?" I breathe out. "It doesn't even matter. Because even though my relationship with Logan might not be perfect, at least he's loyal. At least he isn't picking up random girls on the side of the road--"

Colt's hand slams against the steering wheel, proving I've struck a nerve, but when he opens his mouth to reply, I cut him off again.

"No. You don't get to talk right now."

"I'm sorry? I don't get to talk?" He scoffs.

"No. No, you don't get to talk," I argue.

"Why not, Sunshine?"

"Because every time you do, every time we have an actual conversation, you make me question things, and I'm *tired* of questioning things." I shake my head and run my fingers through my wet, stringy hair, tugging on the roots while praying for the strength to get through this conversation. "I'm not a quitter, Colt. I'm not like you and hockey. I'm not going to simply give up on something."

He jerks away as if I've slapped him, but I don't stop. I *can't* stop. The words tumble out of me, one after the other. "My relationship doesn't have to be perfect for me to want to save it."

"And if he isn't willing to save it with you?" Colt challenges. He leans closer, his breath mingling with my own until I feel like I can't breathe without breathing him in instead of oxygen. And I definitely need some freaking air if I have any hope of clearing my head of what Colt's doing to it.

His gaze is hot with irritation and passion as he stares at me, making me feel like I'm burning alive, even though I'm soaking wet and shivering from the wind and rain outside.

"If he torched whatever shitty relationship you're still clinging to, expecting you to save it all by yourself, what then? Huh, Ash? What then?"

"It isn't torched--"

"Trust me, Sunshine." He laughs. "It's fucking charred beyond repair."

Like a knife is in my chest, I breathe shallowly, refusing to rub at the ache or acknowledge how freaking close he hit the nail on the head. I simply look at him. Stare at him. His stubbled jaw. The slight divot between his brows from frowning. The dark glint in his gaze I've been dreaming about since the moment we first met.

What's he thinking?

Why did he come to pick me up?

And why does he make me feel this way?

It isn't fair.

His attention drops to my mouth. He's so close. So freaking close, I can almost taste him. If he leaned in a little closer--

A loud, jarring sound has me flinching as his phone lights up in the cupholder, breaking whatever weird spell had been cast over his truck and bringing me back to reality.

Unlike Logan, Colt's notifications are set to show a preview of the message instead of keeping it private. It shouldn't surprise me, but it does.

It's Mia.

Mia: Don't worry, boyfriend. I'm not going anywhere without you.

Boyfriend.

23
ASHLYN

I gulp and lean back in the leather seat, putting some distance between Colt and me. The cold pierces the back of my head from the window, bringing an ounce of clarity. And boy, do I need it.

I can't be here.

Fumbling for the door handle, I shove it open as Colt reaches for my wrist and stops me.

"Where the hell do you think you're going?" he demands.

"I can't do this with you."

"We're not doing anything--"

"We're doing everything!" I yell, my emotions clogging my throat. "You have a girlfriend--"

"She's not my girlfriend, Ash."

His grasp disappears from my wrist as I yank my arm away from him. I grab his phone from the cup holder and shove it against his chest. "She called you her fucking boyfriend, Colt."

The rain is coming down in sheets, but I don't give a shit. After unfolding myself from the passenger seat, I slam the truck door and stomp down the road toward home when hands grab me from behind.

Colt twists me around, forcing me to face him as the water sticks to his long, dark lashes, dripping down his cheeks and off his chin while his headlights cast a glow around us.

"Let me go," I seethe.

"Get in the truck, Sunshine."

"I *can't*." My voice cracks, and I flinch in response, a wave of shame flooding every inch of me. Because it's true. I can't get back in. I can't keep playing this game. I can't keep wanting someone who isn't mine––who belongs to someone else.

I…*can't.*

The hardness in his gaze softens as Colt cups my cheek and forces me to look at him, my heart breaking with every brush of his skin against mine. "Get in the truck, Ash. I'm not gonna let you walk home in the rain when it's dark outside."

"I can't be alone with you." The declaration hurts. It hurts so damn much, I'm grateful for the rain. Grateful for the disguise it gives my tears as they cling to my lashes.

He drops his arm to his side and heads in the opposite direction of his truck parked on the side of the road.

"Where are you going?" I yell. His clothes are already soaked. The thin cotton sticks to his back, highlighting every tense muscle as he walks away from me.

He doesn't face me but calls over his shoulder, "I'm walking home."

"Colt!"

He turns around but continues walking backward, putting more distance between us. And it hurts. The distance. The finality in every step taking him further from me when all I want is to pull him closer.

"Get in the truck, Ash," he yells over the pouring rain.

"I'm not going to take your car."

"Yeah, you are," he calls back. "Drive yourself home. Take a hot bath. I'll figure out how to pick up my truck later."

"Colt--"

But he turns around, giving me his back again. Picking up his pace, it turns into a light jog, and he runs down the road.

Shoving my soaked hair away from my face, I race back to his truck and turn the heat on full blast. I'm drenched. Cold. And blown away by his thoughtfulness while hating it too.

Because Colt Thorne isn't thoughtful. He's reckless and selfish and arrogant. He's the guy making out with random women in the hall at a party. The guy who hits on his friend's girlfriend in the middle of the night because he knows he's attractive enough to get away with it.

Colt isn't the guy who rescues a girl on the side of the road before walking home alone in the rain. He isn't the guy who tells them to take a hot bath, or they look pretty in a dress without any intention of taking it off them later.

He's--my attention slides to the empty cup holder where his phone sat with the message from my best friend.

He's not mine.

This is so messed up.

24
COLT

My feet pound against the treadmill in rhythm to Eminem's "Lose Yourself" as I stare blankly at the wall in front of me. I've been running for an hour. My legs are sore, and my lungs are screaming at me to stop, but I don't. I keep running. Keep pushing myself. Keep shoving aside the way Ash looked at me in the truck last night. The way she called me a quitter. The way she shoved the phone into my chest after seeing Mia's text.

The way she ended things between us before we even had a shot at seeing where it could take us.

Theo approaches me from the side of the gym where the weights are located and taps his earpods, motioning for me to take mine out.

Grudgingly, I pull them out of my ears and program the treadmill to slow down as Theo waits for me to catch my breath.

"Yeah?" I ask between gasps of air.

He checks the treadmill's dashboard and sees how many miles I've run, giving me a wary look. "You all right, man?"

"Yeah. Fine," I pant. "Why?"

His eyes remain narrow slits, but he doesn't call me out for why I've been beating the shit out of my body for the past hour on the treadmill. "Practice starts in a few, so I'm gonna get my skates. You good here?"

I nod, indecision niggling in the back of my mind. So I can't talk myself out of it, I ask, "You think your coach will mind if I join?"

He raises his eyebrows. "You wanna get on the ice?"

"Sure. Why not?"

I can see his skepticism as soon as the words roll off my tongue.

Why not?

Maybe because I haven't touched the ice since my dad died. Because I obliterated my future after his accident. Because I retired from hockey and everything to do with the sport when I turned down my scholarship and burned my pads in a dumpster behind my house.

That's why he's surprised. Why he's looking at me like I've grown a second head. And I don't blame him. No one understood why I left after my father passed. Even I didn't understand. I loved hockey. My dad loved hockey. But it was too much after the accident. It hit too close to home. I could barely get out of bed, and I was expected to skate? To go to practice when Coach Thorne wasn't there to critique our plays? It was bullshit.

And it wasn't fair.

But Ash was right last night.

I shouldn't have given up. I shouldn't have quit. Despite the pain, the blood, the sweat, and the tears that went into becoming the player I was, I loved it. And no matter how much time or distance has passed since I've been on the ice, I still love it. Still miss it.

And I think it's time I stop running.

"Come on," Theo says when he realizes I don't have the desire to analyze the reasoning behind my decision. He pulls the red cord connected to the treadmill and moves aside so I can jump off. Then, he guides me into the guy's locker room and says, "Let's find you a pair of skates."

25
ASHLYN

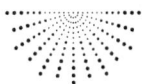

As I round the corner onto my street, my heels dig into the ground, and I stop short.

My car is sitting in the driveway. It's parked next to Colt's black truck. I'd been meaning to drop it off at Logan's house, but since I've been avoiding anything and everything to do with the Taylor House--and everyone who lives there--I hadn't gotten around to it yet.

Apparently, a certain someone decided to take the situation into his own hands.

Great.

Squeezing the straps on my backpack, I trudge up the steps to the porch and push open the front door as dread fills my system.

Please don't be here. Please don't be here, I silently pray to whatever god might be listening.

My heart plummets to my stomach.

"Hey!" Mia calls from the couch as *The Office* flickers on the television screen behind her.

My attention darts to Colt on the cushion next to her. I

can't stop myself. He looks tense. Wary. Like he's been caught doing something he shouldn't.

With a fake-ass smile, I close the front door behind me and reply, "Hey guys."

"How was class?" Mia asks.

"Fine." I slip off my backpack and grab the handle on top of it, letting the weight ground me.

"Colt returned your car," she adds.

"Saw it." I pause, glance at Colt, and drop my gaze to the ground. "Thanks. I'm, uh, gonna…leave you two alone. So…yeah."

Without a backward glance, I head down the hall toward my bedroom, anxious to get the hell out of there. When I reach my bedroom, the backpack slips from my fingers and falls to the floor next to the door with a heavy thud.

Knowing Colt's dating Mia and seeing it firsthand are two very different things. At least they weren't kissing, right? I mean, I'm sure they have. Honestly, they've probably done a lot more––Mia isn't exactly a nun. It's good, right? That I didn't walk in anything too scarring.

And I'm happy for them. I'm happy they're happy and are getting along, and––*dammit!*

I rub at my sternum, trying to ease the ache in my chest as I collapse onto the side of my bed and close my eyes.

Shit, it hurts.

It shouldn't, though. I shouldn't care. So, why the hell do I?

A quiet knock makes my head snap up, and I drop my hand to my lap as if I've been caught doing something I shouldn't. You know, like licking my wounds when I definitely shouldn't have any in the first place.

Colt's leaning against the doorjamb. Watching me, though I can't read his expression.

"Can I help you?" I ask, my voice full of sarcasm.

"Hey," he mutters, scratching his temple with a crooked finger.

Really? We're gonna go with nonchalance?

No, thank you.

Cocking my head to one side, I say, "You shouldn't have fixed my car."

"Felt like the least I could do."

"It wasn't your job."

"Didn't need to be," he argues.

Gah! He's so...infuriating!

Part of me wants to smack him, while the other wants to kiss the crap out of him. Obviously, the latter isn't exactly an option, which leaves me where, exactly?

Oh. I know. It leaves me sexually frustrated and pining after a guy who's only in my house because he's dating my best friend.

Fan-freaking-tastic.

"Fine," I grit out.

On shaky legs, I stand up, walk toward him, and bend down, picking up my backpack next to the entrance while ignoring how close Colt and I are standing. The metallic zipper sounds like nails on a chalkboard as I open my bag, searching for my wallet inside. "How much do I owe you?"

"You don't owe me anything."

My nostrils flare, and I pull out my blue wallet but realize I only have a couple of twenties in cash.

Great.

Dropping it back into the backpack, I let the bag fall with a thud at our feet and pull out my phone from my back pocket. "What's your Venmo account?"

"Not necessary." He pushes himself away from the doorjamb until he's towering over me.

I can feel his breath tickling the wisps of hair on top of my head, proving how freaking close we really are, though I don't look up as I unlock my phone and find the Venmo app. "Will you simply answer the question, so you can get back to your girlfriend?"

"She's not--"

"Stop." With my chin to my chest, I force out a slow breath. "Just stop. Stop lying. Stop twisting things. Stop messing with my head. Tell me how much I owe you, go back to Mia, and leave me alone."

"Ash." The pleading in his voice almost does me in, but I stay strong, refusing to look at him. "Fine. Three hundred should do it, right?"

"Ash," he repeats.

"Not enough? How 'bout five? Does five hundred sound fair?" I delete the previous three digits from the app and jab at my screen, typing in five-zero-zero.

He takes my phone from my grasp and puts it behind his back. "Ash, stop."

Glaring up at him, I seethe, "Give me my phone."

"Not until you promise to let the car be a gift, and you won't pay me back."

"You don't own me. I can do whatever I want."

"Then, you can say goodbye to your phone," he counters, his jaw ticking as he looks down at me, his gaze flashing with determination.

Annoyed, I reach around his taut torso, scrambling for my phone behind his back, but he keeps it away from me in some messed-up version of keep-away.

"Give me my phone," I demand.

"Not until you promise you won't pay me back."

I scramble for the cell again, but he jerks it away. "Look, it's not a big deal--"

"It *is* a big deal," I argue, reaching for my phone again, but he simply twists away from me, using his own body as a barrier between me and my cell until my front is nearly plastered to his, and our arms are tangled together.

"Give me my phone," I spit.

He lifts his arm above my head, using his height to his advantage as he leans his head closer to mine. "Let me do this for you."

I rise onto my tiptoes, reaching for my stupid cell when my breasts brush against his chest, sending a jolt of electricity between us. And I know I'm not the only one who feels it.

Shit.

Dropping my hand to my side, I rock back on my heels and put an inch of much-needed space between us and fold my arms. "Why?" I demand. "Why do you want to do this for me?"

"Because I want to," he deflects, looking down at me, his eyes shining with *something*, though I can't place what it is.

"Why?" I repeat. But I don't know what I'm expecting to hear. And honestly, I'm not even sure I'm talking about the stupid car anymore.

I wanna know why he won't leave me alone. Not only physically but also emotionally. Because I can't stop thinking about him. Where he's at when I'm not with him. What he's thinking. If the feelings are mutual, or if I've made up the chemistry between us.

It's confusing. And draining. And I don't know how to cope with it or how to make it go away. I feel lost. And more alone than I've felt in my entire life.

"You can't keep doing this," I murmur.

"I'm not doing anything––"

"Bullshit," I spit. "You can't keep messing with my head. You can't keep betraying Mia––"

"I'm not betraying her."

"Just stop," I seethe. "Stop lying."

"I'm not lying."

"Bullshit." I shake my head. "This is all bullshit." I step away from him and find his keys on my nightstand. I march back to him and shove them against his chest. "Here. These belong to you. Oh. And one more thing." I take his T-shirt folded on top of my dresser, the same one taunting me since our little encounter in his hallway, and offer it to him.

But he doesn't take it.

"I gave it to you," he replies.

Like some silent battle of wills, I push it to his chest, but he lets his arms hang limply at his sides, refusing to give in.

"Fine." I slip past him and march down the hallway toward Mia, using the sweetest, most sincere voice I can muster. "Hey, Mia! I almost forgot. Colt wanted me to give this to you." I drop the shirt on Mia's lap and look over my shoulder at him. "Right, Colt?"

His lips are pulled into a thin line, and he's glaring at me, but he doesn't say a word.

Sensing the animosity between us, Mia interjects, "Uh… thank you?"

Satisfied, I slip past a frozen Colt in the hall and close my bedroom door behind me. Quietly. Carefully. So he won't know how angry––how *jealous*––I really am.

But my pride over finally beating Colt at his own game only lasts for about two seconds. It fades away, replaced with longing and regret.

Because what just happened between us? It feels a lot more final than what I'd been hoping. But isn't it what I want? To finally end this stupid charade?

I don't know anymore.

And my victory?

It doesn't taste sweet.

Actually, it tastes like shit.

I hate it.

26

ASHLYN

I skipped the last tutoring session with Colt.

I also returned the twenty dollars Logan Venmoed me for the Uber I stood up.

He hasn't texted me since. He hasn't come over. Hasn't tried to reach me. I'm not surprised.

I turn off the water in the shower and dry my body with the white terry-cloth towel on the rack in the bathroom.

It's past midnight on a Thursday night--er, Friday morning, I guess. I should be sleeping. Or studying. Or binge-watching a show with Mia and Kate. Or mending things with my boyfriend. Or ending things with him. I should be doing a lot of things. Instead, I'm here. In the shower. Washing away an unproductive day while the memories of Colt Thorne cling to my skin.

Forcing my limbs to move, I wrap the towel around my chest and knot it above my breasts. I'm brushing my hair when my phone dings with an incoming text.

The words blur with my confusion, and the brush clatters to the floor, slipping from my grasp as I read the message.

Logan: I found someone else. We're over.

I blink, convinced I've read the text wrong. Convinced it was sent to the wrong person. Convinced someone did something to my phone and changed Logan's number to mess with me. To see how I would react to something so delusional, so completely ridiculous.

Because there's no way this message is real.

Logan: I found someone else. We're over.

I slam my phone against the counter, my insides hot with rage.

Years.

Years of building a relationship, and he ends it with less than ten words in a text message? Whatever confusion I'd been harboring inside of me boils into full-blown fury.

How dare he!

I stab at my phone, typing a response but end up dialing his number instead. He thinks we're going to have this conversation through text messages?

Bullshit.

The call goes straight to voicemail.

Frustrated, I hang my head and press the corner of my phone against my forehead, forcing slow, controlled breaths.

Breathe, Ash. Breathe.

It's going to be okay.

Ya know what? Screw it.

Like a bull in a China shop, I rummage through my dresser and throw on a pink tank top and shorts. Once my lady bits are covered, I grab my keys and book it to my car, dialing Logan's number for the umpteenth time, but it goes straight to voicemail. Again.

Of course, it does.

I don't care about my relationship with him anymore, but I'm not letting the coward get away with breaking my heart over a text.

It's bullshit.

But what I hate even more? How I can still hear Colt's warning when he asked if I was the only one willing to save my relationship with Logan.

I stop short in the driveway and look at my car parked out front. My car that became the catalyst for so many screwed-up emotions I can barely look at it right now.

I'm too pissed.

At Colt for fixing it in the first place.

At Logan for his stupid text message.

I'm pissed at a lot of things.

And I'm done ignoring them.

Ripping open my car door, I climb inside with one goal in mind.

It's time I stop running.

It's time to face the truth.

27
ASHLYN

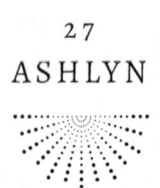

My damp hair hangs in ropes down my back as I shove my car into park and stomp toward the Taylor House. By some miracle, there isn't a party tonight. The house is dark. Empty.

Part of me wonders if it's because Theo knew I'd wind up here after Logan's message *if* Logan had the decency to tell his best friends about our break up in the first place.

And it's a big if.

But if Logan did tell them, Theo probably knew I'd cause a scene. And if he's adamant about anything, it's keeping the drama away from the Taylor House, so he can focus on random women, copious amounts of alcohol, and hockey.

Well, fun fact, boys. I'm about to rain fire and brimstone on the Taylor House.

You ready?

I yank my hair into a high, messy bun without giving a shit what it looks like and bang my fist against the front door.

When it stays closed, I start yelling, "Logan fucking Cameron! Open this door right now!" I slap my hand against the hard surface again. "I'm not even kidding, Logan! You broke up with me in a text message? Are you freaking kidding me right now?!" My hand aches as I pound my fist against the door again. "I'm not leaving until you have the balls to--"

The door swings open, and I stumble back and straighten my spine.

"Can you keep your voice down?" Colt looks around the porch and over the dark street. "You're gonna wake up the neighbors."

"I don't give a shit about the fucking neighbors, Colt," I seethe, ignoring his mussed hair, lack of shirt, and the same freaking gray sweatpants from the first time we met in his kitchen. "Where's Logan?"

He rubs at his tired eyes. "Logan?"

"No, I'm looking for the tooth fairy," I spit. "Why the hell do you think I'm here?"

With an exhausted sigh, he squeezes the back of his neck, his bicep bulging as he answers, "He isn't here."

"Where the hell is he? You know what?" Without waiting for an invitation, I storm inside the house like a raging bull, ready to tear apart anything and everything standing in my way from confronting Logan and demanding an ounce of respect to end our relationship the way it deserves.

In. Freaking. Person.

"Sure, come on in," Colt mutters under his breath, the door softly clicking closed behind me.

"Where is he?" I repeat as I scan the dark family room and empty kitchen. Logan's nowhere in sight.

Pinching the bridge of his nose, Colt lifts one shoulder into a shrug. "Look, I dunno where your boyfriend is. I went to bed and woke up with you pounding on the door and throwing a fit on my porch like a toddler."

"Throwing a fit? Wow. Thanks, Colt. Way to validate my

feelings. And he isn't my boyfriend anymore," I add, folding my arms and tucking my hands into the crooks of my elbows to keep them from shaking. But I'm fuming. Hell, I'm more than fuming. I'm burning up inside.

Colt's eyes widen in surprise, which only pisses me off more.

"Did you know?" I demand, marching closer to him. But he doesn't retreat. If anything, he looks ready to go to battle, daring me to push him when it's clear he hasn't been sleeping well.

Little does he know, I've already been pushed past the edge. And right now? I'm falling, blindly reaching for anything to keep me from crashing into the inevitable truth.

Logan was cheating on me.

And I was too stupid to see it for myself.

Colt looks down at me, the same dark, flinty gaze of his making my stomach flip-flop, but he stays quiet.

"Did you know?" I repeat, refusing to back down.

"Know what, Sunshine?"

"Did you know he was cheating on me?" The words taste bitter as they roll off my tongue.

I lick my lips and hold onto my anger, even though I can feel it transitioning into despair and hurt. But I don't want to hurt right now. Not with Colt standing in front of me, witnessing how pathetic I really am. I shove the feeling aside as I picture Logan screwing someone who isn't me. I lift my chin, ready to go head-to-head with anyone who will listen.

"Did you know he was sleeping around, Colt? Is it why you kept messing with my head? Using me like a freaking yo-yo? Playing with my emotions? Because you knew Logan didn't love me anymore? Is it why you've been so hot and cold? And if it is, why the hell didn't you tell me? I had a right to know." My nose wrinkles in disgust as I shake my head. "You know what? I think that's even worse." I laugh, though there isn't any humor in it. "You had nothing to gain by keeping it from me--"

"He's my friend, Ash."

I scoff and stand on my tiptoes, closing a bit more of our height difference, though it doesn't make me feel any less small. "And what am I? Huh, Colt? Your plaything? Your tutor? What am I to you? I wanna know--"

His mouth slams against mine, taking my breath with it as he slips his tongue between my lips and tangles his fingers in my damp hair. I moan at the contact, opening my mouth wider for him. Letting him take what he wants, how he wants it.

He tastes amazing. My toes curl as his other hand slides along my lower back and presses me against him. Hot. Needy. Kisses. I feel like I can't breathe. Like I'm out of control. Out of my freaking mind. Because he tastes good. Better than I imagined. Better than anything I've ever experienced.

I moan and dig my fingers into his biceps. Lost. Yet more at home than I've ever been before I realize I'm kissing Colt. Colt Thorne. The same Colt who's dating my best friend.

"Stop." I push at his chest and jerk out of his grasp, my chest heaving as I press my fingers against my bruised lips. But it doesn't erase his taste or the memory of his hands on me from seconds ago, or the fact his lips don't belong to me. They belong to Mia.

"What did I do?" I breathe out.

Reaching for me again, he murmurs, "Ash--"

"No." I step back. "You're dating Mia!"

"We aren't dating--"

"Bullshit," I spit. "I can't believe I kissed you." My legs are like Jell-O as I continue my unsteady retreat until my back hits the wall behind me and steals the air from my lungs. "I came here to confront Logan for cheating on me. I couldn't believe he'd do it. That he'd betray me like that. And I..." I slide onto my ass and pull my knees to my chest. "I kissed you. I kissed my best friend's boyfriend. I'm just as bad as Logan. Hell, I'm worse. I can't--"

"Ash." He squats next to me on the hardwood floor, grabs my face, and forces me to look at him. "I'm not dating Mia."

I shake my head, but he keeps his grasp firm. "Don't lie."

"I'm not lying."

"She called you her boyfriend."

"Ash--"

"She called you her boyfriend," I repeat, my voice rising along with my panic and disgust.

Desperate, he says, "It's not what you think."

"What is it?" I demand, well aware of how insane I must sound right now, but I can't help it. I stabbed my friend in the back. I can't believe--

"It's fake," he blurts out.

I shake my head, convinced I'm hallucinating. "W-what?"

"My relationship with Mia," he clarifies. "It's fake."

"That doesn't make any sense," I whisper.

"Shorty's been messing with her, okay? He hasn't been leaving her alone. He's been following her home from work, showing up at her classes, and a bunch of other shit. After I broke up their argument at SeaBird, Shorty made some smartass comment to her about me only wanting to get into her pants and I wouldn't be interested in having an actual relationship with her. *No one* would be interested in having a real relationship with her. So, she lied. She said we were dating. Said we're together."

My mouth opens with another rebuttal on the tip of my tongue, but I stop myself. I knew Shorty was messing with Mia. Maybe not to this extent, but I knew something was up. But if that's the case, why didn't she tell me? I scramble to put the pieces together, attempting to decipher fact from fiction, but it's too convoluted, too messy to make any sense.

Shaking my head back and forth, I press my fingers to my lips and whisper, "You're lying."

"I'm not lying, Sunshine."

"Why do you call me that?"

His expression softens into a ghost of a smile. One barely there, yet somehow reaching his eyes. "You're a ray of sunshine, Ash. You're the only thing I've been looking forward to since I moved back. Maybe even before then," he admits, his eyes going hazy. "Since my dad died."

I sniff, refusing to give in to the sweetness of his sentiment. Because I can't. I can't care about his past the way I want to. Because he isn't mine. And if there's any chance of it changing, I need answers. And I need them now.

"Then what happened?" I demand. "You...agreed to fake-date Mia?"

"She took me out to dinner. Asked if I would cover for her. I agreed."

"Why?"

"Because the only girl I really wanted was in a relationship with my friend." He rubs his thumb against my cheek. "I wouldn't have kissed you if I was in a real relationship, Ash. I'm not a cheater. And you're not in a relationship now, either," he reminds me. "We've done nothing wrong."

My tongue darts out, and I lick my bottom lip as I give in and lean into his touch while refusing to acknowledge how good it feels. How good *he* makes me feel.

"Why didn't you tell me?" I force out. "About Logan. About Mia."

"I felt like it wasn't my secret to tell."

"And Logan?" I push.

He hesitates, letting out a sigh. "My history with Logan is complicated. We've been friends for years. Had each other's back through everything. He said he was done having anyone else on the side, and I wanted to believe him."

"But why?" I choke out. "If you wanted me, why would you want to believe him?"

"I didn't want you to get hurt, Ash. And you wanted Logan," he reminds me. A bitterness seeps into his words, and his shoulders slump slightly. "When I found he was cheating again, I gave him a week to come clean, or I'd do it for him."

Chewing on the inside of my cheek while refusing to acknowledge how painful it is to hear Colt say the truth aloud, I choke out, "When did you tell him?"

"The night your car broke down."

"Is that why you were so frustrated?"

He nods. "I didn't want you to get hurt."

I blink back my tears and suck my lips between my teeth as his words wash over me, and I admit, "I am hurt."

"I know, Ash," he murmurs. "I'm sorry."

"You lied."

"I know," he repeats. "But I didn't mean to. I didn't want to."

I shake my head. "I thought you were with Mia. Part of me *still* thinks you're with Mia," I clarify.

"I'm not with Mia, Ash. I promise."

"Even if you're not, I just got out of a relationship. It's not like I can dive right into another"--I wave my hand at him--"*something* with one of my ex's friends."

"Ash…"

"I gotta go, Colt."

"Ash," he begs. But he doesn't say anything else. I think part of him knows how impossible this situation is, the same way I do.

I push myself to my feet, ignoring how weak my knees feel as I walk toward the front door.

He doesn't stop me.

But as I back out of the driveway, there's a silhouette in the family room window, and I know it's him. Like I know in my gut, whatever's going on between us is far from over.

The question is…how long will it last until it inevitably ends?

28

ASHLYN

I couldn't sleep. Too many what-ifs were fluttering through my mind like a group of caged bats to let me do anything but overanalyze my relationships with every single person I care about.

And after how I left things with Colt?

This sucks.

By the time 8:45 a.m. rolls around, I've already made bacon, scrambled eggs, and french toast. I'm also two seconds from knocking down Mia's door and demanding answers because even if I don't want to admit it, my trust in men is at an all-time low. And if Colt's lying to me about his relationship with Mia? I'll be wrecked.

"Do I smell breakfast?" Kate asks as she walks into the kitchen.

The girl is responsible with a capital R and is always in bed by ten, hits the gym by eight the next morning, and is sitting front and center in her first class by nine. To be honest, I feel like our paths haven't even crossed in weeks.

Motioning to the smorgasbord on the stove, I tell her, "What's mine is yours. Come eat."

She rounds the kitchen island and peruses her options, asking, "What's the special occasion?"

"Logan and I broke up."

With a piece of bacon two inches from her mouth, she freezes. "Yikes."

I let out a breath of laughter, and it feels good. To laugh. To not be sad for two seconds of the freaking day. To be reminded the world isn't going to stop turning because my asshole ex broke up with me over a text message.

"Something like that," I admit, rolling my eyes.

"Do you want me to skip class? We can talk about it."

"I'm okay," I lie.

Unconvinced, she props one hand on her hip while pointing the strip of bacon at me. "You sure?"

"Positive. We should've broken up a long time ago."

"I agree," she returns with a smile, popping the bacon in her mouth. "But still," she argues, her mouth full of food. "You know I'm here for you, right?"

"I know."

She swallows. "Do you want me to egg his house or something? Maybe figure out how to slip him some Ex-Lax into his morning cup of coffee? 'Cause you know I will."

"Thanks. But seriously. I'm all right."

"Hmm." She grabs another strip of bacon and takes a bite while giving me the side-eye. As she chews, she starts dishing up a small portion of French toast, slathers it with butter, and sprinkles cinnamon and sugar on top.

When she catches me staring, she asks, "You sure you're okay?"

"He was an asshole who was cheating on me, so yeah. I'm fine." I lift my chin toward her breakfast. "Do you want any syrup?"

"Too messy. Besides, if you're sure you're all right and

don't want to give me all the gory details yet…" She pauses and waits for my reply.

"Maybe later."

"Then, I gotta get to class," she finishes. "But you should text me if you want to talk. I know I overpacked my schedule this semester, and things are crazy, but I'll always make time for you guys, okay?"

With a nod, I pull her into a quick hug and shove her toward the door. "Ditto. Now, get out of here. We'll talk later."

As the door closes behind her, I check the time on my phone and tap the corner of it against my chin. Part of me wonders if I should let Mia sleep, but the other part is too anxious to care.

After piling up a stack of French toast, eggs, and bacon onto a plate, I open her bedroom door without bothering to knock.

"Rise and shine, Mia," I say, though I'm not brutal enough to flick the lights on.

The lump on her mattress groans as Mia's head pops out above the mess of sheets. "What time is it?"

"Nine a.m."

"What?" she screeches, fumbling with her eye mask until she can see me. "Nine in the morning? Did someone die?"

I laugh and sit down on the edge of her bed. "No. No one died."

But someone might if they don't spill the beans soon.

"So, why are you waking me up so freaking early?" She opens one eye. "And do I smell bacon?"

With another laugh, I take one of the three strips on the breakfast tray and put it in my mouth, letting the salty goodness roll over my taste buds, humming, "Mm-hmm."

She pushes herself up, rests her back against the headboard, and reaches for the tray, resting it on her lap. "Now *this* is how you wake a friend up." Another piece of bacon disappears from the tray as she shoves it into her mouth and licks her fingertips. "So good."

"Glad I could be of service."

"Now, if you could tell me *why* you made bacon and woke me up before noon when I don't have any classes, that'd be great," she quips, slicing off a bite of French toast soaking in syrup with her fork and knife.

"What's going on between you and Colt?"

She stops mid-chew, her gaze darting over to me. She sets her fork and knife back on the tray while looking guilty as hell.

"Why do you ask?" she questions.

"Because I want to know."

"There's not much to tell."

"Mia," I warn.

"Fine. We're dating. Nothing too serious or anything, but yeah."

"And you and Shorty?" I prod.

Like a scared little girl, she fidgets with the napkin, twisting it between her fingers until I'm pretty sure only tiny shreds will be left if I don't take it from her soon.

"Tell me," I push, grabbing the napkin and tossing it onto the tray.

"Nothing's going on between me and Shorty. We broke up. I started dating Colt. End of story."

"Colt explained things a little differently."

Her breath hitches. "You talked to Colt?"

"Yeah. I did."

"Why?"

"Because Logan broke up with me over a text message last night, and when I went to confront him, Colt answered the door instead. And then, I kissed him. Or he kissed me?" I shake my head. "It doesn't matter. What does matter is I kissed him for a whole two seconds before realizing I was kissing my best friend's boyfriend, and I felt like absolute crap, so I pulled away and had a mental breakdown on the first floor of the Taylor House."

She gasps and reaches for my hand, squeezing it tightly. "Oh, Ash, I'm so sorry."

"*I'm* sorry," I reply. "I shouldn't have kissed Colt, or let him kiss me, or…" Again, I shake my head. "Everything was so…*complicated*. And it happened so fast, and I was hurting, and--"

"And he told you the truth," she finishes, her skin paling.

"His version of it," I answer quietly. "But I'd love it if you could confirm it for me."

She sets the tray on her nightstand and pats the bed beside her, so I climb onto it, resting my back against the headboard until we're side by side.

With her head on my shoulder, she murmurs, "Shorty's been following me. Or at least, he was until I blurted out I was seeing someone else. He didn't believe me, so I convinced Colt to be my fake boyfriend. And because he's an absolute gentleman, he agreed to play along."

"Why do you think Colt agreed to do it?"

She hesitates. "He said it was because he has a little sister, and he'd want someone else to step up and help if she was in the same situation." She lifts her head and looks at me. "It didn't hurt that the girl he really wanted was already in a relationship, and he didn't feel like sleeping around anymore."

"Don't say that."

"I'm serious," she replies. "There's only so much to talk about when Colt drives me home from work or when we're hanging out and watching movies to help solidify our little scheme. He likes you. And take it from someone with personal experience…he's thoughtful and kind and will make an excellent boyfriend. It's a shame I have to break up with him now."

I sit up and turn to her. "You don't have to break up with him."

"Yes, I do. You said so yourself. You and Logan broke up. You're officially on the market."

"I'm not on the market."

"Yes, you are."

"No. I'm not," I argue.

"Ash--"

"Mia," I mimic, using her same tone. "I'm not going to jump from one relationship to the next, especially not with my ex's best friend. You know I'm not that kind of girl."

"One. Baloney. You most definitely are that kind of girl."

"No, I'm not."

"Yes, you are," she argues with a laugh. "You've only been with one guy, and his name starts with an L and ends with asshole."

I snort.

"You were made to have relationships, Ash. There's nothing wrong with it. And there's a great guy who'd kill to be in one with you. Sure, he's friends with your ex, but it's not the end of the world."

"One, baloney," I say, using her word choice from seconds ago. "You have no idea whether or not Colt would kill to be in a relationship with me. And two, even if Colt *does*, he's already in one with you," I point out.

"Ash--"

"Yes, I know it's fake," I interrupt. "But I'm not going to let you break up with him and pop back up on Shorty's radar because I feel something for Colt. It isn't fair to you. And honestly? I don't know if it's fair to Colt either."

"What do you mean?"

"I don't know," I admit. "I don't know what I want. Logan

hurt me, Mia. He broke my trust *badly*. And yeah, Colt and I have some off-the-charts chemistry when it comes to physical stuff, but emotionally? I'm scared to let down those walls again. What if it blows up in my face?"

"You won't know until you try."

"Yeah, but in order to try, I'd have to put Colt's friendship with Logan on the line, along with putting you in a not-so-great position with Shorty."

"Do you, though?" she asks.

"What do you mean?"

"What if…" She taps her fingers against her lips, thinking. "What if Colt and I keep up our charade of dating while you and he figure out where you want your relationship to go? You know, whether you guys can open up to each other emotionally or if your connection is purely physical."

I cringe. "Sounds messy."

"Maybe? Maybe not. You guys can hook up, have all the rebound sex you want, and if it turns into more, Colt and I can stage a fake breakup."

"Which puts you back on Shorty's radar," I point out.

"My fake relationship with Colt is going to have an expiration date anyway. It's not like I'm going to be able to convince him to marry me or something. He's a good guy, Ash, but he's not that great."

I laugh. "But what about Colt's friendship with Logan?"

"You already know Colt would be willing to put his friendship with Logan on the line since he kissed you."

"Which shouldn't have happened," I mutter.

"Why not?" she challenges. Reaching for her fork, she stabs another piece of French toast and shoves it in her mouth. "You said he kissed you after you and Logan broke up. In my book, you guys did nothing wrong. And like I said, you aren't even saying you want to jump into a relationship or anything. You only want to test the waters. There's nothing wrong with that."

Chewing on the pad of my thumb, I let the million potential obstacles roll through me. Finally, I ask, "Do you think Colt would go for it?"

"To get in your pants?" She quirks her brow. "Yeah. I think he'd go for it."

Another laugh escapes me. "Mia."

"You know what I mean," she argues. "The question is, when are you going to talk to him?"

"No idea. We have a tutoring session in a couple of days, but I don't exactly want to run into Logan at his place, so…"

"You shouldn't let Logan control you like that."

"I'm not letting him control me."

"You're refusing to meet at his house all because he lives there. That's letting him control you."

"Says the girl who's fake dating a guy to keep her ex off her back?" I challenge.

Her nostrils flare, but she doesn't deny it. "Fine. What if you guys come here?"

"And you'd be okay with it?"

She gives me a look like I'm crazy and asks, "Why wouldn't I be?"

"I don't know?"

"We aren't really together," she reminds me for the hundredth time. "I have no claim over Colt Thorne. And I don't want to have any claim over Colt Thorne. Invite him over. See what he thinks about your idea."

"About us hooking up without a title?" I grimace, the idea leaving a bad taste in my mouth. "You know what would happen if someone found out. They'd think he was cheating on you with me. It would make everyone look bad."

"Everyone but me," she teases.

"Mia…"

"I'm kidding. And even though you make a good point, I think it's still worth the risk. Don't you?"

I bite my lip. "Maybe?"

"Maybe?" Her perfectly plucked brow arches.

"Okay, yes. I think Colt's worth the risk. The question is, does he think I am too?"

"Only one way to find out." She stabs a piece of cold French toast. "Now, get out of here so I can enjoy my breakfast."

I take a step toward the door as she calls out, "Wait!"

"Yeah?"

She throws off the sheets with a soft whoosh and heads to her closet, rummaging through it for a few seconds. When she finds what she's looking for, she tosses me a grin over her shoulder and throws me a white ball of cotton fabric.

"What the...?" My voice trails off as I straighten the material and lift it in the air. "Colt's shirt? Really?"

She grins back at me. "Thought I'd hold onto it in case you needed it. You're welcome, by the way."

Tucking it over my arm, I roll my eyes. "Whatever. Enjoy your breakfast."

"Enjoy your orgasms when Colt sees you in his shirt!" she calls as I walk out of her room.

I cover my face and laugh.

Whatever.

29
COLT

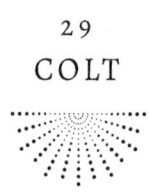

Ash and I haven't spoken since I kissed her, and she pushed me away. I told her how I felt, and she went home. I didn't reach out to her afterward. Didn't think I should, no matter how much I wanted to.

She texted me yesterday, though. She invited me to her place for the tutoring session so she wouldn't run into Logan.

But the text was short. Detached. And it didn't tell me anything about what she's thinking after her conversation with Mia.

Which means I'm flying blind.

And I hate flying blind.

Tearing my attention from her bedroom window, I climb out of my truck and lock the doors. Trudging up the steps, my senses are on full alert. After a few soft knocks against Ash's door, it opens with a quiet squeak.

"Hi," Ash greets me, her baby blue gaze dropping to the floor. Shy. Unsure. Sexy as hell.

"Hey."

She steps aside but doesn't say a word, letting me into her apartment as Mia appears from the hall.

"Hey, Lover Boy," she says when she sees me as she grabs her purse from the coat rack next to the door. "I'm going out. You two have fun." Her attention shifts from Ash to me, and she winks, slipping out the door without a backward glance.

"Everything good?" I ask as I watch her disappear down the stairs toward the driveway.

"Mm-hmm," Ash hums. She wrings her hands in front of her. Realizing she's fidgeting, she forces herself to stop and motions to the kitchen table. "Wanna take a seat?"

My brow quirks, but I head to the table, letting her take the lead, but I'm not sure she knows where to go from here. The truth is, neither do I. As I pull out the chair, the legs scrape against the laminate floor, sounding like rumble strips on the highway in the otherwise silent room.

I wait, suffocating in Ash's presence. I want to kiss her. I want to ask if we're okay. If she's upset I kissed her. If she spoke with Mia. If she's talked to Logan. I want to ask her a lot of things, but I stay quiet, forcing myself to let her take the lead even if it kills me.

"Can I, uh, get you anything to drink?" she offers.

"I'm good, thanks."

"Okay." She rocks back on her heels. "Are you hungry or anything?"

"Just ate."

"Got it."

"You gonna take a seat, Ash?" I challenge, turning in my chair to face her fully. "You're making me nervous."

She looks like a scared little mouse. One who will scurry off in the opposite direction if I'm not careful. I've never seen her this nervous. It's adorable as shit. And surprisingly, it gives me hope.

"Oh. Sorry. Of course." She sits across from me and folds her arms.

"You sure everything's good?"

"Yup. Everything's...great."

"You talk to Logan?" I prod.

She shakes her head, her anxiety dimming into sadness. "No. I haven't seen him since before I showed up on your doorstep the other day."

"Neither have I," I return. "I think he knows I wanna beat the shit out of him."

Her gaze flicks to mine as she registers my comment. The makeup around her eyes is darker today. More pronounced. Her lips are a shade darker, too, like she's wearing lipstick or lipgloss or...something. I scan her up and down. Actually, she looks more put together than I've seen in a long time, but effortlessly so. Like she wants to look like she woke up that way, but it's an illusion. One I could die in if she'd let me.

Fucking beautiful.

If only I knew what was going through her pretty little head.

"Why do you want to beat the shit out of Logan?" she asks when she catches me staring.

Jealousy floods my system as his name rolls off her tongue, and I shift in my chair, resting my elbows on the dark oak table. "Because he hurt you."

She nods, not bothering to deny it.

"But I kind of want to buy him dinner too," I add.

She tilts her head to one side, surprised. "Why?"

"Because he was too much of a dumbass to see what he was leaving behind."

Her tinted lips lift into a smile. "I think that's up for debate. But thank you."

Not up for debate, I want to argue, but instead, I ask, "Did you talk to Mia too?"

She nods.

"And?"

"And she's on my list for not telling me about Shorty's advances," Ash replies. "But she did corroborate your story."

My heart pounds a little harder. "Yeah?"

She nods again. "Yeah."

"And?"

"And she's happy to let you out of the fake relationship whenever you want." She bites the pad of her thumb, her baby blue gaze glued to a knot in the stained table separating us. Finally, she peeks up at me again, her lips parting slightly. "She also said you're allowed to hook up with whoever you want despite your fake relationship, so…I guess we're both off the hook for the kiss."

"Good to know."

"I'm sorry I freaked out," she adds. "And…I guess I wanted you to know I liked it. The kiss. And since we're off the hook now…" Her voice trails off, and she licks her lips, looking so damn innocent but curious too.

And it's the way she says it. With an undertone of some kind. Maybe it's the spark in her eyes. Maybe it's hunger in my own. But I feel like a switch flipped. Like she's given me a green light. Like all she needed was for Mia to give *her* the green light. And now that we have it, I'm going to take full advantage.

"Is that right?" I muse, pushing to my feet.

My footsteps are slow and controlled as I round the table.

Ash's gaze is on me. Curious. Hesitant. Nervous. Her breathing is shallow as I grip the back of her chair and turn it so her knees aren't tucked under the table anymore. Now, she's fully facing me. Her lips slightly parted. Waiting to see what I'm going to do next.

Good question, Ash.

I know what I want to do. The question is, will she let me?

"Seems like you and Mia talked about a lot of things," I mention.

She swallows. "We did."

I slide onto my knees in front of her and skim my hands from her knees to her outer thighs. "Tell me, Ash. Since we're off the hook for the kiss, do you think Mia would mind if I took it a step further with her friend?"

"I…" Her voice catches in her lungs, and she licks her lips. "I think she'd be okay with whatever."

"Whatever?"

She gulps. "Yeah. Whatever."

"Like this?" I rise onto my knees, sliding my hands along her bare arms, over her collarbone, and up her neck to grasp the back of her head. My hold is firm as I pull her closer to me. Without hesitation, she gives in, allowing me to position her any way I please. And shit, does she please me.

She feels like silk against my palms. Soft. Supple. I want to wrap her around me. I want to be buried inside her. I want her skin to rub against mine. To feel her fingers scrape against my back.

I want it all.

"Yeah," she breathes out, her eyelids heavy with lust. "I think this is fine."

I smile and close the last inch of distance between our mouths, swallowing her gasp as our lips connect.

She tastes as good as I remember. Like honey and vanilla. Like heaven. My heart beats faster, and my blood rushes south. I slip my tongue into her mouth, and she sucks on the tip, pulling a groan out of me. It's funny. This is only a kiss. A fucking kiss and I'm on my knees, begging for more. For anything she'll give me.

I could kiss her all day. No food. No sleep. I don't need anything else except her mouth on mine.

My aching cock screams in protest as I smile against her lips.

I stand corrected.

If I'm being greedy, I guess I need one more thing. I need Ash naked so I can worship every inch of her the way she deserves.

My fingers slip down her arms, and I cup her breast in my hand, squeezing over her soft cotton T-shirt. Her whimper is quiet and addictive as she arches her back and wraps her arms around my neck. Desperate. Needy.

Freaking perfect.

Even though it kills me, I let her go and trail my hand down her lithe body, grasping her hip and tugging her to the edge of the chair.

She complies, her greedy mouth taunting mine as she lifts her hips, searching for friction.

I got you, Sunshine.

With deft fingers, I undo the button of her jeans and slide her zipper down as she shimmies out of her pants and underwear, using my shoulders as leverage. Tearing my lips from hers, I put my head on her sternum and nuzzle her perfect tits, breathing in her scent. As she catches her breath, her chest rises and falls. Like she's preparing herself for what's to come. And so am I. Because I've been dreaming about it for weeks.

"Lay back, Ash," I order.

"Colt," she breathes out, watching as I slide down her body and sit on my haunches. Her knees are locked together, and her fingers are pressed to her bruised lips. Watching. Waiting to see what I do next. She looks like a wet dream. Innocent. Vulnerable. Ready to be taken. To be worshipped.

"Let me be a gentleman, Sunshine."

DON'T LET ME FALL

Her mouth tilts up, and she rolls her eyes.

I touch her knees, gliding my hands over her silky smooth thighs before retreating to her calves. Her muscles soften, and I do it again, slipping my hands up her knees and to her hips, then sliding back down. With every pass, she relaxes, her curious stare setting me on fire as she spreads her thighs and gives me a glimpse of her perfect center.

When it comes into view, my mouth waters, and I lean in, peppering kisses along every inch of her skin—nibbling at the soft patch of flesh between her thigh and core. Sucking on her lips, I kiss the most intimate part of her. My cock aches as I lick her slit, greedy for more. With a moan, her fingers tangle into my hair, and she urges me closer.

And fuck, do I want to get closer. I want whatever she'll give me. Because this? This is more than sex. It's Ash. And the way I feel about her? Nothing comes close to it. I want to prove it to her.

Frustrated by the angle, I grab her thighs and toss her legs over my shoulders, lifting her ass off the chair. Then I eat at her like a starving man. And I *am* starving. But not for food. I'm starving for her. I have been since the moment I saw her at the stoplight in her car. And nothing could've prepared me for how addictive she tastes. With the tip of my tongue, I swirl her clit, and she moans, the sound loud but breathy as she twists her hips, fucking my face until her juices are dripping off my chin.

I've never been so turned on in my entire life, but I don't want it to stop. I want to live like this. To die like this.

"Colt." Her fingers thread through my hair, tugging at the roots until I'm pretty sure I'll have a bald spot. "Shit, Colt. Keep doing that. Yes. Right there, Colt. Right. Freaking. There."

Her head tilts back, and her muscles tense beneath my touch as she comes against my mouth with a scream.

I keep lapping at her as she comes down from her high, transforming into putty in my hands. As I get to my feet, she smiles up at me, practically drunk on her orgasm.

"Do you have any idea how good that felt?" she asks.

I chuckle and scrub my hand against my sore scalp. "I have an idea."

She laughs and stands up, her lower half still naked, as she grabs the hem of her shirt and tugs it over her head. With her perfect breasts teasing me through her white, lacy bra, she drops the shirt and steps closer to me, pressing her front against mine. Every curve. Every inch of heated skin. Every piece of the girl I've been lusting after is in front of me. Mine to explore. Mine to take. Mine to savor.

I wrap my arm around her slender waist as she undoes my jeans and slips her dainty little hand into my boxers, squeezing the base of my cock, sliding to the tip, and rubbing her thumb against the head of it until it's fucking weeping.

With a groan, I drop my forehead to Ash's and close my eyes. "You trying to kill me, Sunshine?"

Her laugh is light and makes my chest tighten. "Simply trying to repay the favor. Tell me, Colt. How do you want me?"

Fuuuuck.

30
COLT

The sound of Ash's innocent little voice giving me free rein makes me almost come in my pants against her hand. I grab the back of her head and shove my tongue into her mouth, imagining how good it would feel against my dick while walking us both to the wall. When her back hits it with a soft thud, I grab her wrist and turn her around.

"Hands on the wall," I growl.

She does as she's told.

"Spread your legs."

Again, she listens and peeks over her shoulder, arching her back and giving me a glimpse of how mouth-watering she really is.

"Do you have any idea what you do to me, Ash?" I mutter under my breath as I shove my jeans down, pull out my dick, and rub my hand against it a few times before remembering protection.

Shit, I almost forgot.

I pull a condom out of my wallet and slide it on my swollen cock as Ash bites her bottom lip.

With her eyes glued to my dick, she whispers, "Want to know a secret?"

I step closer and rub the head against her slit. "What?"

"You were right," she breathes out. "In the hall that night. I imagined you. What it would feel like to have you inside of me. To have your lips against mine. Your--" She gasps as I push myself into her, her breathing staggered but laced with need. Resting her head against her forearm on the wall, she catches her breath. "You have no idea how good this feels."

"Trust me," I grunt, forcing myself to stay calm as she adjusts to me being inside her. "I know how good it feels. What else did you imagine?"

"This," she whispers, rolling her hips against mine, silently urging me to continue. "I imagined this. What it would feel like to stretch around you. To hear your groans. To feel you. All of you. The way you'd whisper my name."

I reach my arm around her torso and grab her wrists, forcing her to stand so her back is pressed to my chest. Then I breathe her in. Soak her up. Commit every detail to memory while my cock begs me to thrust into her. To chase the oblivion I know is imminent. But I don't want to. Because I don't know if this will be the last time. And now that I've had a taste? I'm not sure I can go without it again.

Without *her*.

She shifts her hips. "You're killing me, Colt."

I press a kiss to her bare shoulder. "Hands on the wall, Ash."

With spread fingers, she rests her hands against the wall. I grab her waist, retreat a few inches, and push into her again. Over and over, I thrust. She gasps. I groan. She pants. And even though I don't want it to end, I drag my hand down her front and pinch her clit, almost blacking out as her core clenches around me.

Fucking perfect.

Her orgasm pushes me over the edge, and I come hard, pulsing into her with only the thin piece of latex separating us. And for the first time ever, I hate the thin piece of latex. Because even after being this close to her, it isn't enough. I want more. I want it all.

I want *her*.

All of her.

The good.

The bad.

The ugly.

A sheen of sweat clings to her brow as Ash peeks over her shoulder at me and smiles. Her smile. It could light up the world. It's been lighting up mine since the moment we first met.

"Whoa," she breathes, letting out a light, breathy laugh.

I pull off the condom, toss it in the trash beneath the sink, and pick her up, carrying her to the couch.

She laughs a little harder and smacks my shoulder while shaking her head. "Carrying me? Really?"

"Always a gentleman," I quip.

"Mm-hmm," she hums. The sound goes straight to my dick.

"I helped you get off. Twice," I clarify.

"Almost three times," she notes, patting my chest as I sit on the couch, keeping her cradled against me. "Don't worry, though. We'll work on your stamina."

I snort. "Glad I can be another project for you."

She kisses my nose and gives me the same innocent smile but stays quiet as the high from our orgasms slowly fades to the background, and the aftermath of what we did rises to the surface.

I just fucked my best friend's ex.

Shit.

31
COLT

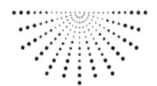

Ash's cheeks are still flushed as she presses her hands to them, her eyes glassy and bright in the middle of her family room. And I want to know what she's thinking. Especially after everything we did. But I don't ask. I simply wait, dragging my fingertips against her thighs as she straddles my hips on the couch.

"We had sex," she murmurs a few seconds later. There's a touch of awe in her voice. Like she's surprised.

With a low chuckle, I brush the hair sticking to her forehead away from her, her skin like silk beneath my fingertips. "Yeah, Sunshine. We did."

"No, but like...*we* had sex," she repeats, emphasizing *we* as she waves her hand back and forth between us. As if I don't get it. As if I can't feel the weight of what we did. Together. After months of build-up. Months of want. Need. It finally happened.

"Yeah. Yeah, we did," I murmur, running my hand up and down her spine as I settle further into the couch cushions, my muscles spent.

Her mouth opens again to argue her point, but a light

laugh spills out, and she covers her face. "Oh, my hell. We had sex. You and me. After all the chaos and the drama and the obstacles and the build-up and…everything. We finally had sex. In my kitchen, mind you. I… Holy shit, Colt. We had sex."

She's cute when she rambles. She's cute all the time. But right now, especially. When her face is pink, her hair is mussed, and her cheeks are pinched from grinning. She's the most beautiful thing I've ever laid eyes on.

Tilting her chin up, I force her to look at me. Her long hair tumbles around her shoulders, a soft smile on her lips, and my chest aches at how gorgeous she really is.

"You okay with it, Sunshine? That we had sex?"

Her soft breath fans across my cheeks as she leans closer and presses her forehead to mine, breathing me in as her pulse flutters in her neck. It's intimate. Something I haven't really felt since high school.

But I like it.

I like *her*.

"Yeah, Colt," she whispers, her elation morphing to acceptance and awe. "Yeah. I'm okay with it. Don't get me wrong. I know this is only a casual hookup and everything, but it's still surreal, ya know? I've only ever been with Logan, so this?" She pecks at my lips again. "This is crazy for me. I just had a casual hookup with Colt Thorne, and I'm kind of reeling from it."

My arms tighten around her, and her muscles soften against me. "Is it all you want? For this to be nothing more than a casual hookup?"

I don't know why I'm disappointed, but I am. All she wants is a casual hookup? Does she even know what those are? The girl screams innocence and commitment louder than a blow horn, for chrissake.

Her teeth dig into the pad of her thumb for a few seconds.

She drops her hand to her lap and shrugs one shoulder. "I think it's all I can handle right now. Especially when you factor in Shorty and Mia and Logan--"

"That's what this is about?" I ask, a sharpness tainting my words. But it's too late to reel it back in. I sit up a little straighter. "Logan? You're kidding me, right?"

Damn, it burns.

She leans away from me, putting a few more inches of space between us. "You're his best friend, Colt. Can you imagine what he would do or how he would act if he found out we hooked up? Especially when he knows I've only ever been with him until today? He'd be pissed--"

"Then, let him be pissed, Ash. He lost you. It's on him. Not me. Not you. *Him*."

"I know," she murmurs, dragging her hands along my shoulders, brushing her thumb against the dip in the center of my brows as if her touch can erase it. "And I don't regret it. Logan and me breaking up. You and me and"--her baby blues flick to the kitchen--"everything that happened. I don't regret any of it." Her gaze meets mine again as she runs her tongue along her lower lip. "But I don't think I'm ready for *complicated* quite yet, assuming you'd even want *complicated* with me." She shakes her head and rolls her eyes. "Forget I said the last part. I guess I'm trying to say I think you and me doing anything other than casually hooking up would get complicated, and I'm not ready for it. But I like what we did. Without the drama or the chaos or...any of the other stuff. Only me and you. Having fun. Studying. And occasionally giving each other orgasms. Does that sound good to you?"

No, it doesn't sound good. It sounds miserable. Which is ironic, considering my past. But she's right about Mia and Shorty. She's right about Logan. She's right about pursuing anything other than a casual hookup turning our worlds upside down. What she doesn't understand is...I'd be okay with it.

"Hey." She cups my cheek and gives me another smile, leaning closer and kissing me. It's soft. Sweet. Innocent. But laced with hesitancy. Like she's scared she offended me or hurt my feelings or something. Probably because Logan was an ass to her and made her walk on eggshells during the last few months of their relationship. But what do I know?

Still, the idea he tainted her, made her question whether or not she's allowed to voice her own opinions or say what she wants without repercussions leaves a bitter taste in my mouth. And not even her kiss can erase it.

"What did I do wrong?" she whispers, sensing my disgust.

My forehead falls to hers. "You did nothing wrong, Sunshine."

"I can tell you're mad--"

"I'm not mad at you, Ash."

She bites her lower lip, not moving as she watches me, trying to read my thoughts, but I don't let her.

With a firm pat against her thigh, I say, "Go get dressed, and we'll study for the test."

"You sure?"

"Of course."

"Okay." With a soft, vulnerable smile, Ash presses a quick kiss to my cheek. "Thank you."

But as she goes to climb off my lap, I grab her wrist and keep her in place. "One more thing."

"Yeah?"

"I don't mind *complicated*. Not if it's for something I want."

Her soft gaze searches mine, a hint of vulnerability slipping past her post-orgasmic haze. "What do you want?"

I want you, I almost say but stay quiet and smirk back at her, knowing she isn't ready for the truth. Not yet. Because she's right. She just got out of a serious, long-term relationship. She needs time to wrap her head around anything different. And I don't plan on going anywhere.

"I want you to stop overthinking what we did and go get dressed." I let her go, and she stands up, glancing over her shoulder toward where I'm sitting on the couch one more time as she disappears down the hall in search of clothes.

32
ASHLYN

We spend the rest of the day studying, and I'm reminded of how smart Colt really is. So smart, in fact, as he slips his textbook into his bag, I point out, "You're smart."

He pauses and looks at me. "Thank you?"

"No, like *really* smart."

"And it's surprising?" he counters with a dry laugh, though he almost looks shy. Humble. Like the compliment is off-putting somehow.

"I mean…" I puff out my cheeks. "I guess I thought…"

"What?"

"I guess I assumed you flunked out of your other school, which is why your mom had to call the dean and everything."

With a shrug, he finishes packing his backpack, zips it up, and slings it over his shoulder. "It's one of the reasons."

"But you're smart," I repeat.

"I wasn't failing because I didn't know the material, Sunshine."

"So, why were you failing?"

"Same reason I initially quit hockey."

"And that is...?"

He shrugs again, but I can tell I'm close to touching on a dangerous topic, and if I'm not careful, he'll close the door, locking away himself and the *real* Colt Thorne I'm dying to know. But I'm too curious to stop myself.

"Tell me," I beg.

"It's not a big deal."

"Then, you shouldn't mind telling me."

He looks down at the table and tucks his hands into his pockets, refusing to look at me while leaving my hands itching to pull him into a hug, though I have no idea why.

"I guess I felt like I didn't deserve to be successful," he grits out.

I shake my head, more confused than ever. "Why?"

So many emotions flash across his face. From resentment to discomfort, to defensiveness, to an overwhelming resignation breaking my heart. He leans closer and presses a soft kiss to my cheek.

"Thought you didn't want *complicated*," he reminds me with a teasing grin, his cocky mask pulled firmly into place.

Aaaand there it is—the proverbial door closing in my face.

"Guess I'm curious." I rub my hands along my bare arms and fold them across my chest. "You're a mysterious guy, Colt Thorne."

"Not really."

"Uh, yes," I argue. "You can have anything you want--any future you want--if you went for it, and yet I can see you putting up barriers for yourself."

He scoffs. "What barriers?"

I bite my lip to keep from blurting out a half dozen examples. Like the fact he quit hockey during his senior year even though he was made to be on the ice. I know because I Googled him after we first met. I saw a few ESPN spotlights but closed the browser quickly because I didn't want to intrude on his private life. But still. It was a barrier. Something keeping him from having what I *know* he wanted.

Or maybe I could mention the barrier he put up when he moved as far away from his friends and his family as possible, then showing up with a chip on his shoulder and a shady excuse as to how he wound up back here when I know for a fact, graduating from college isn't exactly on his to-do list.

Or I could always point out how he hit on the *one girl* who was off-limits when we first met because he knew I wouldn't cheat on Logan. That right there was a barrier. Something to keep him from getting what he wanted. *Me.* Even if it was only physical.

But the most recent example involves a certain test, along with a certain grade I know isn't accurate. Especially after studying with him today.

"Professor Buchanan contacted me last week," I tell him. "Did you know? He mentioned you failed your last test when I know for a fact you understood the material. So, the question is, why? Why would you fail on purpose?"

He sighs and pinches the bridge of his nose, realizing he's been caught. "It's not so simple, Sunshine."

"Or maybe someone's *making* it complicated," I tease, but there's an undertone in my words. A sense of worry. "Tell me this. What do you want to be when you grow up? You know, other than insanely good looking."

He chuckles and rounds the edge of the table, approaching me. "I dunno. Why?"

"Because you're smart. Talented. A hard worker."

"And insanely good looking," he reminds me with a smirk.

I snort and rise onto my tiptoes. "Obviously." My lips press against his for a quick kiss. I pull away and add, "Which is why it doesn't make any sense you'd fail your classes on purpose. The only person it hurts is yourself."

He frowns, whatever amusement from two seconds ago disappearing. "Maybe I deserve to be hurt."

My breath hitches, and I pull back. "Why would you say that?"

Clearing his throat, he rocks back on his heels. "Thanks again for today."

"Colt--"

"Want to get together again tomorrow? For another study session?"

I wave my hand toward my closed laptop and textbook on the table beside us. "You already know the material, remember?"

"I think I could use a few more study sessions."

I roll my eyes. "I think you're full of crap."

He grabs my hips, touching me again, and I hate how much I like it. How much I crave it.

"And *I* think I like you, Ashlyn."

My chest swells with emotion, nearly clogging my throat, but I swallow it. Because I hate how he can't see what I see when I look at him. How he still paints himself as the villain when I've seen firsthand, he's the opposite. How I might say I don't want *complicated*, but part of me is terrified it's because of the walls he's keeping between us. The secret I know he's keeping close to his chest and the realization he doesn't owe me anything, especially not the opportunity to climb those walls or to let me in.

"When can I come over again?" he prods.

"To study?" I challenge.

"If that's what it takes to be with you, sure," he offers.

"So, you admit you're all caught up on the material?"

He hooks his finger beneath my chin and tilts my head up until we're eye-to-eye. "I'm admitting I like you and want to see you again. If it's under the guise of a tutoring session, I won't complain…as long as I get to see you."

"Just *see*?" I cock my head to one side.

He leans forward and touches his lips to my exposed neck. It isn't a kiss, though. Only a brush of his lips. A taste.

"Whatever you'll let me do, Ash."

"No strings attached?" I breathe out, trying to focus on the conversation at hand and *not* the way his breath feels against my flesh.

But it's pretty damn impossible.

Besides, I'm not sure who I'm asking. Because I definitely feel the pull when I'm with him. The desire for those *strings to be attached*. It's like we're being sewn together with every moment we spend in the same room. But as soon as we start to get close, one of us pulls out the scissors and makes a cut in our progress.

It's infuriating.

He hesitates, not kissing my neck but not pulling away either. Like he's frozen. Like he's considering my comment about no strings attached from every angle. Finally, he bites my neck softly, scraping his teeth against my sensitive skin as my breath catches in my lungs. I should push him away. I should put some distance between us. I should set some boundaries. I should be smart. I should do a lot of things.

What I *shouldn't* do is lean into him, savoring the feel of his hardening length against my belly or the way his fingers flex against my hips.

"Like I said, Sunshine," he growls against my throat. "Whatever you'll let me do." He kisses my neck again, then pulls away, albeit grudgingly. "I'll tell the guys I'm coming over here to watch a movie with Mia or something. We won't even have to use the excuse I'm a dumbass, and it'll help sell my relationship with Mia to Shorty. Does tomorrow work?"

"I can't."

"Why not?"

"Well, for multiple reasons, actually."

"Such as?"

"For starters, I'm afraid I might like you too much to keep this casual, and I'm not sure I have the strength to take on *complicated* right now. But also because it's Mia and Kate's night off. We were going to binge on ice cream and reality TV."

"What? No pillow fight too?"

I laugh, grateful he brushed aside the whole *I might like you too much* word vomit I spewed and decided to cling to the whole *girls' night* portion.

"Maybe," I reply.

"Can I join?"

"For a girls' night or a pillow fight?"

"Whatever you'll let me do."

Another laugh bubbles out of me, and I shake my head. "It's girls' night."

"So?"

"So, it's *girls'* night," I repeat, emphasizing *girl*. "You're a guy."

"I'll bring ice cream," he offers.

I pop out my hip and cross my arms, my gaze narrowing. "What kind?"

"I believe you mentioned Ben & Jerry's?" He quirks his brow.

My mouth twitches, but I hold in my amusement. "What flavor?"

"Half-Baked?"

"That's Mia's favorite, not mine."

"All right." He taps his finger against his chin. "How 'bout Cookie Dough?"

"Kate prefers Brownie Batter but close."

"I'll keep that in mind," he mutters. "So, not cookie dough for you either?"

"Nope."

"Hmm... Maybe you're a Tonight Dough kind of girl? Definitely not fruit. You like to indulge in the rich stuff. Am I right?"

"You're getting closer, but I'm not going to tell you unless you guess it." I open the front door, and he steps onto the porch with his hand wrapped around his backpack strap, showcasing the veins along the back of his hand.

"All right, Sunshine. I accept your challenge and will see you tomorrow night."

"That wasn't an invitation!" I call to his retreating form, but he ignores me and saunters down the stairs toward the driveway.

As I close the door quietly behind me, I can't stop the smile from spreading across my face. Surprised but grateful for how we ended things. But I think it's why I like him. Because he sees me. He knows how to talk to me. To handle me. Sometimes, I'm afraid he might even know me better than I know myself. And while it's a little terrifying, there's comfort too. If only it wasn't so *complicated*--me and Colt-- I'd jump in with both feet.

Crazy.

Leaning the back of my head against the door, I close my eyes and mutter, "See you then."

33

COLT

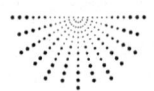

The bass is thumping as I step down the stairs, weaving around a couple of people dry humping next to the railing, almost tripping on a full cup of alcohol someone put on the bottom step for safekeeping.

I shake my head and pick it up, taking it back to the kitchen, where more people and more booze are littered everywhere.

As I dump the liquid into the sink, a deep voice calls, "Yo, Colt!"

I turn around and nod my greeting at Shorty and Graves, who are looking at me from the middle of the family room. The crowd parts like the Red Sea as they walk toward me. Shorty's a big guy. But we haven't really spoken since I intervened at SeaBird, which is probably what he wants to talk about despite how long ago it was.

"How you doin', man?" he asks as he refills his red Solo cup with whiskey, splashing half of it onto the floor.

He's drunk.

Tongue in cheek, I drop a couple of napkins onto the

floor and wipe up the spill with the toe of my shoe as I answer, "Not bad. You?"

He shrugs. "Been better."

I nod as Graves flanks my other side and pours himself some soda.

Not drunk.

Noted.

My attention shifts from Shorty to Graves' cup and back again. "Sorry to hear you're not doing so great, Shorty."

"Yeah, me too." He steps a little closer and chugs a few sips of whiskey from his cup, wiping his mouth with his hand. "Not sure if you know this since we didn't really get to talk at SeaBird or at practice the other day, but Mia and I go way back."

"She mentioned it."

"Did she also mention she promised I'd be the only guy for her?"

"Girls promise a lot of things, Shorty." I tilt my head up and meet his gaze, refusing to eat up this bullshit intimidation tactic.

"You two serious?" he demands.

"I'm hanging out with her tonight," I lie. Although, it's sort of the truth. Ash, Mia, and Kate are having a girls' night, and since I plan on crashing it, we'll all be together.

"You'd be smart to move on," he warns, crowding me against the table.

"I know you're used to getting what you want on the ice, Shorty."

"And off the ice," Graves clarifies, crossing his meaty arms as he closes in on me a little more. The guy's built like a tank. But he's slow. Slower than me, anyway. I grab a bottle of beer from the table. Something solid. Something heavy. And shift it from one hand to the other while acting like I have all the time in the world.

"I know professional teams are scouting you," I continue, ignoring Graves completely while keeping him in my periphery in case he decides to do something stupid. "I know you think you can push people around because you're big and scary. But Mia's allowed to do whatever the hell Mia wants to do."

"And if she doesn't know any better?" Shorty challenges.

I shrug one shoulder. "She learns from her mistakes. Take you, for example. She learned she wants nothing to do with you." His hands clench into fists, daring me to continue. "She also learned how bad it would look if the golden boy who's being recruited by the NHL had some less than savory skeletons in his closet. Such as stalking. Or a restraining order. Or hell, maybe even an image or two of a bruised, innocent girl who can't be more than a third of his size. What do you think?"

If looks could kill, I'd be curled up on the floor as Shorty towers over me, his nostrils flaring and his face red with anger. "She'll be sick of your pussy ass within a month. And when she comes crawling back to me, I'm gonna love fucking the memory of you right out of her mind."

Well aware I'm playing with fire, I pat his shoulder like I would a dog who brought me the ball during fetch. "And if that day comes, and she comes back to you on her terms, have at it. But only if Mia decides she wants you. We clear?"

He scoffs but nods. "Sure thing, Colt. Have fun on your date."

I smirk up at him. "Don't worry. I will."

34
ASHLYN

"You really think he's going to come?" Mia asks, her feet propped on the coffee table as she flips through Netflix.

"No idea," I answer.

We haven't talked since our little tutoring session slash hookup. No texts. No Snapchat. Nothing.

I think he's trying to give me space since I said I want no strings attached, but there's a little voice inside my head arguing a different story. Telling me he's gotten what he wanted. Telling me he doesn't need to see me again now that he knows what it's like to be with me.

I shake my head and tell the voice to shut up.

"I still can't believe you guys got it on in the kitchen," Kate adds beside her.

I cover my face and fold in half on the couch, resting my head on my knees. "I know!"

"Like seriously," Mia adds. "You couldn't have made it to the bedroom or something so I didn't have to think about you two going at it on the same table where I eat my Lucky Charms?"

"Technically, we didn't do it *on* the table," I point out when a knock on the door interrupts me.

I stare at it for a solid five seconds.

Kate asks, "Do you want me to get it?"

With a soft shake of my head, I push myself up and walk to the door. "I got it." I swing the door open and say, "Hi."

"Hey." There's a grocery sack hanging from one of Colt's arms and a pint of Half-Baked ice cream in the other. His dark, wavy hair hangs over his forehead, and he gives me a smile that makes my stomach tighten as his warm gaze flicks over me. "I believe I owe a group of ladies some junk food for letting me crash their girls' night."

"Damn straight!" Mia yells from the couch.

Colt chuckles and pecks my cheek like it's the most natural thing to do as he comes into the townhouse. I bite my lip to keep from grinning like a loon at the simple yet toe-curlingly sweet sign of affection as whatever condescending voices plaguing me since we hooked up are wiped out with a quick brush of his lips. He tosses the pint of Mia's favorite ice cream to her. "M'lady."

"Sir," she returns with a grin.

"Miss Kate," he adds, digging out the Brownie Batter ice cream I'd mentioned.

"Why, thank you."

"Two down, one to go," I note, folding my arms.

"You're really gonna make me guess your favorite flavor?" he asks, giving me the side-eye.

"Consider it payment for letting you crash our girls' night."

He grins. "Playing hardball, huh?"

I lift my brows but don't back down.

"All right. I'll play, Sunshine." Colt opens the grocery bag and walks to the table as I follow behind, peeking around him to get a glimpse of what's inside. "I grabbed every flavor they had at the store, except the plain flavors, 'cause if you're gonna go with Ben & Jerry's, you're gonna want all the stuff they add to the ice cream. Let me see." He rummages through the bag a bit more. "All right. You didn't sound too thrilled about Cookie Dough or Tonight Dough, but how do you feel about"––he retrieves a pint and shows it to me––"Oat of this Swirled?"

I snort and shake my head.

"Okay, okay." He sets it on the table and takes out another pint. "Maybe a little Chubby Hubby? Eh? Eh?"

I shake my head again.

"Ooookay. Let's see what else we have in here." He dives in for another pint. "How 'bout some Chunky Monkey?"

"Wrong again!" Mia calls from the couch, clearly enjoying her entertainment for the evening.

"All right, last guess," Colt concedes. "And not because I didn't buy four more flavors, but because I'm pretty confident about this one."

"Oh?" I challenge, a slow smile spreading as I wait for Colt to fall flat on his handsome face.

"Mint Chip," he announces, unveiling the pint of ice cream from the grocery sack like it's the grand prize on a gameshow. "It's creamy. It's refreshing. You get those nice little chocolate chunks." He pinches his finger and thumb together to prove his point. "It's not too out there or overloaded with stuff you don't need. It's simple yet satisfying. Am I right?"

Kate and Mia slow clap and push to their feet, giving Colt a standing ovation.

"Bravo, Colt!"

"I'm officially impressed!"

I bite back my grin and motion to the pints of ice cream littered across the kitchen table, refusing to give in no matter how adorable the guy is. "You really think all of this is going to fit in my freezer?"

One of Colt's arms snakes around my waist as the other offers the mint chip pint for me to take. "Nah, but I think we can make a pretty decent dent in the stash."

"You think?"

He leans in and kisses me again. Nothing over-the-top, but somehow more sweet and affectionate than I ever could've expected. Even when he pulls away, his taste still lingers on my lips, making me crave him even more than if he'd never kissed me at all.

"And on that note, we're gonna head out," Mia says as she and Kate reach for their jackets on the coat rack next to the door. "But thanks for the ice cream. Until we find another roommate to take the fourth room, my funds are too tight for junk food."

"Where are you going?" he asks, letting me go. "It's girls' night."

"No, it's *date* night," Kate argues as she motions to Colt and me. "Obviously."

"*Girls'* night," Colt repeats. "I asked if I could join it, not cancel it. Stay. I even promise to keep my hands to myself."

"You? Keep your hands to yourself and simply hang out?" Mia challenges. "I mean, I get us doing that"––she waggles her fingers between them––"since it's basically what we've been doing for weeks. But you and Ash?" She shakes her head. "Not possible, buddy. Go have fun, you two. But if you decide to have sex again, can you do it in Ash's room? I'd like to *not* taint the couch if possible." She swings the pint of Half-Baked back and forth in goodbye and opens the front door. "See ya later."

"Wait!" Colt yells. "Only girls' night attendees get ice cream. You wanna pass up on girls' night, you gotta pass up on Half-Baked and Brownie Batter." He stretches out his hand, leaving the palm face up to collect payment.

Mia scoffs and turns around. Exchanging glances with Kate, she asks, "Are you serious?"

"Those are the rules, ladies. Come hang out with us."

Kate frowns. "But..."

"I'm not trying to steal your friend away," Colt argues. "At least not until after you guys convince me what's so great about *The Bachelor*."

Mia exchanges another quick glance with Kate, smiles, and turns to me. "Oh, honey, your boy toy has so much to learn." They head back to the couch and turn on the first episode.

We spend the rest of the night talking, laughing, binging ice cream, and soaking up snuggles until Mia and Kate yawn a few hours later and go to bed.

Then, Colt and I taint the crap out of the couch while he makes me eat crow for my stamina comment yesterday.

After three orgasms and a sore va-jay-jay, Colt kisses my forehead, tucks us both in with a blanket, and snuggles up next to me.

And the crazy part? The annoying voice in my head who's been screaming at me about how unlikely my *whatever-this-is* with Colt could work out? She hasn't made a peep.

It's one of the best nights of my life.

35
ASHLYN

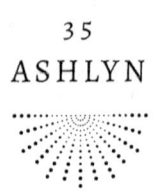

When my phone vibrates against the bathroom counter, notifying me of a message, I slide the mascara wand back into its tube and look at the text.

Colt: Hey.

The butterflies in my stomach bat their wings, and I bite my lip to keep from grinning.

Me: Did I just get a text from the infamous Colt Thorne?

Colt: You're surprised?

Me: I thought you hated texting.

Colt: I do hate texting.

Me: And yet, here we are.

Colt: I'm at the gym with the guys and figured texting might help us fly under the radar easier.

Me: Look at you, Mister Smarty Pants. You also mentioned you only text if you're looking for a hookup. Does this mean what I think it means?

Colt: It means I kinda miss you, Sunshine.

My cheeks pinch from grinning so hard as I give up trying to keep it at bay as I scan the message again.

I kinda miss you, Sunshine.

It's been three hours. Three. Not ten. Not twelve. We fell asleep on the couch, tangled in each other's arms. He snuck out around seven in the morning so he wouldn't have to do the walk of shame in front of Kate or Mia. The fact he's already reached out? And he admitted he misses me?

Swoon.

Me: Kinda miss you too.

Colt: Do you have any plans tonight?

Me: Nope. Only hanging out, catching up on The Bachelor, and binging leftover ice cream. Wanna come over?

Colt: Yeah. Need me to bring more ice cream?

I snort.

Me: Pretty sure we're good on ice cream for the foreseeable future, but I'll let you keep the brownie points for your thoughtfulness.

Colt: You know me. Always a gentleman. ;) I'll see you tonight.

Me: See ya.

I stare at my phone for another thirty seconds. Shoving the swell of butterflies aside, I finish getting ready for the day. My hair is already pulled into a high pony, but my makeup is only half-done, thanks to Colt's interruption. With a wistful sigh, I untwist the mascara wand and get back to work.

"All right. Colt has my approval," Mia says a few seconds later. She's resting her shoulder against the bathroom doorjamb with her arms folded.

I laugh and swipe the mascara wand against my upper lashes. "Glad he gets your stamp of approval."

"It won't let him off the hook for tainting our couch, though."

With a snort, I cover my mouth and mutter, "Oops."

"Seriously. You owe me one. Or five," she adds. "However, I do have one question."

"Yes?"

"Are you guys *always* going to hang out here?"

I shrug one shoulder and continue with my makeup. "I have no idea. Why?"

"I'm curious how squishy it's going to be once we finally get a fourth roommate. Don't get me wrong. I don't mind having him here," she adds. "But hiding away and pretending Colt doesn't share a wall with Logan--let alone a childhood full of memories--isn't exactly going to work for you in the long run, is it?"

"Wow, Mia," I interrupt, turning to her with a look warning her to tread carefully. "Way to call it like it is."

She raises her hands in defense. "I'm just saying!"

"It's only been a couple nights," I argue.

"No offense, but I think this has been going on a lot longer. I can see you like him, Ash, and there's nothing wrong with it."

"But shoving it in Logan's face *is* the right way to go about this? Especially when Colt and I aren't even officially dating?" I shake my head and get back to my mascara. "You're making things complicated."

"No, I'm trying to prevent the inevitable fallout. Even if you're only casually hooking up with Colt, and there aren't any real, long-lasting feelings there––which I think is a load of crap––Logan shouldn't have the power to prevent you from hanging out at Colt's place. Even if it's only for a fake tutoring session, it still isn't fair. And I promise I'm not saying this to be selfish and claim our apartment as my own either. I'm seriously only looking out for you."

I know she is. Mia isn't selfish. But it doesn't make her point any easier to swallow. The idea of seeing Logan again after our shitty breakup is…well, shitty. And it's not like I'm not over him or anything. I'm pretty sure I'd been getting over him even before he ended things. But is it so wrong to want to leave my past in the past?

Then again, if it were so important to me, I'd probably be smart enough to pick someone who isn't friends with Logan to hook up with. And I would if Colt weren't so freaking charismatic. So, the joke's on me, I guess.

I twist the cap on the mascara and set it on the counter. "Thanks," I mutter. "And you're right. I'll see what I can do."

She smiles and pushes herself away from the doorjamb, swaying closer and pulling me into a hug.

I love Mia's hugs.

Because they're rare.

And special.

I guess I can blame her father's death for that one. Well,

her father's death and Shorty's borderline abusive behavior. Her walls have always been high, but by some miracle, I was able to scale a few of them. And I wouldn't change it for the world.

"Love the crap out of you," I murmur.

"Ditto." She pulls away and smiles. "Seriously, though. You and Colt are adorable together. As soon as you give the word, I'll stage a break up with him, and he'll be all yours."

A loud knock echoes from the front room, interrupting us.

"I'll get it," Mia says as she heads down the hall to answer it.

There are hushed voices, but I can't make out what anyone's saying or who's at the door, so I peek down the hall to see if I can catch a glimpse.

When I do, my breath hitches.

Shorty's here. And he looks *pissed*. He's towering over Mia, his face hard and red as he says something in a low voice. Mia shakes her head and takes a step back, her hand wrapped around the edge of the door as if it's the only thing keeping her from collapsing onto the floor. Like a snake, his hand darts out, and he grabs Mia's arm, wrenching her closer to him and out of my line of sight.

Shit.

I take a step back into the bathroom so I won't be caught snooping as I search for a solution that doesn't wind up pissing off the hockey player in our foyer even more.

I need to do something, though.

With a deep breath, I pretend to be oblivious to the shitstorm brewing at the front door and yell, "Hey, Mia!" I pop my head back into the hallway. "Colt's calling you!"

The door swings further open, and Shorty's grasp on Mia's arm disappears as I head toward them with a smile. "Oh. Hey, Shorty."

"Hey, Ash," he returns. "Sorry about you and Logan."

"It's fine. We weren't exactly meant to be. What are you doing here?"

"Wanted to say hi to Mia." He tilts his head toward her, and she rubs her tender arm.

"Apparently, she's a hot commodity today," I reply, turning to Mia. "I told Colt you'd call him right back."

With a fake-ass smile, she says, "Nice chatting, Shorty. I'll see you around."

"Yeah," he grunts. "You will." Then he heads down the steps.

Mia closes the door, turns the lock faster than a tornado in Texas, and rests her back against it.

"Mia," I start, but she holds up her hand.

"Not now."

"You should call the police."

"He's been staying away. Today was a fluke."

"And if I hadn't been home to save you?"

"I would've figured it out."

"Mia…"

"Do you mind if I ask Colt to drive me to work?" she whispers.

My expression falls, and I pull her into a hug, ignoring her straight spine and the way she refuses to accept my embrace. Because her walls are up again, and she won't take them down until she's ready.

"Yeah, Mia," I murmur, forcing myself to let her go. "Give Colt a call. I'm sure he'll be happy to help."

With a weak smile, she mutters, "Thanks."

36
COLT

Theo and Depp are laughing as everyone puts on their gear while Graves makes some dumbass comment about his date tonight. It's good to be back here. In the locker room. Hearing the team shoot the shit.

It's easy.

Comfortable.

I've missed it.

Theo asks how Graves convinced a girl to go out with him, and everyone laughs again as Logan sits down on the bench near my locker.

I glance his way, adjusting my elbow pads and tugging my practice jersey over my head. We haven't talked much since the night of the storm. Pretty sure he's been too busy getting laid.

"Good to have you back, Colt," he starts.

I lift my chin. "Thanks."

"Like the good ol' days, right?"

Chuckling, I mutter, "Not exactly."

"You gonna play in Saturday's game?"

I shake my head. "Nah."

With a knowing nod, he mutters, "I get it."

"Yeah."

"Theo and I are gonna grab drinks after practice. You should come."

Shrugging one shoulder, I lie, "Uh, yeah. Maybe. Mia and I might be hanging out, but--"

He laughs. "That's one thing I don't miss. Having to check in with Ashlyn anytime I--"

My phone rings, interrupting him.

"One sec," I mutter.

As I dig it out of my bag, Logan stands up and says, "We'll catch up later," as he walks back to the bench by his locker, grabs his helmet, glove, and stick, and disappears through the exit toward the rink.

As I watch him go, I answer the call and keep my voice low. "Hello?"

"Hey," Ash murmurs. Her voice is quiet but rushed. Like she's nervous. *Scared.*

I sit up straighter, my senses on full alert. "Hey. What's up?"

"I know it's none of my business, but did Mia tell you about her run-in when you dropped her off at work?"

"No?"

"I'm seriously going to strangle the girl," Ash mutters under her breath, adding, "Shorty showed up at our place earlier. I don't think Mia wanted me to tell you, but he grabbed her, Colt. He grabbed her wrist, and it freaked me out."

"He did what?" I growl into my cell as the rest of the team ties their skates and starts heading to the rink.

"I know Mia won't want to make it a big deal, and I know it isn't your job to protect her," Ash adds, "But he grabbed her arm, Colt. And if I hadn't been here…"

My blood boils as I find Shorty in the room playing with his phone. Like he didn't scare the shit out of Ash and Mia. Like he didn't show up on their porch earlier today. Like he wasn't acting like a fucking caveman, using his size to intimidate an innocent person.

My hands clench around my cell, threatening to crack the screen as I grit out, "I'll take care of it."

"Colt!" Theo yells, oblivious to my phone conversation. "Coach wants to talk to you."

"Coach?" Ash asks, her voice cracking through the cell speaker.

I pinch the bridge of my nose. "Uh, yeah. I've been practicing with the team."

"Holy crap, Colt! That's huge."

The rest of the team files out, and I watch them go, clearing my throat and turning back to my locker. "Uh, yeah. Thanks."

"Are you officially on the team now? Like, are you playing in the games and stuff? Why didn't you tell me? Can I come watch? I'd love to show the *team* my support if you know what I mean."

I can hear the smile in her voice, and it only fans my guilt.

"Can we talk later?" I ask, keeping my voice low.

She pauses. "Oh. Yeah, of course. Are you still planning on coming over tonight? You know…to study," she teases. It eases the tightness in my chest.

I chuckle and glance around the empty locker room when Coach Sanderson yells from his office, "Thorne! Now!"

"Gotta go." I hang up the phone, shove it in my locker, and walk into his office.

"Close the door," he orders.

I do as I'm told and sit down on the seat across his desk littered with trophies, Expo Markers, and a couple of pucks.

With his fingers steepled in front of him, he stares at me for a solid minute. Finally, he asks, "So?"

"So?" I repeat, shifting in my chair.

"So, can I rely on you?"

"For...?" My voice trails off.

"You've been practicing with us for weeks, but you're refusing to play a real game, and you won't let me put you on the team roster. Since you didn't play for any previous colleges, you can be a walk-on, Colt. You know this."

"Yeah, I know. I'm..." I scrub my hand over my face. "I'm not ready yet."

"Bullshit. I've seen you at practice. You're already better than the majority of your teammates."

"I meant up here." I tap the side of my head, and he nods his understanding.

Adjusting his red and black LAU hat on his bald head, he asks, "And what will get you ready up there?"

"I dunno," I answer honestly. "But if I can't practice with the team anymore––"

"You know you're always welcome, Thorne."

I scratch my jaw, unsure what to say. "Thanks."

"Did you know I knew your dad?" he asks. "Before?"

Before.

It's such a fucked up terminology.

Before he died.

Before I killed him.

Before my world turned upside down.

Of course, I knew.

We'd been talking about me playing for LAU for years before everything went down, and I flew to the opposite side of the country to escape. Pretty sure it was Sanderson's connection to my dad that convinced the dean to let me on the student roster in the first place after I screwed up at Dixie Tech. But what do I know?

Ignoring his question, I reply, "Can I ask your opinion on something, Coach?"

"Sure thing. What do you need?"

"Shorty's an abusive asshole and is stalking his ex. I wanna know how you think I should handle the situation."

His eyes widen in surprise. "That's a serious allegation, Thorne."

"It's true," I argue. "Her name's Mia Rutherford. She doesn't want to go to the police. She thinks ignoring the situation is going to work, but I don't think it will. I know scouts are watching Shorty play, and I wanna know what I can do to get him to leave her alone. If there's anything *you* can do to get him to leave her alone."

He tosses his hat on his desk and holds his head in his hands as if he's been blindsided. "Shit, Thorne."

I shrug one shoulder, unsure what he wants me to say.

He looks up at me again. "And she doesn't want to involve the police?"

"No."

With a sigh, he rests his elbows on the table and taps his steepled fingers against his frown. "All right. I'll take care of it."

"You will?"

"Yeah."

"Thank you." I stand up and wipe my palms against my pads.

"And, Thorne?" Coach says.

"Yeah?"

"You're a part of this team. Even if you decide you don't want to play a single game. You can count on us. All right?"

I nod, surprised by how much it means to me. "Thank you, Coach."

"Now, get out there. You're late for practice."

37
ASHLYN

Ignoring the problem is healthier than facing it, right?

Okay, I'm not that ridiculous. But seriously. What's wrong with going with the flow instead of overanalyzing every single thing in one's life?

Honestly, I'm going to go with nothing. Nothing's wrong with it. Nothing's wrong with sleeping with the same guy over and over without needing to discuss a future or a label or anything else at all. Only when the next hookup will be, and if we should grab food before or after.

This is why I most definitely should *not* have my feelings hurt over something as stupid as hockey.

But if hockey's as stupid as I'm trying to make it out to be, why do I care Colt didn't tell me he was on the team again?

Oh, I know. Maybe because I stuck my head in the sand more times than I can count when I was with Logan, and I don't want my--whatever I have--with Colt to end up the same way.

Which means I need to be assertive. I need to express myself. Even when it's hard.

Collapsing onto the couch, I send Colt a text before I can talk myself out of it.

Me: Hey. Are you still coming over after practice? I kind of miss you.

I hit send, drop my cell onto my lap, and reach for the remote as the front door opens.

"Hey," Kate greets me.

"Hey," I return, glancing over my shoulder. "You're home early."

"Yup. Gotta get ready for my date." She bounces her eyebrows up and down.

I clap my hands and pull my knees under my butt so I can face her fully, grateful for the distraction. "You have a date?"

"Yup. He's cute too."

"And his name?" I ask.

"Wes."

"And how did you meet mister Wes?"

"He likes to come to the restaurant."

"Ooo, is he a good tipper?" I ask.

She laughs and nods. "Yes. And when the last tip had his number on it, I had no choice but to text him."

"Obviously," I agree as I glance at my darkened cell phone screen, revealing zero texts from a certain someone. But I shouldn't be expecting one. He's at practice.

I shake off the thought and add, "So. How do your parents feel about this little date?"

With a sigh, she rounds the couch and collapses onto the cushion next to me. "They don't know yet."

"Ooo brave," I note. Kate's relationship with her parents is complicated. While mine are absent most days, her parents are hands-on with a capital H. But I don't blame them. Not with her history.

"Or stupid," she counters, resting her head in her hands.

"You gonna tell Wes about…everything?"

"Discussing chronic diseases on the first date might be a bit much, don't you think?" she mutters into her hands.

"Good point." I bump my shoulder against her, causing her body to sway while alleviating a bit of the weight in the room. "You should go get ready. Don't wanna be late for your date."

She sits up and presses her hands to her knees, her fingers flexing against her black tights as she pushes herself to her feet. "Right. Or I could stay with you, and we could watch the Kardashians."

My nose wrinkles. "I don't think I can handle any more drama today."

"Why? What happened?"

"Nothing," I lie, too exhausted to give her all the gory details.

She quirks her brow. "Liar."

"Let's just say our dear Mia needs to figure out what to do with Shorty as soon as possible."

"Why? Because you wanna officially claim Colt for yourself? Because if that's the case, you have my full support. You two are adorable together."

"It's not that," I argue. "Especially not when I just caught him lying to me."

"What?" she screeches.

"Okay, fine. Technically, he wasn't lying. He was…" I shove my hair away from my face and blow out all the oxygen in my lungs. "*Blah.* I don't want to talk about it. Right now, I want to focus on Mia."

"What about Mia?" Kate prods.

"Shorty showed up on our doorstep earlier today."

I swear her eyes almost pop out of her head. "Are you serious?"

"Yup."

"Why does everything happen when I'm not home?"

"Consider yourself lucky," I mumble, annoyed.

"What happened?"

"Honestly? I don't even know. Like I said, Shorty showed up on our doorstep before Mia's shift, said something to her, and grabbed her arm."

"He grabbed her?"

"Yeah. And it freaked me out." I sag further into the couch, my body feeling drained. It's exhausting trying to keep everyone happy. Trying to take care of everyone. Trying to help everyone. I breathe out a sigh and put my feet on the coffee table, stretching out and letting go for a second.

"Holy crap, Ash," Kate replies. "Did Mia call the cops?"

"No. But I *did* use Colt as her scapegoat when Shorty was here. Thankfully, it worked, and he left. But still."

With a frown, Kate sits back down and pulls me into a side hug. And it's nice. To not be the only one carrying the load anymore. To talk to someone. To voice my fears aloud. To have someone…listen. And if Kate's good at anything, it's listening.

"I know you love Mia like a sister," Kate murmurs, "and I know you want to protect her by letting her borrow your boyfriend--"

"Colt isn't my boyfriend."

"He would be if you let him," she argues. "But my point *is*…Mia's used to handling the world on her own. And you're used to being Mother Goose and swooping in to help anyone and everyone whenever you can."

"So?"

"So, I think Mia needs to reach out to someone who can actually help her, and you need to *not* swoop in and try to fix everything," she explains gently. "Especially when it's out of your control."

With a frown, I ask, "And you, oh wise one? What do you need to do?"

"*I* need to get ready for my date and not freak out." She presses a loud, smacking kiss to my cheek and stands. "Wish me luck."

"Good luck," I mutter as she heads to her room, but she stops, turns around, and faces me again.

"And, Ash?" she adds.

"Yeah?"

"I also think you should give Colt a chance to explain himself for whatever lie he might've told you."

"Yeah, yeah," I deflect.

"I'm serious," she returns. "Colt seems like a good guy. I don't want your shitty past with Logan to taint what you could have with Colt if you gave him a real shot."

Then, she heads toward her room, and I'm too dumbfounded to stop her.

38
COLT

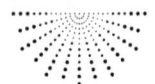

Every muscle in my body aches as I trudge up the steps and knock on Ash's door.

When it opens, she frowns, surprised. "What are you doing here?"

"You invited me," I remind her.

"Right." With a weak smile, she glances over my shoulder and scans the sidewalk while opening the door the rest of the way. "Come on in."

"Everything all right?" I ask as she folds her arms, rubbing her hands up and down them.

Looking small.

Fragile.

"Uh, yeah," she lies.

Snaking my hand around her waist, I bring her closer and kiss her softly, melting a bit of the iciness between us.

"Missed you," I murmur against her lips.

She closes her eyes and sighs. "Missed you too."

There's resignation in her words though.

I pause, pull away, and look down at her. "What's wrong?"

"Nothing."

"Talk to me, Sunshine."

"It's nothing," she repeats, avoiding my gaze.

"Ash," I warn.

"I..." She sighs and folds her arms again, putting some distance between us. "Can we talk?"

"About what?"

"About hockey?" she suggests.

I shake my head, ignoring the ball of lead in the pit of my stomach. "What about it?"

"Why didn't you tell me you're on the team?"

"'Cause I'm not. Technically."

"*Technically?* I thought you said you were at practice?"

"I was," I return, grabbing her hand and guiding her to the couch. I have a feeling I'm gonna need to sit down for this.

"How are you not *technically* on the team?" she asks, keeping a few inches of distance between us. Like she's guarding herself even though I know I've done nothing wrong.

Jaw clenched, I grit out, "Because I don't want to play in any of the games."

"Why not?"

"Because I'm not ready," I answer. "And what's with the interrogation? It's only practice."

"But it isn't *only* practice," she argues. "I..." She chews on her lower lip, her gaze darting around the room as she looks anywhere but at me.

"What's wrong?" I demand, too exhausted to tiptoe around shit today. Practice was hell. I was too busy worrying about her, Shorty, and Mia to focus, and my teammates took full advantage by putting me in my place.

I felt like a rookie on the ice.

It sucked.

"Logan never wanted me at any of his games," she whispers. "At the time, I thought it was because he was superstitious and didn't want me to rock the boat or anything. But later, I realized it's probably because of all the puck bunnies in the crowd. You know, the ones he'd been sleeping with behind my back. He didn't want me to run into any of them." She runs her fingers through her hair, pushing the long waves away from her face as she shakes her head in disbelief. "Like, how shitty, right? How naive can a girl be? I know I should've questioned things. I know I should've called him out for his crap, but when you're so used to being an afterthought like with your own parents, it's hard to push it aside and stand up for yourself, but that's not the point. My point is, Logan didn't want me to have anything to do with hockey--which is a big part of his life, mind you--all because his side pieces liked to hang out at the rink."

I feel like I've been slapped, and I flinch back a few inches, rubbing my hand over my face, defeated. "You think I have a side piece?"

"I think I don't know what to think," she admits, her eyes glassy. She blinks the moisture away. "I think I'm probably going to have trust issues for a while, thanks to Logan, and I think I'm being ridiculous because we aren't even really a couple, so it's not even possible for you to have a side piece. But it still hurts."

"Ash--"

"I feel like you lied to me."

"I didn't--"

"You did, though. Maybe not explicitly, but you kept me in the dark on something kind of a big deal for you. It hurts. How could you not tell me you're on the team?"

"Because I'm not on the team," I repeat, cradling my head in my hands. This can't be happening. We can't be fighting over something as stupid as hockey.

"Yeah. Well. It seems like you kind of are. And I know you don't owe me anything, but it hurt to find out the way I did."

I look up at her again. "Ash--"

"Look. If I learned anything from my shitty relationship with Logan, it's I need to voice my needs. I need to stand up for myself. I need to express myself. So, that's what I'm trying to do. And what I need right now is honesty. Can you give it to me?"

It hits me then. We aren't fighting because of hockey. We're fighting because Logan's an ass, and she's learning how to trust again.

But she's talking to me about it.

She's trying to be open. To be honest.

And I've been an ass for not doing the same.

I cup her cheek, dragging my thumb along her sensitive skin. "There is no one but you, Sunshine."

Sucking her bottom lip between her teeth, she bites down hard, causing the flesh to turn white from the pressure. I pull it out of her mouth with my thumb and caress it softly.

"I'm moving at your pace because I think it's what you need and because Logan was shit at giving you any control in the relationship. But I'm in this, Ash. You and me. No one else."

"Promise?" she whispers, squeezing her eyes shut.

I nod and lean closer, kissing her softly. "Promise."

She lets out a shaky breath. "Okay."

"Yeah?" I tilt her head up and make her look at me.

"Yeah." She smiles, and whatever doubt had been clouding her eyes when I first showed up disappears. And I'm surprised by how much easier I can breathe with it gone.

"I'm sorry," I add.

She nods. "Me too. I didn't want you to feel like you were being interrogated."

"I get it," I return, leaning in to kiss her again. To make sure we're okay. Because the idea of losing her? It's starting to hurt more and more.

39
ASHLYN

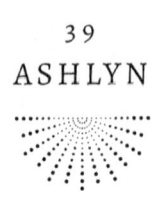

"Where exactly are you taking me?" I ask as Colt weaves his car through traffic. We've been sneaking around for weeks, and while it's been fun and exciting, it's been a little exhausting too. So much so that Colt showed up on my doorstep this morning and announced he was taking me somewhere. And now, here I am, in his car, on my way to who knows where. The weather is beautiful, though. We have the windows rolled down, making the car ride feel like a breeze. In fact, it almost makes up for his lack of transparency.

Almost.

Colt's hand is on my thigh, and he squeezes it softly, looking free and at ease for the first time in...ever. Sunglasses cover his eyes, but his mouth is tilted up in a smile. He's happy. If only I knew where we're going.

"Seriously, Colt. You're killing me," I tell him.

He turns off the freeway.

"We're already here? So wherever you're taking me isn't too far. Hmm." I tap my finger against my chin. "Good to know."

"Patience, Sunshine," he reminds me.

"Patience is for suckers." I look out the passenger window at the trees lining a neighborhood street, searching for clues, but I come up empty. "Seriously. Where are we?"

"It's Sunday."

"So?"

"So, on Sundays, my family has brunch. Remember?"

"Y-your family?" I stutter, pulling my sunglasses a few inches down my nose to peek over the edge of them.

He grins shamelessly. "The one and only."

"You're taking me to meet your family?"

"Is that a problem, Ash?"

Grimacing, I answer, "Well...no?"

And yes, I think to myself. We aren't a couple. We're only messing around. Okay, we're doing more than messing around. We don't have any labels--we *can't* have any labels--so, why would he take me to meet his family? It's official. I'm freaking out.

When I'm silent for too long, he points out, "You don't sound so sure."

"You know what I mean! Meeting the family is kind of a big step considering our circumstances, isn't it?"

His grip tightens on my thigh, the heat from his palm warming me all over again and turning my insides to mush. "My mom wants to meet you."

"She knows about me?"

"Someone recommended I reconnect with her more now, with me living closer and all," he reminds me.

"Well, yeah, but I didn't know you'd talk about *me*." I point to my chest to prove my point.

Another laugh slips out of him. "Why are you surprised?"

"I dunno? I thought we were keeping this casual."

He glances at me again, lets my thigh go, and rests his wrist on the steering wheel. "It's only brunch, Ash."

"*Only* brunch?"

"Yeah. Not a big deal."

"You sure?"

"Yes."

"And you felt like having me tag along was a good idea because…?" I prod, still confused, as I wipe my sweaty palms against my jeans.

With another glance my way, he sighs. "I like you, Ash."

"I like you too."

"Keeping this thing a secret has been driving me insane, though. I wanted a normal morning for once. Where we could be ourselves."

My chest pinches with the sweetness overload, and I almost swoon while sitting in the passenger side of a truck belonging to the most amazing guy I've ever met.

Seriously. How did I get so lucky?

And yet here he is, wanting to introduce me to his family.

"I get it," I reply. "And I want us to be able to be ourselves too." The soft breeze through the window ruffles his short hair while making him look straight out of a magazine or something. I tear my attention from the sight and try to focus on the conversation at hand instead of how freaking attractive the guy is.

"But meeting your family?" I say. "It still feels like a big deal."

"Did you not want me to tell my family about you?" he asks, his confidence slipping.

I shake my head. "It isn't that."

"Does your family not know about me?" he pushes. Like he's trying to understand my side of things, and it makes me melt a little more.

But I swear this guy has to think I'm a basket case.

Scrunching up my face, I shove aside my embarrassment and rip the truth off like a Band-Aid.

"My family doesn't know about a lot of things in my life. We don't exactly talk much."

There. I said it.

"Did they know about Logan?" he challenges.

"Barely. And even then, most of the time, they didn't even remember his name. They'd call him Luke or Landon or Lance. Anything with an L they considered a success."

"No shit?" He laughs.

"It isn't funny."

"It's kind of funny. Besides, my family's a lot cooler than Logan's. You'll do fine."

I cringe. "And if I never met Logan's family?"

He turns to me, his eyebrows practically reaching his forehead. "You never met Logan's family?"

"Nope."

"But you were together for years."

"Guess I'm not parent material. I mean, if I can't even make my own mom and dad like me…"

"Hey," he scolds. "Be nice to my Ash."

"*Your* Ash?"

His mouth lifts on one corner, but he doesn't deny it. "I'm serious. Be nice. I don't want to hear you saying things like that. My parents––my mom," he corrects himself, clearing his throat. "She's going to love you."

My chest cracks as I hear his Freudian slip, and it makes me cave almost instantly, putting aside my insecurities to be a rock for the man beside me.

Reaching toward him, I touch his knee. "You're right. I'm probably making this out to be a bigger deal than it needs to be. Like you said. It's only brunch."

"Yeah." He gives me the side-eye again. "Only brunch."

He turns down another street lined with white mailboxes and picket fences, showcasing the perfect suburban neighborhood. He pulls into the driveway of a red brick house with black shutters.

"We're here."

40
ASHLYN

We walk up the steps to Colt's childhood home side-by-side as my anxiety eats me alive. It's a beautiful brick two-story house with a porch swing and a large maple tree out front. There's also a welcome mat, and a little wreath with Easter Eggs glued to it is hanging on the door.

It's adorable.

And a little intimidating.

Colt pushes the front door open without knocking and presses his hand to my lower back so I don't bolt in the opposite direction. The scent of cinnamon and vanilla tickles my nostrils as Colt guides me inside.

"Colt?" a soft, feminine voice calls from further in the house.

"Hey, Mom," he yells back. "We let ourselves in."

"We?" another voice calls as a girl with red, messy curls and a baseball cap pops her head around the corner. "Ooooh. Someone brought a friend."

"Blake," Colt greets her, less than amused. "This is Ash. Ash, this is my little sister, Blakely."

I wave my hand. "Hi."

"Hi. Nice to meet you." She pops back around the corner. "Mom! She's cute and totally out of Colt's league."

I slap my palm over my mouth and bite back my laughter as Colt rolls his eyes.

"We can still hear you," he says, leading me the rest of the way down the hall. Family pictures are hung on the walls, and I stop in front of a more recent one. Colt looks almost exactly the same, and so does his little sister. Two other men who look strikingly similar to Colt flank the sides of the photo while an older man and woman stand in the center.

"That's my dad," Colt says when he catches me looking at it.

I smile and glance at him. "His genes must've been strong because all of you look like him."

"Yeah." Colt chuckles. "My mom used to always complain about how she did all the hard work by carrying us for nine months, yet he's the one who gets the credit for our good looks."

"And big heads!" an older woman with red hair and a round face adds, appearing in the hall with an apron around her waist. She wipes her hand on it, pulling Colt into a hug. "I didn't know if you'd make it."

"I said I'd try," he reminds her.

"And I'm glad you did." She lets him go and turns to me with a warm smile. "I'm Becca Thorne, Colt's mom. Obviously. You can call me Mom, Becca, Mrs. Thorne--whatever makes you comfortable. Nice to meet you."

"Nice to meet you too," I reply.

Like I'm one of the family, she pulls me into a hug after letting Colt go and whispers, "I've heard a lot about you, Ashlyn. It's nice to finally put a face to the name." When she lets me go, she shoos us into the dining room. "Now, let's eat while it's hot. No one likes a cold pancake."

"They're the worst!" Blakely adds. She's already sitting at the table with her plate full of bacon, eggs, and pancakes smothered in butter and syrup.

"Did you save any for us?" Colt asks, pulling out my chair.

I sit down and smile up at him as he takes the seat next to mine and across from Blake and his mom.

"Har, har. I ran eight miles this morning. You'll have to cut me some slack for being the only one in shape around here."

Colt hands me a plate of pancakes and dishes out two for himself. "Blakely's training for a marathon."

"A marathon?" I repeat.

Blakely nods and shoves a bite of sausage into her mouth.

"That's awesome," I tell her. "My roommate convinced me to do a 5k once, and I almost died."

With a laugh, Blakely stabs her fork into a pancake and takes another bite. "Sounds like your roommate and I could be friends."

"Definitely. She's a sucker for a good running partner, and since I failed spectacularly during our freshman year, she'd kill to find a new one."

"Well, I'll have to hit her up next semester."

"Yeah, Colt mentioned you're transferring to LAU."

"Yup. That's the plan. Don't get me wrong. I've loved going to the community college while living with Mommy Dearest--"

"You mean babysitting me since all my boys left me?" Mrs. Thorne quips.

Blakley laughs, but Colt isn't half as amused as she explains, "But I am excited for a legit college experience. I need to find a place to live, though."

"We have a spare room," I offer. "Actually, you'd be doing us a huge favor. Tutoring doesn't exactly pay well, and even though Mia works her butt off at SeaBird, and Kate, my other roommate, has a scholarship, we've been looking for a fourth roommate to help share the load. So, if you're interested…?"

"Really?" Her attention shifts to Colt. "You'd be cool with it?"

"To be fair, I thought the alternative would be you sharing a roof with Theo."

Her nose scrunches. "Ew. No. That bossy manwhore can stay as far away from me as possible, thank you very much."

"Language," Mrs. Thorne scolds.

But Colt and Blakely ignore her, and Colt teases, "Come on. You love Theo."

Blakely glares back at him. "I love Teddy about as far as I can throw him."

"Teddy?" I whisper to Colt, leaning closer to him at the dinner table.

"Theo hates being called Teddy," he answers. "Which is why she does it."

"Ooooh," I reply, the pieces clicking together.

"Actually. Scratch that," Blake continues. "'Cause I've been lifting weights lately. I love him *less* than I can throw him. Which is saying something, since even with the weightlifting, I'm still insanely weak," she adds with another laugh.

Her pancakes are already soaked, but she picks up the syrup and pours more on them as if the stack is Theo's head, and she's hoping he'll drown in it.

Seriously. The girl must have the metabolism of the Energizer bunny.

"Blake doesn't like being told what to do," Colt explains.

"Yeah. And since I already have three overbearing older brothers, I do *not* need another one. Most of your friends are cool and hands-off like Logan or any of Knox's friends, but whenever Teddy comes by, he likes to be an asshat who thinks he can tell me what I can and can't do. No, thank you.

Au revoir. See ya later." She takes another bite of pancake and grinds her teeth.

"That's kind of funny," I admit.

Blake frowns, pausing mid-chew. "Why?"

"Because I most definitely have *not* gotten that vibe from Theo. He's like the most laid-back, loosey-goosey guy I've ever met."

"Until Blake's around," Colt jokes. "Honestly, it's refreshing. At least I know there's one guy who won't want to sleep with you next semester."

"Colt," Mrs. Thorne warns.

He laughs. "Sorry, Mom, but it's the truth."

"Mm-hmm," she hums, clearly unamused, as she slices a piece of cantaloupe into a dainty little bite with her fork and knife.

"But back to the point," Blakely continues. "If you really are looking for a roommate, I'm not even kidding. I would love to apply or"––she waves her fork around––"whatever."

"Yeah, for sure. I'll get your number from Colt and get it all taken care of."

"Seriously?"

I nod. "Yeah. Happy to help."

"Thank you."

41
ASHLYN

The rest of brunch is spent laughing, talking, and soaking up each other's company. Which is weird. And comfortable. It's like I've already been accepted. In fact, it's so easy, so effortless, I'm kind of blown away, and I love it more than I want to admit.

Growing up with my parents was kind of the opposite. Not that they didn't love and accept me, it was simply...different. I felt like I didn't fit in. Like I was too uptight for their hippie ways, too busy clinging to structure and bedtimes to appreciate their namaste outlook having little to do with rules or guidelines and more to do with finding your own path. The only problem was, my own path didn't jive with theirs. It led me to crave rules and structure more than my next breath and only pushed my parents further away, convincing them I could take care of myself and I didn't need them anymore.

But today? With Becca and Blakely? It was different. Easy. Maybe it's because I *don't* need them––hell, I barely know them––but I was embraced, regardless. And it's exactly what I needed.

As I help wash the dishes in the kitchen with Mrs. Thorne, Colt and Blakely are moving some boxes into the attic for her.

Becca slides the last skillet into the soapy water and grabs a dish towel from the hook beside the sink.

"I want to thank you," she says.

I glance back at her, surprised by the sincerity in her voice. "For what?"

"For helping Colt with his grades. My nosey mama heart hacked his online portal his first day at LAU, and I've been monitoring his grades ever since. Don't worry. Colt knows," she adds with a wink. "But Professor Buchanan updated the scores on his latest test earlier this week. Colt scored ninety-seven percent."

"He did?"

My chest swells with pride as Mrs. Thorne grins back at me.

"Yes, he did. I don't know what you did or what you said to convince him to start trying again but thank you. From the bottom of my heart, thank you."

I bite my lip, too stunned to know what to say. "I didn't do much," I hedge.

"And I beg to differ," she counters. "He likes you, you know."

I smile back at her. Scrubbing at the skillet with the cleaning brush, I admit, "I like him too."

"It's nice to see him smile again."

There's a sadness tainting her words. I glance over at her and swipe some hair away from my forehead with the back of my soapy hand. "Oh?"

"Yeah. When his father died, I was afraid he'd never smile again."

Well, shit.

With my heart in my stomach, I chew on my lower lip and offer, "I'm really sorry, Mrs. Thorne."

"Don't be. It isn't your fault."

"Your son told me the same thing when I found out about his dad and apologized," I tell her.

She laughs. "I guess we're two peas in a pod."

"I guess you are. But I *am* still sorry. Even though it isn't my fault," I clarify, rinsing the skillet under the water and handing it to Mrs. Thorne so she can dry it. "It still sucks."

With a sad smile, she takes the cookware and wipes it dry with the dishtowel. "Yes. Yes, it still sucks. Thank you, though. For pushing him to come to Sunday brunch again. Since Knox and Garrett have been out of state, it's been Blakely and me. Reconnecting with Colt after his father's death"--she pats my soapy hand--"it means a lot to me."

"I think it means a lot to him too. And thank you for raising Colt the way you have."

"He's quite the gentleman," she agrees, and I bite the inside of my cheek to keep from snorting. Thankfully, Mrs. Thorne doesn't notice and adds, "They had a good example in the home, you know. Their father was a gem."

"If he was anything like Colt, I believe it.".

"He was a lot like Colt." She sniffs and pats the corner of her eye with the edge of her dishtowel. "Those two were close. They'd talk for hours every Sunday, watching whatever game was on for the day. Didn't matter what sport. They just liked talking. It was adorable."

My heart aches at the pain in her voice, but I don't comment on it. Instead, I give her a smile and say, "Sounds like it."

Wiping the cleaned plates on the drying rack with a fresh towel, she adds, "How 'bout you and your family? Are you close with them?"

I hide my frown behind a fake smile and avoid her gaze. "Not exactly."

"Oh?" I can hear the question in her voice. The way she doesn't want to dig but is also curious enough to wait out the silence to see if I'll give in to it.

Lips pursed, I grab another dirty plate from the side of the sink and scrub it as I explain, "I'm an only child. And my parents are great but a little...hands-off, I guess. I think they were excited to have their freedom again once I moved out." I rinse the plate under the water, hand it to Mrs. Thorne, and grab another one, scrubbing it with a bit more elbow grease than the previous ones. "I see them around the holidays and stuff. But even if they lived close, I don't think we'd have traditions like Sunday brunch or anything."

The leftover syrup mixes with the soap bubbles as I dip the plate in the hot water, avoiding Mrs. Thorne--and her pity--at all costs.

"Well. I hope you know you're always welcome here," she returns.

I peek up at her and smile, even though I know she's only being nice. I'm her son's...whatever I am, for Pete's sake. What else is she supposed to say?

"Thanks," I reply. "I appreciate the invitation."

"Always."

After rinsing the plate under the faucet, I hand it to Mrs. Thorne, and she dries it in silence, lost in her head as the minutes tick by.

But I'm okay with it. The quiet. It's comfortable, even. Nothing like anything I ever experienced with my parents, and the realization makes me sad, but I don't focus on it.

Once I'm finished, I drain the dirty dishwater, wash my hands, and am turning off the sink when she stops me.

"He really cares about you, you know. I can see it in his eyes. When his first girlfriend cheated on him, I knew the walls around his heart would be hard to break down. But it seems you managed to scale them completely."

"I don't know about that."

Her knowing smile makes my heart rate spike when she replies, "I do."

And even though I've deflected her more times than I can count, I can't help but hope she's right.

It terrifies me.

42
ASHLYN

I'm still not sure how I wound up on my ex's doorstep, yet here I am, trying to move forward with his best friend, who's fake dating my best friend to protect her from one of his teammates.

Since, ya know, it makes perfect sense.

But after meeting Colt's mom and sister and learning more about his father and all the pain he went through, it's past time to face a few demons. One of which is towering over me.

Hello, Taylor House. Please play nice today.

Puffing out my cheeks, I shift the strap of my backpack a little further onto my shoulder and ring the doorbell.

Heavy footsteps echo through the opposite side before the door swings open.

"Hey, Ash," Theo greets me. "Come on in. Colt's jumping out of the shower."

"Oh." I squeeze the backpack strap until my knuckles turn white and peek around Theo's massive frame. "I can wait in the car or something--"

"Logan's not here."

"Oh," I repeat, letting out a sigh of relief.

"Come on in." He pushes the door open the rest of the way and adjusts his baseball cap on his head. Pretty sure he's always wearing it, and it's not because he's going bald or anything. He actually has a head full of thick, curly hair, but the old baseball hat is part of his identity now. Hell, it's his trademark. I zero in on the worn bill while avoiding the giant elephant in the room threatening to choke me.

This is so freaking awkward.

As if Theo feels the same way, he clears his throat and adds, "I think it's shitty what Logan was doing behind your back."

I fold my arms and rock back on my heels. "Yeah. Me too."

"He can be a dick sometimes, but I hope you don't hold it against him."

I smile tightly but stay quiet.

"So, have you been dating anyone else yet? Or--"

"Hey, Theo. Give the girl some space, yeah?" Colt calls as he skips down the stairs, rubbing a white towel over his still-damp hair. How the guy manages to look so effortlessly sexy all the time is beyond me, but I'm not about to complain, especially when he's saved me from the most awkward conversation I've ever had.

Thank you, Colt!

"Hey," I say when he reaches the main floor.

He tosses the towel over the railing and smiles. "Hey."

My fingers itch to touch the hair falling on his forehead, but I dig them into my folded arms instead.

"Hey," Theo interjects. "I was wondering if Ash would want to get together as friends or something with you and Mia."

Colt's brows reach for his hairline. Theo adds, "Like I said. Only as friends, Ash. I know I'm a catch and all, but I don't date my friends' exes. It'd be weird."

I laugh, my attention shooting to Colt for a split second as I rock back on my heels. "And asking them to hang out *isn't* weird?"

"I mean, Mia's dating Colt, and since you're Mia's best friend, and I'm Colt's best friend, and Logan's been too busy hooking up with anything that walks to hang out with––"

"Theo," Colt barks, glaring at him.

Theo grimaces. "I didn't mean––"

"I know what you meant," I mutter.

Seriously, though. Kill me now.

"Sorry," Theo apologizes, visibly cringing as he adds, "Anyway, Ash. You could do a shit-ton better than Logan. We'll find you someone."

"We?" Colt interjects, clearly unamused.

Theo's head bobs up and down. "Yeah. Come on, Colt. You know I'm an excellent wingman. Let's hook this little lady up with someone." He tosses his arm around my shoulder and tugs me into his chest like we're a couple of buddies. "Maybe go to a bar, scout out the options and shit. How 'bout tonight? Broken Vows and Fender Hayes are in town. They're supposed to play at SeaBird for a little reunion gig. And you can bring Mia. It'll be fun."

"Mia's actually related to Fender Hayes," I mutter, "But…"

"No shit?" Theo returns. "Come on. Now we *have* to go. Maybe she can introduce us to the band." He nudges Colt with his elbow while Colt scrubs his hand over his face, his tongue in his cheek as he looks at me, still pinned against Theo's chest.

"I don't, uh…" He pauses, looking panicked. "Ash? What do you want?"

"Me?" I peek up at Theo, who's basically got me in a headlock at this point, and force a smile. "I think I don't have much of a choice."

"Hell, yeah." Theo lets me go and slaps his hand against Colt's shoulder. "Let's do it tonight after your study session."

Then he walks upstairs without a care in the world, oblivious to the wrench he just shoved between Colt and me. Which sucks. Because after Sunday brunch with his family, things almost felt real between us. With no barriers. No secrets. Nothing but a perfect, genuine relationship...no one else knows about.

Hello, reality, you heartless bitch.

Chewing on my lower lip, I open my mouth, snap it closed, and head to the kitchen, unsure of what to do or say while still absorbing the shitstorm thrown at me.

This is bad. This is very bad.

"Ash," Colt murmurs behind me. He looks pissed.

I turn on my heel and throw my hands into the air. "What the hell was that?"

"I could ask you the same question."

"So we were both blindsided back there?"

He scrubs his hand over his face. "Apparently."

I drop my backpack onto the ground, collapse onto a chair, and pinch the bridge of my nose. "And if I don't want to be set up?"

"Theo's a stubborn ass. Once he gets an idea in his head--"

"He keeps pushing it until everyone around him gives in," I finish for Colt. "Yeah. I know. Just witnessed it. Thanks for standing up for me, though."

"What else did you want me to do? You're the one who wants to keep this private, Ash." He wags his finger between us.

"You're the one dating my best friend--"

"*Fake* dating," he growls.

I glare back at him, my frustration boiling in my veins. "Feels pretty real at this moment."

"You know that's bullshit," he counters.

He's right. I do know it's bullshit. But I'm too pissed off to care. I feel like everything was great at his mom's house, and yet, here we are, traveling back in time where we aren't a real couple. We're only hanging out and hooking up under everyone's noses. I don't know what to do about it. With my lips pressed together, I try to rein in my temper, but it feels useless.

"I gave you an opportunity to back out," he adds a little more carefully this time. "You decided not to take it."

"Oh, so this is my fault?"

"It's Theo's fault," Colt clarifies. "Actually, it's not even his fault. He's trying to be nice."

"Yeah. Well, little does he know, he kind of put a damper on my day, so..."

Colt comes closer and rubs his hands up and down my arms. Comforting me.

"You don't have to go," he murmurs.

"And what about you?" I peek up at him. "Are you going to take Mia on a fake date to convince your friend––who's *also* friends with Mia's ex––you two are together?"

"I dunno," he admits. "I didn't exactly think he was going to corner you when you walked in."

"Yeah, well, he did, and now, I'm going to go on a fake double date with my best friend and the guy I have a thing for while my non-date tries to play wingman. Does it sound fun to you?" I seethe, stepping away from Colt and pacing the kitchen like a caged bull. "This is ridiculous."

"There's a solution, you know," Colt mutters, closing a bit of the distance between us. Again.

"Don't say it."

"Ash--"

"I'm serious, Colt." I stop pacing but fold my arms and lean against the kitchen counter. "Don't say it."

He steps closer. "Ash. I like you. You know I do."

I do know it. And I like him too. Way more than I should. Which is why this entire situation is so freaking difficult. It's why I want to hide away in one of our bedrooms and pretend none of the chaos outside can reach us. Because as soon as we leave the safety of our own rooms or his childhood home, it does. The chaos twists what we have into something that feels like it can slip out of our grasp at any second. And I really don't want to lose it. To lose *him*.

"I like you too," I whisper. The words terrify me no matter how many times I voice them aloud. "But it doesn't mean I want you to break up with Mia all because we got cornered into going on a double date. She needs you right now."

"Ash."

"We'll simply pretend nothing is going on between us, and we'll have you and Mia make goo-goo eyes at each other all night. It'll be a real hoot," I say sarcastically.

"And when Theo tries to hook you up with someone at SeaBird?" Colt growls, stepping closer to me. "How am I supposed to pretend then?"

I shrug one shoulder. "I'm sure you'll think of something."

"Ash--"

"I gotta go, Colt."

I grab my backpack from the floor and try to slip past him, but he grabs my arm, holding me in place. His warm breath tickles the top of my head as I keep my gaze glued to the ground.

"You're not allowed to be mad at me," he rasps.

"Let me go."

"You're not allowed to be jealous, either."

I know he's right, but it doesn't stop the sting of truth from hitting its target. I am jealous. I'm jealous Colt could have any girl he wants, yet I'm too scared about letting him in to claim him as my own. I'm jealous that I've been in this position before. That I've wanted to run away so many times, and he's always reached out to keep me from running. To keep me from hiding from my true feelings, which are more real than I'd like to admit. To anyone, let alone myself.

"Tell Theo I'll meet him at SeaBird," I whisper.

"Ash." His grip tightens around my bicep, tainting his touch with frustration. "Tell me we're good, or I break up with Mia."

I look up at him, my eyes glazed with fear. "You know you can't do that right now."

"Has she seen Shorty since your place the other day?" he challenges.

"Not that I know of, but we both know Mia likes to play all the drama close to her chest."

He curses under his breath and scrubs his hand over his face. Defeated. Angry. Resigned. "I can't be her scapegoat forever, Ash. I already talked to Coach, and he said he'd take care of it."

"Did he, though?" I ask.

He shrugs, unsure. "She should call the police. Get a restraining order or something."

"I told her the same thing, but she said she was taking care of it."

"Is she?" he pushes.

I slip out of his grasp. "I dunno, but I don't think right now is the time to rock the boat, either."

"So, where does it leave us?"

With a quick peek over my shoulder toward the staircase,

I rise onto my tiptoes and brush my lips against Colt's. "I'll see you tonight."

"What about the tutoring session?"

I sniff and squeeze my backpack strap a little tighter. "I don't really feel like studying right now."

And I leave.

43
COLT

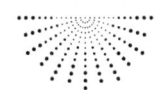

The place is packed. Everyone is shoulder to shoulder, and I'm pretty sure we're breaking a few fire codes in here. Mia's uncle is part of the band, and since he let us in the back door, he apparently doesn't give a shit about fire codes.

"Hey, Mia," he greets her, pulling her into a hug.

She smiles and squeezes him back.

With a wave of her hand, she says, "Everyone, this is Fender, my uncle. Fen, this is Ash, my best friend and roommate. And Theo, a friend from LAU. And Colt." She pauses, and Theo barrels toward Fender, offering his hand.

When Fender takes it, Theo explains, "Colt is Mia's boyfriend. Nice to meet you, man. Love your music."

Fender chuckles and slaps his hand against Theo's back as he looks me up and down with more curiosity. "Boyfriend, huh?"

Hooking her arm around my bicep, Mia leans her head against my shoulder and smiles. "Uh, yup."

"And why hasn't your aunt heard of him?" Fender asks.

"Because Aunt Hadley's a Nosey Nelly."

He chuckles again and nods. "Good point. She'll be pissed she missed you. I thought you weren't coming until tomorrow's show?"

"Theo suggested we swing by tonight, too, and since you're kind of family and all…"

"Kind of?" Fender quirks his brow and steals another hug from her as Ashton, one of SeaBird's managers, catches us near the back door.

"Fen, you gotta get on stage," he interrupts. "And you," he adds, talking to Mia. "I thought it was your night off."

"It is, but since this ol' lug"--she elbows Fender in the ribs--"decided to play a show, I thought I'd come support him."

"Ah, got it. All right, I'll tell Sonny you'll be right there," Ashton says to Fender and heads into a back room around the corner.

Once he's gone, Fender points at me. "Treat her right." Then he points at Mia. "Tell your aunt you have a boyfriend, and bring him to dinner before the show tomorrow night so she can meet him."

He doesn't bother to ask if Mia will listen as he gives us his back and heads into a room with the rest of the band without another word.

"Man, I still can't believe you're related to a rockstar, Mia," Theo gushes.

But Mia doesn't answer him. She's too busy looking like she might puke, and Theo's too distracted by the buzzing crowd to notice.

What the hell?

It feels like the pressure from everything is finally coming to a head, and it's only a matter of time until it pops.

And based on Mia's pale cheeks and shallow breathing, it might be sooner rather than later.

My attention darts to Ash. She's hiding in the shadows of

the hall, isolated a few feet away from us. Though I can't read her expression from the lack of light, her arms are crossed, and she almost looks...numb.

It kills me.

"Hey, will you guys find a place to stand while Ash and I grab the drinks?" I ask Theo and Mia.

With a quick glance at Ash, Mia hooks her arm around Theo's the same way she did to me a few minutes ago. "Sure thing." She leads Theo through the crowd, giving Ash and me some privacy.

"Ash--"

"We'll talk about it later." She squeezes past me and heads to the crowded bar, lifting her finger to grab the bartender's attention while ignoring me completely.

She's pissed. And she has no right to be. Which she already knows. But the truth doesn't make me feel any better. And I don't think it's making Ash feel any better, either.

But seeing Ash hurt like this?

I can't take it.

Not anymore.

The place is so packed, no one notices as I slip my hand around her waist, pin her back to my front, and lean in close enough to whisper in her ear. "I'm ending it with Mia tonight."

She peeks over her shoulder at me, causing my lips to brush against her cheek as panic settles into her bones. "You can't--"

"I know it hurt to watch, Ash. Wanna know how I know?" I squeeze my fingers against her. "Because I had to see you with Logan for weeks. And sure, my relationship with Mia is very fake, but when everyone else thinks it's real, it's easy to fall down the same rabbit hole. I refuse to let you think I want anyone else but you. Do you understand?"

"We're only hooking up," she argues.

I rub my cock against the curve of her ass, loving the way her breath hitches as the band rushes on stage behind us and the audience begins cheering.

But I don't turn around.

And neither does Ash.

We're lost in our own little world.

And thankfully, the crowd is too distracted to notice us.

"Don't get me wrong, Sunshine. I love fooling around with you, but I think we both know there's more to this than sex." I slide my hand lower, cupping the apex of her thighs with my hand as Broken Vows starts their first song.

The melody is energized, with a strong bass causing the people around us to start dancing right away. Ash wiggles her hips into me, rubbing against my cock and my hand cupping her sex, searching for friction.

"It's only sex," she whimpers. Hell, if I hadn't been watching her mouth, I doubt I would've heard her. Instead, the words shoot straight to my dick, making me harder than I swear I've ever been in my entire life.

Her eyes are closed, and her head is tilted toward the ceiling, but she doesn't stop rubbing herself against me. Subtly. Tiny movements driving me insane.

Leaning closer, I bite her earlobe and whisper, "Think you can come right now, Sunshine?"

Another whimper.

I add more pressure with my hand, and she grabs my wrist. Whether it's to make me stop or keep me from retreating, I'm not sure. I relax my fingers, testing her, and she slips her hand over mine, pressing her fingers against my own. Urging me on.

"You want me to keep going?" I rasp against the shell of her ear.

She tilts her head to the side and rolls her hips a little more.

As I suck at her neck, she becomes a little bolder. A little more greedy. And I know she's close.

Shit, she's close.

I want to push her over the edge. I want to make her come. I want to brand her. To prove to her I'm the only guy she needs. And this thing between us? It's so much more than sex.

Grabbing her wrist, I twist her around and lead us to the bathroom.

There's a line, but most of the people are too busy enjoying Broken Vows to notice us as I slip inside when the person who'd been using it opens the door.

"What are you--"

I shove Ash against the door and twist the lock with my other hand, gripping her wrists and pulling them above her head.

"Say you're mine," I growl.

"Colt--"

"Fucking say it, Sunshine."

Her lower lip trembles as she breathes out a slow breath but stays quiet.

"You're mine, Ash." I keep her pinned to the door but use my other hand to shove her skirt up and undo my own jeans, pulling my erection out. I rub the tip against her slit, and she moans, shaking her head back and forth as her juices coat me.

"Colt," she moans.

"Say you're mine, Sunshine."

She spreads her legs a little wider, giving me better access to the heat I crave, but I don't give in. I won't until she gives me what I want.

Pushing the head of my dick against her entrance, I tease her, and she hooks her ankle around my calf. Desperate.

"Please," she begs.

"Not until you say it."

"I'm on birth control, and I trust you. Just..." She wiggles her hips and grabs my ass, trying to bring me closer to her, but I pull away and push my forehead against hers.

"Say you're mine, and I'll fuck you, Sunshine." My nostrils flare. "Say you're mine, and I'll give you whatever you want until you're sick of me." My chest heaves. "Say you're mine, and I'll treat you like a fucking queen." My hands flex around her wrists. "But not until––"

"I'm yours."

I close my eyes and thrust into her, savoring her wet heat as it swallows me whole.

Letting go of her arms, I grab her thighs, and she jumps, wrapping her legs around my waist. She's too worked up to take it slow and doesn't complain when I thrust into her again with all of my strength.

Her moans spur me on. Her hot breath against my neck. Her needy whimpers begging me for more. My skin feels too tight as a bead of sweat rolls down my spine. Then, we're coming.

We both fall over the edge at the same time, and she melts in my arms.

This girl.

This damn girl.

She might be the death of me.

But I wouldn't care if she was. Because she's mine now. And there isn't a chance in hell I'm ever letting her go.

With her head on my shoulder, she catches her breath, and I slowly let her slide down my body, already missing her even though she's right in front of me. Once her feet are on the ground, my dick slips out of her. Along with my cum.

Shit. We didn't use protection.

I'd been so caught up, the ramifications were barely a blip on my radar until now.

I grab some toilet paper and help clean her up. Holding her face with my opposite hand, I force her to look at me. "You're on birth control?"

"I said I was," she replies.

I know she did, but I still need to hear it one more time. Because I've never had sex without a condom. I've never been stupid enough to. But it felt good. Not only physically but also emotionally. Like the last of our barriers were finally behind us. And I needed it more than I realized.

With a quick kiss to her forehead, I breathe out a sigh of relief, toss the toilet paper into the toilet, and flush.

Before she has a chance to open the door, I grab her wrist and stop her. "Say it again, Ash."

She looks up at me and rolls her eyes. "You're being ridiculous."

"I mean it. Say it again."

Whatever sarcasm present from seconds ago vanishes, her little tongue darting between her lips to moisten them.

"I'm yours," she whispers.

I lean down and kiss her again, savoring her unique taste along with the declaration like it's a fine wine, surprised by how much I need it. Her compliance. Because this fake dating bullshit while sneaking around behind everyone's back? It's been a bitch. And I'm done hiding.

44
ASHLYN

I can't believe I said I'm his. I mean, I can because he most definitely owns me. But the fact I said it out loud? To his face? After the best sex of my life in a dirty bar bathroom? That was a new low--*high?*--even for me.

The rest of the night is a blur. After being yelled at by Theo and Mia for forgetting the drinks Colt promised, we ordered a round of beers, found a booth at the side of the bar, and settled in. Well, for a little while. Until Theo tried to hook me up with a few random men. Colt intervened and said I wasn't in the mood. Afterward, Theo asked why Mia and Colt weren't dancing. I intervened and said Mia wasn't much for dancing.

Round and round we went, twisting our lies into a web of chaos until Theo found a woman who's a sucker for hockey players, and he went home, leaving the rest of us alone.

Finally.

Don't get me wrong. I like Theo. But he's more of a meddler than Kate's parents, and that's saying something.

As soon as SeaBird's door closes behind him, a serious

Mia leans forward in the booth, resting her elbows on the table, and tells Colt, "We need to break up."

With a dry laugh, Colt puts his arm around me. "Yeah. I know."

She leans back in the booth, surprised. Like she didn't expect him to give in so easily when he's the one helping her out in the first place.

"You do?" she asks.

"Yeah. This has gone too far."

"Agreed." She shakes her head, glances at the now-empty stage, and turns back to us. "I can't lie to my family. It's the one thing I can't do. I didn't think Theo would blurt something out like that. But my aunt and uncle are the greatest. I can't lie to them."

"No one's asking you to," Colt returns. "You should tell them about Shorty too."

Wringing her hands in front of her, she mutters, "I don't want them to worry."

"I'm sure you don't, but they have a right to know," he continues. "And no matter how much you might think we have it under control, Shorty's doing some shady shit, and you deserve better."

"I know." A straw wrapper lies on the table, and she reaches for it. Rolling it between her fingers, she forms a little paper ball, lost in her thoughts and indecision.

"What can I do to help?" I ask.

"Wanna go back in time and keep me from dating Shorty in the first place?" she offers, her smile bleak at best.

She and Shorty have been dating off and on since freshman year when Logan introduced them. It was not long after her dad died, and she was hurting. She wanted someone to swoop in and care for her. Little did she know, she'd attracted one of the most controlling assholes on the planet. And every time she works up the guts to leave him, he reels her right back in. Once, she told me it was easier to be with him than deal with how awful he was when they weren't together.

It broke my heart.

Honestly, I think it's part of the reason I stayed so long with Logan. Because our relationship looked like rainbows and butterflies compared to Mia's. Little did I know how toxic relationships can be. Especially when you're together for the wrong reasons.

With a frown, I pat Mia's hands on the table. The paper straw she'd been messing with rolls toward me. "Unfortunately, I didn't know what you were getting into with Shorty, either, but if I could go back in time, I would."

"You and me both," Mia mutters. "But enough sad talk. It's making me depressed." She slips out of the booth and grabs a glass of water from the table. "Sorry about this." With a quick flick of her wrist, she splashes it in Colt's face and yells, "We're over!"

She stomps away, leaving me alone with Colt.

"I guess that's one way to end a relationship," I mutter, barely holding in my laugh as the water drips down his face and off his chin. The bartender, Sammie, walks over with a towel.

"Damn, Colt. You okay?" she asks.

He takes the towel, wipes off his face, and hands it back to her. "Yeah. I'm good. Thanks."

With a grimace, she prods, "I guess that means you and Mia are through?"

Colt looks toward the exit and back at Sammie. "Guess it does."

"I'm sorry."

"I wouldn't worry about it, Sammie." He squeezes my thigh beneath the table, and warmth spreads through my chest as Sammie takes the damp towel, excuses herself, and walks away to help another customer.

"I guess that's that," I announce, surprised by how easily something as daunting and crippling as their fake relationship was simply...canceled.

Lifting his glass, Colt clinks it against the neck of my beer and says, "To new things."

I smile and raise my bottle, almost giddy. "To new things."

And we both drink.

45
COLT

The house is dark as I step inside and lock the door behind me. Giggles echo from the first floor, probably belonging to one of Theo's or Logan's one-night stands, but I'm too exhausted to investigate.

I really need to order a pair of noise-canceling headphones.

Pulling out my phone, I bite the bullet, order a pair on Amazon, and slide it back into my jeans when the kitchen light flickers on.

"Hey, man." Logan lifts his chin and grabs a beer from the fridge. "Want one?"

I shake my head, surprised to find him down here.

After popping the cap off with a bottle opener, he sits down on a barstool by the kitchen island and points toward the second floor, where a girl is chanting, "Yes. Yes. Yes!"

"Are my girls as loud as this?" he asks.

I chuckle and sit down next to him. "Sometimes worse."

"Shit." With another dry laugh, he swallows down some of his drink.

"Surprised you don't have company tonight," I add,

cracking my knuckles and resting my hands on the cool granite.

He smirks back at me. "She had to go home early."

"Ah. Makes sense." I laugh. And it's real. Because I don't worry about how it might affect Ash anymore.

He dips his head in confirmation, taking another swig from the bottle.

"How've you been?" I ask. "I haven't really seen you outside of practice."

"Yeah. Been busy with my newfound freedom and shit."

"Glad you're staying busy."

He nods and settles back into the barstool, stretching out his legs. "I never thanked you, by the way."

"Thanked me?" I ask.

"For pushing me to tell Ash. It's nice. Not sneaking around anymore," he clarifies, lifting his almost empty drink in a cheers motion. "That shit can weigh a guy down."

"I can imagine," I mutter as he finishes his drink and sets it down on the counter. "Listen, I wanna talk to you about something."

His brows raise. "Yeah?"

"Yeah. I'm dating Ash."

His smirk slips, and he sits forward. "What?"

"I'm not telling you this to make you jealous or get your permission. But you're still one of my best friends, even when you're an ass," I clarify, trying to lighten the mood. Sobering slightly, I add, "And you deserve to hear it from me."

His eyes look almost hazy as he stands up, walks back to the fridge, and opens another beer. Quiet. Almost robotic. The refrigerator door closes softly as he turns around and faces me, his expression unreadable.

I don't know what he's thinking. What he's feeling. But the silence is weighted. Heavy. Like a storm ready to break at any second. His jaw ticks as he avoids my gaze, drinks his beer in one go, and sets the empty bottle on the counter right next to the first.

Slow. Controlled. Deliberate.

"What about Mia?" Logan asks, his hollow voice breaking the silence.

"She and I broke up."

"And she's cool with you dating her friend?"

"Took it better than I ever would've expected," I reply.

With a sharp nod, he clears his throat but doesn't look at me. "Kind of an asshole thing to say. That you aren't asking for my permission."

"If I did, would you give it?" I counter.

He shrugs one shoulder, scratches his jaw, and drops his hand to his side. "Probably not."

"Then, I guess it's why I didn't ask permission."

He scoffs, lifts one brow as if to say, *touché*, and asks, "How long?"

"Made it official tonight," I answer.

"And before?"

"She came over the night you two broke up. She was looking for you. Wanted answers."

"And you gave them to her. Didn't you?" He scoffs again, unable to help himself. "You were always an asshole, Colt. I guess I shouldn't expect anything different, huh?"

I ignore the sharp pain in my chest but don't bother to defend myself. Because he's right. I was a shitty friend for going after someone who wasn't mine, let alone someone who belonged to one of my best friends. Ash and I might not have hooked up until after Logan ended things, but I still crossed the line with her. Still wanted more from my buddy's ex. That's on me.

"I'm sorry, Logan."

His head hangs between his shoulders as he looks at the

ground. He scrubs his hands over his face again and pastes on a stupid, fake-ass smile. "You know what? It's fine. She and I weren't happy anyway."

I stay quiet, refusing to confirm his assessment even though he isn't wrong. They weren't happy. I could see it. Theo could see it. *Everyone* could see it. But seeing her happy with me? It's gotta be a shitty hand to deal with. Seeing your ex with a stranger is one thing. Seeing them with one of your best friends?

It's a bitch.

"You should invite her over," he decides. "You know, so we can sweep the past under the rug. Turn over a new leaf."

I cock my head. "You sure?"

"Yeah. Sure."

"All right," I reply. "Maybe after spring break or something."

"Good."

Without another word, he leaves the kitchen, his footsteps echoing up the stairs while leaving me hollow inside.

Because even though he was an ass and we had our own problems, I didn't want to hurt him. I only wanted to move on. Who would've thought it would be with his girlfriend, though?

Karma really is a bitch.

46
ASHLYN

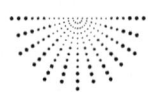

"Why are your boxes so heavy?" Mia groans, helping Blakely move another box in from the U-Haul parked out front. Colt insisted they could fit all of her things in the back of his truck, but Becca thought it was better to rent a trailer and be safe rather than sorry.

Blakely squints and reads the chicken scratch scrawled along the cardboard box in Mia's arms. "Probably because you grabbed a weight box."

"A weight box?"

"You know, full of weights. It's not my fault I can't afford a gym pass."

"Those are weights?" I ask.

"Yeah. My mom let me take the weights from home," Blakely replies.

"There are weights in this thing?" Mia screeches.

Blakely grins back at her. "Only a few."

With a thud, Mia drops the box into the center of the spare bedroom and wipes her forehead with the back of her hand. "And this, my friends, is why I stick with running. Because weights are a bitch."

"A bitch that's awesome," Blakely argues. "But so is running. Did you sign up for the marathon we talked about the other day?"

After brunch with Blakely, I got her number from Colt and passed it along to Mia and Kate to see what they thought about Blakely renting the spare room. By the time I got home, Mia was cracking up at a TikTok Blakely had sent and gave her stamp of approval. Since then, a group chat was created, and Blakely's been accepted into the fold like she always belonged here.

"There's a marathon?" Theo interrupts from the doorway, carrying in Blake's mattress like it weighs less than a couple grocery bags. He leans it against the door and folds his arms.

"Maybe," Blakely replies. "I'd invite you to join us, but you don't run."

"I don't need to."

"Cardio's good for your body, the same way weights are good for your body," Blakely points out, tossing a quick glance at Mia to make sure she's listening.

I almost laugh but choke it back as Theo pushes himself away from the wall and stalks closer to Blakely. "I get my cardio in ways other than running."

"Such as?"

"I skate, and I fuck."

Blakely snorts. "Of course, you do. But now that I know they're on the official approved Teddy regimen, I'll be sure to give them a try since I'm at college like a big girl."

"You don't skate."

"You're right." Blakely clicks her tongue against the roof of her mouth. "I guess I'll have to focus on the fucking part."

His gaze drops to her mouth as the curse slips past her lips, leaving Mia and me exchanging glances of curiosity.

Hot damn.

Pretty sure the sparks flying between these two could cause a full-blown inferno.

I'm also pretty sure the two of them are oblivious to Mia and I still standing in the same room with them. Since Theo's blocking the doorway, we can't exactly escape or give them privacy, which means...

"Should I pop some popcorn?" Mia mutters under her breath, sidling up next to me.

I swallow back my amusement and wait, unsure where to look or what to say. Theo growls, "You think your brother would let any guy around here within a ten-foot radius of you?"

"You're within a ten-foot radius of me," she points out, lifting her chin in defiance.

"Yeah, and I'll kill anyone who thinks they can get past me to get closer to you."

She scoffs. "So, what? You're my own personal bodyguard now?"

"Just like high school," he confirms.

"It's funny. I don't think I saw *brooding hockey player slash bodyguard companion* on the pamphlet when I signed up for LAU, so I think I'll pass." She pats his chest. "Thanks, though."

He chuckles and steps closer. "You think I'm gonna give you a choice, Blake?"

"I don't need a bodyguard, and I sure as hell don't need another brother, Teddy."

His nostrils flare at the nickname, but he doesn't comment. "You're right. What you need is a chastity belt. I'll see what I can find on eBay."

"Always a peach. To be fair, I believe you're the one who felt like enlightening me on your approved cardio activities, so--"

"Yo, Theo!" Colt grunts, his arms full of a nightstand. "Where've you been?"

Theo stares down at Blakely for another beat. Turning around and facing Colt, he apologizes, "Sorry. I got"--he exhales through gritted teeth and shakes his head--"distracted."

Once the nightstand is in place, the guys bring up Blakely's bed frame and put everything together. Meanwhile, I pick up pizza, grateful for the reprieve. Because whatever was going on in there? It was a hot mess.

47
ASHLYN

"So...where exactly are you taking me?" I ask. The sun is high in the sky, and the freeway is buzzing from excited college students anxious to get where they're going to celebrate Spring Break, and Colt and I aren't any different.

He surprised me with a weekend getaway, and I'm *so* ready to put away my books, catch a few rays of sun, and soak up my days and nights with the guy beside me.

Ever since SeaBird last week, things have been...freaking perfect.

His familiar sunglasses are propped on his nose, and his hair is a mess of waves from running his hand through it. But it's his corded forearm resting on top of the steering wheel and the carefree smirk that does me in.

Like he has a secret.

And I want to know what it is.

"Seriously," I prod. "Where are you taking me?"

"You packed the things I told you?" he asks.

"Most of them."

His brow quirks. "What'd you forget?"

"I may have misplaced my slutty lingerie and edible underwear."

With a dry laugh, he shakes his head and sticks out his lower lip in a pout to make any toddler proud. "Party pooper."

I roll my eyes and reach over to him, booping his bottom lip with my index finger. "I think you'll survive, mister."

"Barely."

A few minutes later, we pull off the freeway and take a winding road through the city and turn into a warehouse district, leaving me with more questions than answers.

As I peek out the passenger window, I murmur, "Seriously, though. Where the hell are you taking me?"

He parks and pulls the keys out of his truck, his eyes glazed as he studies the building in front of us as if it holds a ghost. And his earlier carefree attitude? It seems to have evaporated into a plume of smoke.

"Colt, what's wrong?" I plead quietly.

He exhales slowly but doesn't take his eyes off the building. "This is it."

"It?" I glance at the gray building surrounded by a sidewalk and concrete steps. There isn't anything special about it. Nothing to make it stand out or look unique in any way.

"The rink where we were supposed to be." He swallows thickly. "It's where my team practiced when I was a kid. I knew it like the back of my hand and told my dad I'd meet him here for the last game of the season, but Dad knew I'd be late. My girlfriend, Brooke, had been out of town. She'd gotten home the night before, so I went to her parent's house to see her before the game during my senior year. My dad was pissed I was late and missed the bus with the rest of the team. Like I said. I told him I'd meet him here, but he let the bus leave without him and waited for me at the house. By the time I pulled into the driveway so I could grab my gear, he was furious."

"Colt." I reach over the center console and place my hand on his, though it doesn't put a dent in his haunted gaze.

"We were fighting on the way to the game." He sniffs, then exhales long and slow. "I didn't even see the semi before it hit us on my dad's side. He died on impact. And me?" Grabbing my hand, he tangles our fingers together and squeezes. Like I'm the only thing keeping him present. In this car. Instead of being lost in the memory of the worst day of his life. "I walked away with barely a scratch, Ash. I replay the drive all the time. I replay the whole day," he clarifies, his body oozing with disgust.

"It wasn't your fault, Colt."

"I know," he rasps, glancing at me with a weak smile. "But every time I got on the ice after the accident, I couldn't stop replaying the day. How it looked. How it sounded. Even how it smelled."

"It's why you quit," I whisper.

With a slow, jerky nod, he keeps staring at the building, unable to look away. "Yeah, Sunshine. It's why I quit."

My heart cracks, and I drag his hand into my lap, desperate to comfort him. To take away his pain. "I'm sorry."

"I know." He tears his gaze from the building and squeezes his eyes shut, wiping away the moisture from his tear ducts. Clearing his throat, he looks at me with red-rimmed eyes. "But I want to thank you."

"For what?" I whisper.

"For convincing me to play again."

"I didn't--"

"You did. The night of the storm. You reminded me of what my dad used to always say... He didn't raise quitters. So, I picked my ass up again and strapped on my skates the next day. And even though it killed me a little to be on the ice, it brought me back to life too. Without you, Ash, I don't think I'd be where I am. I wouldn't be kicking ass in school. I wouldn't be on LAU's hockey team. I wouldn't be starting in the final game this season--"

"Colt!" I almost squeal. "You're gonna play in a game?"

He nods, a slight tinge of pink sneaking through his olive skin. "On one condition."

"What condition?"

He brings my hand to his mouth and kisses the back of it. "You come to every home game."

My eyes crinkle in the corners, and my cheeks pinch with happiness as I fight the urge to jump into his lap and kiss the crap out of him. But I can't help it. My enthusiasm. Not only for me but also for Colt. Because he's been through the wringer. And seeing him pick up the pieces and fight for what he wants? It's the most beautiful thing I've ever witnessed. And it makes me feel like the luckiest girl on the planet.

"You know I wouldn't miss them for the world," I reply.

"Good. You can sit next to my mom and Blakely. But I'll warn you. They aren't against facepaint."

I throw my head back and laugh, surprised by how good it sounds. "I'll keep it in mind."

"Good." He squeezes my hand again. "Now, come on."

48
ASHLYN

After another quick kiss to the back of my hand--as if Colt can't help himself--he lets me go and climbs out of his truck. I watch him round the front, open the passenger door, and offer me his hand. Once my feet are on the ground, he grabs a duffle bag full of his hockey gear from the back of his truck, and we walk inside.

The place is pretty big. The walls are all gray cinder blocks, but jerseys are hanging from the ceiling from different state teams, along with scoreboards on both sides of the room. It's big. Somewhat bland. And definitely daunting.

As Colt rents some ice skates for me from the rental booth, my nerves finally get the best of me, and I blurt out, "I feel like you should know I've never skated."

He stops, his jaw almost unhinged. "Are you shitting me?"

Cringing, I wipe my sweaty palms against my jeans, eyeing the ice rink like it's Mount Everest. "Nope."

"You dated Logan for years, and he never took you skating?"

"Nope," I repeat, popping the 'p' at the end while fighting

off my embarrassment. Because seriously, how pathetic, right? We dated for years, and he never took me ice skating. It was something he clearly enjoyed doing, and he never shared it with me. I still can't believe how oblivious I was. How backward my perception of a healthy relationship was. It blows my mind and makes me a little sad, too. But at least I get to experience the real deal with Colt. I can't believe how different it is this time around.

"No shit?" Colt asks.

"Stop asking!" With a laugh, I press my cool hands against my hot cheeks. "You're gonna make me self-conscious."

His chuckle is low but warm as he guides me to a bench along the outside of the rink and starts lacing up my rental skates for me.

"I'm surprised," he admits.

"And why is it surprising?" His calloused fingers are mesmerizing as he loops the shoelaces around the hooks, keeping the boot tight and secure around my foot. There's something so sexy about a guy who knows what he's doing. And clearly, Colt's in his element.

"Because I had no idea Logan was such a dumbass," he returns as he finishes lacing my skates and kisses my jean-covered knee, looking up at me. "How could he have not taken you skating?"

I shrug and watch him exchange his Nikes for skates, recognizing I'm definitely sitting next to the most attractive guy I've ever laid eyes on. The confidence. The bad boy smirk. It's official. He's the whole enchilada, and for some reason I still can't understand, he's here. With me. About to teach me how to ice skate. When I realize I'm staring, I clear my throat and smooth out the hem of my shirt, attempting to look busy while scrambling to remember what the hell we're talking about.

Oh. Right. My asshole ex, who never took me ice skating.

"I dunno?" I answer. "I guess it wasn't worth the effort of teaching me how."

"That's the fun part, though," he argues. "You looking like a baby deer. All needy and helpless. Me looking like a badass stag as I help you figure it out. It's frickin' perfect."

I laugh as he stands up and helps me to my feet, guiding me to the rink on--he guessed it--baby deer legs.

"This is *not* easy," I tell him, my ankles wobbling back and forth as I balance on the blades of my ice skates.

"You're not even on the ice yet," he teases. "Have you ever rollerbladed or anything?"

I shake my head but keep my death grip on his hands as I inch closer to the ice rink. "Not really. One bad experience at Amber May's birthday party in third grade was enough to deter me for the rest of my life."

He laughs a little harder. "Come on. Let me show you."

Once we're on the ice, he makes sure I have a firm grasp on the edge of the rink. Then, he skates backward, his blades cutting through the ice and causing tiny divots in the smooth surface as he shows me how talented he really is. Gliding back to me, he takes my hand.

He's right. Watching him look so confident while I'm seconds from falling on my butt is sexy as hell. He owns the rink. Like he owns me.

After a little while, I finally start to get the hang of things and can skate around the oval-shaped rink without clinging to Colt like he's my lifeline. But I'm far from ready to spin around, skate backward, or take the curves at a billion miles per hour, unlike Mr. Hot Shot.

It's fun, though. Comforting somehow. And when my ankles are spent, we turn in my skates, replacing them with my original flats, and head back to his truck.

"Thank you," I murmur.

His boyish grin makes my stomach flip-flop as he glances at me from the driver's seat. "For what?"

"For being perfect."

He chuckles and squeezes my hand. "Far from perfect, Sunshine. But I'm glad you can see past my bullshit. Come on. Let's grab some food."

49
ASHLYN

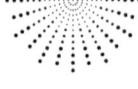

"So," I start, twirling a few noodles onto my fork and taking a bite. The lights are low, and the ambiance is quiet as we eat Italian in a little restaurant called Angetti's.

Colt smirks and watches me chew from across the table, more amused by my lack of question than his own meal.

"So?" he prods when I'm finished swallowing.

"Have you seen Logan much? I know you're on the team and all, but..." I wave my empty fork between us, unable to find the words to express what I really want to know.

"Are you asking if Logan knows about you and me?"

I nod, my stomach twisting at the thought. "You know, since you live with him and all."

"Yeah." Colt smiles, but it feels forced. "He knows."

"Seriously?" I make myself take another bite and try to look natural, but it still feels weird. Talking about Logan. But it's hard to leave your ex in the past when you're dating his friend. When you're dreading the moment you'll run into him again. He feels like a giant elephant in the room that is my relationship with Colt. Like…how am I supposed to handle it?

"Yeah," Colt confirms. "I told him myself."

My eyes bug out, and I nearly choke on my pasta. I reach for the wine glass and take a sip. "Y-you told him?"

"Yeah."

"When? How?"

"Before Spring Break. He had a right to know."

"Don't get me wrong. I know he did. But knowing it and actually being brave enough to say something are two very different things," I point out, smoothing out the cloth napkin on my lap while avoiding his gaze. "So…how'd he take it?"

I don't know why I ask. I shouldn't. It's not like I care, but I also don't want to cause the rift between friends, either.

"Fine," Colt offers.

"Just fine?"

"You thought he'd take it differently?"

I shake my head. "No? But kind of yes too?"

He laughs, and the sound eases the weight on my chest.

"Care to expand?" he asks.

"I mean…we were together for years, Colt. And then he broke my heart, and I wound up dating his best friend? It's gotta be relatively weird for him, doesn't it?"

"Do you want him to be jealous, Ash?" he asks, setting his fork down and reaching for his napkin.

I shake my head again. "No?"

"That a question?"

"No," I say more decisively. "It's a weird situation I've been trying to wrap my head around for weeks. That's all. I guess I assumed it would take him some time to wrap his head around it too? But I don't feel jealous," I tell him. "I feel guilty. For potentially coming between you guys. You two are best friends."

He tosses the burgundy red napkin onto the table and settles back in his seat. "We aren't as close anymore."

"I know. And it kills me."

His brows furrow. "What do you mean?"

"Is it my fault? Am I the catalyst? The reason you two aren't close anymore?"

With a sigh, he mutters, "Ash--"

"You know what I mean, Colt," I argue.

He reaches forward and grabs my hand, brushing his thumb against my palm on the white table cloth as the candlelight flickers off his dark, flinty eyes. "My friendship with Logan was already on rocky ground before you and I were ever a thing. And the way I feel about you?" He shakes his head, torn. "It's the real thing, Sunshine. I'm not going to let anything get in the way of pursuing it. Including one of my friends."

"Are you sure?"

"Yeah, Ash." He smiles. "Never been more sure of anything in my life."

"And Logan?" I push, still anxious. Still unsure. "How am I supposed to act around him now?"

"Be yourself. He said it was okay. And if he has an issue, he can talk to me about it."

"You're sure?"

"Yeah," he repeats, squeezing my hand softly. "I won't let him come between us if you don't."

The air in my lungs releases in a quiet, slow breath, making me feel lighter than I have in weeks. "Deal."

∼

Dinner's delicious, but the company makes it even better. As we reach our hotel room, I pat my stomach and say, "Didn't know you were going to put a baby in me this trip, Mr. Thorne."

His skin turns pale as he chokes out, "What?"

I rub my stomach again, turning sideways to show him my profile. "A pasta baby."

With a quirked brow, he counters, "You think you're funny, do you?"

My teeth dig into my lower lip as I bite back my grin. "Maybe a little. You should've seen your face, though." I do a chef's kiss with my fingers. "Perfection."

He sets our luggage near the window, grabs my hand, and tosses me onto the bed. With a squeal, I laugh, and he pounces on me, caging me in on both sides, running his nose along the column of my throat. I tilt my head to the side and savor his kisses until he replaces them with a raspberry, blowing all the air in his lungs out his mouth and onto my skin until I'm squirming beneath him. Shoving at his chest, I try to get away from him, but he's too strong to let me get far.

"I give up! I give up!" I yell as he continues his assault and collapses onto me.

"I can practice putting a baby in you if you'd like," he jokes.

"No, thank you. Not yet, anyway. I'd prefer to teach a few rugrats for a couple years before going down the mama road. How 'bout you? Do you want kids?"

He nods. "Yeah. I think so. Not anytime soon. But one day."

"So, you're a traditional family kind of guy?" I ask. We probably should've had this conversation at dinner or on the drive home or, hell, maybe a year from now instead of when we're in our hotel room on Spring Break, and he's pinning me to the mattress with a semi-hard erection pressed against my stomach. But hey, who am I to complain?

He brushes my hair away from my face, cradling my head between his palms as he looks down at me. Really looks at me. My heart beats a little faster, and my eyes soften as I'm reminded, yet again, how lucky I am to be here with him.

"With the right girl, yeah," he decides.

I lick my lips. "Interesting."

"Why's it interesting?"

"I sorta had you pinned for the bachelor life."

"Me too…until I met you." He leans down, bracing himself on his elbows, and kisses me. This time, it's less playful. More intimate. Like he's peeling away a piece of me I didn't even know existed, leaving me open and vulnerable beneath him.

I open my mouth and let him in. He takes full advantage, dragging his tongue along mine, dipping in for a taste. My heart rate continues rising, and my clothes feel like they're suffocating me as I wiggle beneath him, gripping the hem of his shirt. He reads my mind and sits up, shedding his clothes, and helps me out of mine. When I'm left bare, he pauses, his mouth turning up in a crooked but soft smile.

"What is it?" I ask.

"You're beautiful, Sunshine."

I bite my lip to keep from grinning like a lunatic. I lift my head and kiss him again.

"Wait here," I tell him, pulling away a few seconds later.

"Ash," he groans, but he rolls aside and lets me slip out from under him.

"Give me two minutes. I have a surprise for you." I dig in my bag and pull out my present for him.

"I hope it's the edible underwear!" he calls as I close the bathroom door behind me.

"Even better!" I return, slipping the gift over my head.

When I step out of the bathroom and into the bed portion

of the hotel room, I run my fingers through my hair and smile as his gaze slides down my body and the white cotton material practically swallowing me whole. The same cotton material that brought us together all those weeks ago. It's crazy how quickly life changes. And this time, it's definitely for the better.

His eyes heat with interest, and he shakes his head. "Is that my fucking T-shirt, Ash?"

"Mia may have returned it." I grin and lift one shoulder. "You like?"

"Get over here," he growls.

With a soft laugh, I jump onto the bed, and he grabs me by the waist, spinning us around until I'm pinned beneath him. Reaching up, I hook my arms around his shoulders and savor our position. His weight feels good on top of me. Every inch of his skin is pressed against mine as I hold him. Him and all of his broken pieces. The bad boy. The once-upon-a-time hockey star. The supposed backstabbing best friend. I hold him to my chest and breathe him in, knowing how easily I could fall in love with him.

How much I want to.

Spreading my thighs, I drag my hands up and down his bare back and cradle him there. With nothing but his LAU T-shirt separating us, I feel like we've never been closer. But I want more. Just like last time. Just like the next time. I need him.

"I want you inside of me," I whisper.

He kisses my neck and snakes his arm between us, dragging his cock between my folds. I angle my hips and lift myself to meet him, but he pulls back. Teasing me. Tempting me. Driving me insane.

"Colt," I warn.

"I wanna make this last, Ash," he whispers, looking down at me. And I know he means more than this moment. More than this sexual encounter. More than this weekend. He wants to make *us* last.

I smile up at him, my chest pinching at the look in his eyes. "Me too."

Leaning down, he kisses me again, teasing my clit with the head of his cock until I'm squirming.

"Please," I whisper when I'm positive I can't take it anymore.

He thrusts his hips and enters me in one swift movement. With a gasp, I arch off the bed as my fingernails dig into Colt's bare back.

I'll never get used to this. The feel of him stretching me. The feel of his weight on top of me. The feel of his breath against my throat. It's perfect. Incredible. Addictive.

We aren't frenzied. We aren't in a hurry to chase our orgasms. We're here to feel. To be. To connect.

And I've never felt closer with anyone in my entire life.

I bite my lip to keep the truth from tumbling out of me as he slowly picks up his pace, causing my breaths to quicken. My fingers bite into his ass, spurring him on. He kisses me again, groaning against my lips the same way I'm moaning against his.

The headboard slams against the wall in rhythm to his thrusts and only turns me on more as he shoves my shirt up, grabs my breast, and squeezes, pinching my nipple into a small bud. Leaning down, he takes it into his mouth.

I gasp. His hot tongue swirls around my nipple, the ache building in my core.

"Please," I beg. "Colt––"

"Wait," he growls.

His hand slips between my legs, and he pinches my clit at the same moment he bites my nipple, sending me spiraling into the sweetest oblivion I've ever experienced.

And he follows right after, pulsing inside me until we're both a spent mess on the bed.

As I catch my breath, he rolls onto his side and tugs me closer to him, but I push my hands against his chest. "I should go get cleaned up."

"Later," he replies.

"Colt--"

"I like the idea of me dirtying you up, Ash. Let me live a little, will ya?"

I laugh and snuggle against him, giving in no matter how insane his request is. Because I like him dirtying me up too. Actually, I like anything having to do with Colt Thorne. And while I used to find it terrifying, I kind of love it now. Our connection. Our talks. Our sex life.

Somehow, Colt's managed to slip past my defenses, making me feel cared for and appreciated in a way I didn't even think was possible.

But I do now.

"You know you're crazy, right?" I ask.

"Mm-hmm," he grunts. The sound rumbles against my ear as he grabs the covers from the opposite side of the bed and flings them over us, turning us into a little burrito. It's comfortable. And quiet. And absolutely perfect. And when I fall asleep in his arms, I realize I've never been happier.

50

ASHLYN

"Hey, Ash?" Colt murmurs against the top of my head.

The morning light is shining through the white curtains in our hotel room, but a quiet peacefulness envelopes us. Like we're cocooned in a fairytale. One I don't want to wake up from. Every inch of my body is exhausted from ice skating and making love, but it kind of feels amazing. The comfortable exhaustion. The slight ache as I stretch against Colt like a cat. The low chuckle rumbling from his chest as he drags his fingers along my bare arm.

Soaking up his warmth, I stifle a yawn behind my hand and croak, "Yeah?"

"I need to tell you something." His voice is still rusty from sleep.

I roll onto my side and peek up at him. "What is it?"

He hesitates and pulls me closer. "I want to be honest."

"About what?"

"Nothing crazy, but I feel like I should come clean."

"About?" I prod.

"I lied to you, Sunshine."

Like a pin to a balloon, the peace encompassing us is popped with five simple words. I push myself away from him, my heart in my throat. He lied to me? When? He can't be serious. There's no way. Not after how amazing this weekend has been--hell, the entire time we've been dating--would he lie to me. Especially when he knows my trust issues with the opposite sex.

No. No, no, no.

There's no way.

He wouldn't lie.

Not to me.

Would he?

"What are you talking about?" I choke out.

"Whoa, Sunshine." When he sees my fear shining back at him, he cradles the back of my head with his hand and rubs his thumb along my jaw, but I don't lean into him. "Calm down. I'm not trying to scare you. We're good. I only want to be transparent with you--"

"Answer the question," I demand. "When did you lie to me?"

He sighs and drops his hand from my cheek. "When I took you to brunch, and you met my family. I lied."

I replay the day the best I can, but nothing sticks out to me, which only feeds my insecurities. Because I didn't spot the lie at the time, which means I must've fallen for it.

My voice is nothing but a breath of fear as I pull up whatever defensive walls still exist inside of me and whisper, "When?"

"When we were in the car. I told you meeting my family wasn't a big deal. It *was* a big deal." He runs his calloused fingers against my bare arm again. Softly. Carefully. Like I'm a China doll he wants to protect. "I've only brought one other girl home. And even she didn't really count."

"Are you serious?" My heart feels like it's still caught in

my throat as I try to calm the hell down. "You scared the shit out of me, Colt!"

"I know, and I'm sorry," he adds. "I felt like I needed to come clean. Especially after last night."

Last night.

The last wave of uneasiness seeps from my pores, and I smile at the memory, my muscles melting as I relax against him. "Okaaaay. So, how does she not count?"

"We went to high school together," he clarifies. "We started dating my junior year, and since we didn't have our own places yet, we'd take turns hanging out at each other's houses. That's why I brought her home."

"So, you didn't love her?" I ask, still reeling from my mini-meltdown. Seriously. This boy deserves to be smacked upside the head for scaring me like he did.

Colt chuckles, the sound low and throaty. "Thought I did."

"Thought?" I push, surprised by my jealousy, though I blame Colt and his terrible timing and cryptic word choices.

Like, for real. When my sanity returns in a few minutes, I'm gonna give him one hell of a titty twister.

"It was complicated. Brooke was the reason I didn't make the bus on game day and drove with my dad instead. And then at his funeral, I found out she was seeing someone behind my back."

My heart shatters. "Colt…"

"When you find out someone's cheating on you, it's hard not to question everything you built together. Every excuse. Every kiss. Every moment."

"If anyone gets it, it's me. At least when it comes to the cheating part," I clarify. "I still can't believe I was so blind to Logan's lies."

"We see what we want to see."

He looks down at me, his eyes shining with something I can't quite put my finger on.

Pressing a quick kiss to his bare pec, I ask, "And what do you want to see, Colt?"

"With me and you?" he questions.

I nod.

His fingers drag through my hair, pushing it over my shoulder as he studies me carefully. "I want to see you in the morning. With your hair a mess and your eyes smudged with yesterday's makeup." I laugh and wipe under my eyes to remove said makeup, but he stops me, his expression softening. "I want to see you in front of a class of kindergarteners, singing the ABCs and yelling at one of them for wiping boogers on their neighbor." My chest swells, and another laugh bubbles out of me. Pushing himself up, he leans his back against the headboard, dragging me with him and tucking me into his side. "I think I might even see you in white one day, walking down an aisle toward me."

My breath catches in my lungs. But I can imagine it. The white flowers. Our families lining both sides of a church. Mia and Kate as my bridesmaids. It's funny. I used to picture Logan up there. Next to the preacher. But the vision was always skewed, and I never understood why it was so hard to imagine it. And it's so much more breathtaking when Colt's face comes into view instead. His same cocky smile. His hair mussed from running his fingers through it. A boutonniere pinned to his dark suit, and his hands folded in front of him as he watches me walk toward him. I can see it all. And it looks good. Great, actually. Like a dream. It kind of makes me want to cry.

Because we haven't even said *I love you* yet.

But I've never been more sure of anything in my entire life.

We've been too busy hiding. Sneaking around. Bending

over backward to keep our pasts from catching up to us when it's our future I want to chase.

"I want to see it too," I admit on a sigh, nuzzling into his chest and soaking up his heat like it's the sun.

"Maybe one day." He drops a kiss to the top of my head and rolls me onto my back, pinning me against the mattress. "But for now, I wanna worship you again, Sunshine."

My laugh turns into a moan as he bends his head and kisses me.

Yes, please.

51
ASHLYN

"Seriously, Colt. You gotta stop surprising me by taking me places," I mutter as the pilot turns on the fasten seatbelt icon and announces we'll be landing shortly. I click my seatbelt into place and puff out my cheeks, ignoring the anxiety in my chest and how close I am to hyperventilating.

"To be fair, this isn't a surprise," Colt returns. He reaches over my lap and slides open the window screen. "You know where we're going." When the different patches of greens and yellows come into view, creating a quilt of my home state, he smiles.

With a scowl, I counter, "Yeah, but I didn't know until you took the exit to the airport instead of the one that led home. Not cool, dude. Not cool."

"We have one more day of Spring Break. I figured your parents would want to see you."

"Yeah, well, you don't know my parents like I do," I mutter, fiddling with the cold metal from my seatbelt.

I'm not annoyed. I'm nervous. Like…really nervous. Which is stupid. I have nothing to be nervous about. So,

Colt's meeting my parents. Big deal. It'll be fine. Totally. Completely. Fine.

Sensing my reservations, Colt tears his attention from the window and touches my hand resting on the armrest between us. Like he knows this is killing me a little bit but is pushing me anyway because it's what he thinks I need. And in a way, he might be right.

Maybe.

His warmth is soothing. The way he brushes his thumb back and forth against my skin while my anxiety eats a hole in my stomach lining.

"You haven't been home since Christmas, Ash. I thought it'd be nice to visit your family," he points out. "Besides, I've been wanting to meet them for a while, and since I knew you'd put it off for as long as possible––"

"I wasn't going to put it off for as long as possible," I argue, folding my arms.

His thick brow arches. "You sure?"

With another scowl, I turn toward him in the gray leather seat, my defenses still raised. "You know my relationship with my parents is…weird."

"And I think it's time we fix it."

"You make it sound so easy." My stomach flip-flops as the plane descends toward the runway, and I gulp, peeking out the oval window toward my hometown.

"No, it's gonna be complicated. But we like *complicated*, remember?" Colt leans forward and presses a kiss to my temple. "If you're gonna push me to fight for the things I want and to build the future I want, I'm gonna push you to have the relationship you want with your parents. Even when it's hard. Understand?"

"But what if they don't want it back, Colt?" I whisper, voicing my fears while hating them more than ever. "A good relationship."

"Sunshine," he groans, tugging me closer to him. It's awkward, thanks to our seatbelts, but I kind of love it too. His desire to comfort me. His need to make things better. To fix things even when they're out of his control. It means he cares. And I love how he cares.

"Maybe they think your relationship *is* good," he argues. "Did you ever think of that? Maybe they don't know there's a problem in the first place."

He's right. My free-loving parents are definitely oblivious. Probably from all the weed in their systems, but what do I know? It doesn't make the situation hurt any less.

"That's even worse," I grumble against him. "Because if they don't see the problem, maybe it's me. Maybe *I'm* the problem."

"Not true."

I roll my eyes and pull away from him, but he grabs my chin and forces me to hold his gaze.

"Don't. Don't belittle your own feelings because you're afraid it'll inconvenience someone else."

"I'm not--"

"You are," he interrupts. "I've seen you do it plenty of times. From Mia and me to Logan, to your parents. You shoved aside what you needed and put them first. Time and time again."

"There's nothing wrong with putting someone else first," I argue.

"True. But there *is* something wrong when you're always the one taking the brunt of it. And since you suck at looking out for yourself, I'm gonna do it for you." He lets me go and settles back into his seat, proud of himself.

My lips purse. "Colt, I'm fine."

"There's nothing wrong with voicing your needs in a relationship, Sunshine. But you put everyone else's needs before your own, and I'm not gonna let you do it anymore."

"So, what are you going to do?"

"I'm gonna support you. And I'm gonna push you to stand up for yourself. And when you can't, I'll do it for you. I'll be your voice. I'll be whatever you need me to be. Understand?"

I glare back at him, but it only lasts for a second. My mouth twitches with a smile. Because he's cute when he cares. And he's even cuter when he cares about me.

He grins. "That's my girl."

52
ASHLYN

"Hey, Mom. Hey, Dad," I greet them when they answer the front door of my childhood home. It's nothing more than a tiny, two-bedroom villa surrounded by vines and shrubbery. There's also a mint green Volkswagen van parked out front, complete with a peace sign sticker and fuzzy pink dice hanging from the rearview mirror. Colt laughed when he saw it, but I told him not to ask.

It feels weird to walk up to my house when I've been gone for so long, and I know Colt notices. Thankfully, he's a gentleman and didn't comment as my hand hovered over the door handle before I lifted it and knocked my knuckles against the bright red aluminum door.

He's also ignoring my death grip on his hand as I introduce him to my parents, who are standing in front of us. "This is Colt Thorne, my boyfriend. Colt, this is Angelica and Wade Peterson, my parents."

Colt offers his opposite hand. The one not being squeezed to death by me. "Mr. and Mrs. Peterson, hello. We talked on the phone yesterday. Thanks for letting us swing by on such short notice."

My eyes widen in surprise. He decided *yesterday* to drag me here? Is Colt serious?

I guess I shouldn't be too shocked. After how perfect everything has been, I can understand why he'd be ready to take our relationship to the next level which, unfortunately, includes a parent meet-and-greet. And since he knew I wouldn't introduce him to my mom and dad without dragging my feet, he took matters into his own hands.

Sneaky bastard.

"You're welcome," my dad returns. "And please, call us Wade and Angelica." He pushes his shaggy gray and brown hair away from his face and shakes Colt's hand. My mom does the same.

"You're lucky we were home. We have a cruise coming up next week," she explains, stepping aside so we can come into the house. "Our shaman is hosting the whole thing. I think it's gonna be a very enlightening experience. Right, Wade?"

"Yes, honey," my dad agrees, pinching her butt. "*Very* enlightening."

Oh, my hell. Could they be any more embarrassing?

The strong scent of weed hits me square in the nose, making it wrinkle as I glance at Colt while praying he doesn't notice. Like I'd warned, my parents have always been free spirits, but telling Colt and having him see it with his own eyes are two very different things.

Part of me has always wondered if that's why I didn't fit in. Why they never bothered to reach out after I moved away. It's not like we have much in common. I'm a stickler for details, and they can barely even remember what day it is most of the time.

Doesn't make it hurt any less, though.

We stride into the house, and Colt wraps his arm around

my shoulders as my mom's attention shifts from him to me and back again.

She smiles.

"I like this," she decides, waving her fingers between us. "How was your flight?"

"It was good," I answer.

"Good. Your father and I were going to grab some lunch. There's a delicious little vegan place a few minutes away." She grabs a tie-dyed shawl from the coat rack near the front door and slips it over her shoulders. "Would you prefer to stay here? I know vegan isn't usually your thing. We can always catch up later."

I flinch back, embarrassed. I mean, it's not like it's a big deal, but we just got here, and they already want to ditch me?

"Actually, I think we'd love to join," Colt replies for me, his hand practically branding my lower back as he looks down at me. "Wouldn't we, Ash?"

Swallowing back my disappointment, I nod. "Yeah, of course."

"Are you sure?" she asks. "The flight must've been long. We can always catch up after––"

"Yeah. We're sure," Colt interrupts.

"Let me, uh, use the restroom. I'll be back in a second." I slip out from beneath Colt's arm and head to the bathroom without a backward glance, trying to keep my pace steady.

I need a minute. To breathe. To wrap my head around the fact we're here, and Colt now has a front-row seat to my less than traditional parents. It's not like they're bad people. I've always had a roof over my head and food on the table. But their love for me isn't like Colt's parents'. And me admitting out loud versus him witnessing it firsthand? Well, it sucks.

This is going to be one long weekend.

53
COLT

"So, Collin," Ash's mom starts when the bathroom door closes. "How did you meet our Ashlyn?"

"Actually, my name's Colt," I correct her. " And we met when Ash was my tutor for a while."

"Colt?" She frowns, her expression flooding with embarrassment. "Yes. I apologize. I'm terrible with names."

"It's fine. Ash warned me you aren't the best with them."

"It's awful. Wade got me this necklace to help me retain information." She toys with a white and orange crystal hanging on a gold chain around her neck. "Unfortunately, names still seem to slip my mind despite the calcite's healing properties. What was her last boyfriend's name again?"

"Lucas?" her dad chirps. "Or was it Landon?"

Tapping her finger against her chin, she narrows her gaze. "Lockland?"

"No," Ash's dad returns, shaking his head. "That wasn't it."

"Logan," I answer. "His name was Logan."

"Right!" Ash's mom snaps her fingers and smiles back at me like I correctly answered the final question on a game show. "I'm impressed you knew that. We didn't have a chance to meet him, but I guess it all worked out in the end, didn't it?"

"It did," I agree.

"But she brought you home," she adds. Her long blonde hair has strings of silver woven through it. It swishes to one side and almost reaches her hip as she tilts her head, and looks me up and down. She's pretty in a free spirit kind of way. No makeup. A long, flowy skirt. She's a flower child through and through, and her husband isn't any different. But if they think I'm not serious about their daughter--or I'm anything like Logan--they're wrong.

"Or, I guess since you're the one who called, you invited yourself," Wade clarifies.

"I did," I announce, shifting my weight from one foot to the other. "I love Ashlyn."

The sentiment feels foreign on my tongue, but good, too. Like I was made to say it. To love her. I probably should've told Ash before blurting it out to her parents, but it's too late now. They need to know my relationship with Ash is the real deal. I'm not going anywhere.

"As do we. She's our strong, independent daughter," Wade announces, tucking his left hand into his tan linen fisherman pants as his eyes light up with pride.

And I think he's telling the truth, which leaves me with a hell of a lot more questions than answers.

It doesn't make sense. How they perceive their relationship versus how Ashlyn does. Not to mention my brief conversation with Angelica yesterday. It felt like pulling teeth to get her to agree to let us stay for a night.

My attention shifts to the still closed bathroom door where their strong, independent daughter is collecting herself after their shitty comment. It's painted with black, yellow, and gold, and the walls on each side of it are decorated with two massive portraits of Native Americans in their traditional headdresses, their faces painted with courage and determination.

I siphon a bit for myself and blurt out, "Do you mind if I ask you something?"

"Not at all," Wade returns.

"Why don't you ever call her back?"

Angelica's brows pinch. "Excuse me?"

"When she calls. When she reaches out. You never call her back. You never ask about her day or how she's doing. You don't even bother to remember her boyfriend's name."

"I--excuse me?" she stutters. Probably surprised by my audacity.

Then again, so am I.

"We even showed up a few minutes ago, and you said you were going to a vegan place, only inviting us to join like it was an afterthought," I continue.

Wade's jaw clenches. "Listen, Collin--"

"Colt," I correct him. "My name's Colt. Although, honestly? I don't give a shit what you call me because I don't care. All I care about is your daughter and her happiness."

"And you think we don't care about our daughter's happiness?"

I scrub my hand over my face, but it's too late to back down, and now that I've opened this can of worms, I'm afraid I've got to see it through. "No, I think you do, but I also think *you* think because Ashlyn moved away, your days of being supportive and present aren't necessary anymore. And I guess, in a way, you're right. Because she doesn't need you. Ash is strong. And independent. And smart. So fucking smart," I add, before I realize I just dropped the f-bomb in front of my future in-laws.

Shit.

I clear my throat and continue. "But she still wants you in her life. She misses you. She wants to be close to you. Even when she's across the country at school. Even when she's taking on the world all by herself. She still wants her mom and dad. I think you need to stop taking it for granted."

Wade's gaze narrows. Not angrily. Almost defensively. "Who says we're taking our roles as parents for granted?"

"No one had to say it. I could see it."

He takes a step toward me. "Listen here--"

"I had to twist your arm on the phone yesterday," I remind them, my attention shifting from one defensive face to the other. "You might not have even noticed, but you had multiple excuses locked and loaded as to why we couldn't come, and you didn't agree until you felt like you had no other choice."

Angelica jerks back as if I've slapped her. "We get busy--"

"I get it," I return. "And if it were one instance, I'd believe you, but it's *all* the time. You want to claim the title of parents without doing any of the heavy lifting anymore. It isn't fair to Ash."

With her lower lip trembling, Angelica toys with the gold strand on her necklace but stays quiet as she leans into Wade's side.

"I'm not going to lecture you anymore because we both know it isn't my place," I add, my tone softening. "But if you care about Ash--and I know you do--you need to start showing it. Not only when it's convenient for you. Not just around the holidays and shit. But all the time. Because I can guarantee one day, I'm gonna propose to Ash. And I know she's going to want you to walk her down the aisle. But only if you've earned the right. And lately? It hasn't been the case."

Wade scrubs his hand over his face and mutters, "Listen, Colt--"

"My dad died during my senior year of high school, Mr.

Peterson. I know what it's like to have too much space. Too much time between conversations. Do you know what I would give for him to be able to call me? To hear his voice again? You guys can still talk to Ash, but you don't." I scoff, blown away by how her own flesh and blood wouldn't want to talk to her every hour of every day. "Life is short, Mr. Peterson. It's *short*. And you don't know when or how it'll end. I know you're not trying to take your role for granted as Ash's parents, but she needs more. She needs to hear how proud you are of her. Not me. I already know she's a badass, and I spend every day reminding her of it. But she needs to hear it from *you* too." I raise my hands in surrender, take a step back, and let out a long, slow breath. "Okay. Now I'm really done. I'm sorry." I force out another breath. "I love your daughter, and I want to make sure she's being treated the way she deserves. That's it. I love her."

The entryway is so quiet I swear you can hear a pin drop. But I keep my mouth shut––because I've already said too much––and wipe my sweaty palms on my jeans.

Waiting.

Just…waiting.

For Wade to punch me in the face.

For Angelica to throw me out of their home.

For both of them to chew my ass out for overstepping my bounds. Because I'm not a dumbass. I know it's exactly what I've done.

But they needed to hear it. The truth.

The good.

The bad.

And the ugly.

No matter how much it hurts.

Angelica laces her fingers through Wade's and brings his hand to her lips as they engage in some kind of silent conversation. He stares down at her, his eyebrows pulled low for a long second. He dips his chin and looks at me again.

Reserved.

Hesitant.

But vulnerable.

"We'll keep it all in mind, Colt," he tells me.

I nod, grateful for his understanding while hiding my surprise at how well they handled my speech. "Thank you."

The bathroom door opens, and Ash strides toward us, her ballet flats scuffing quietly against the hardwood floor as she wrings her hands in front of her, looking like she belongs on another planet compared to the house she was raised in.

Every inch of her clothes coordinates with the style of her hair, or the color of her shoes, while the world around her is mismatched and chaotic but just as perfect.

My mouth quirks up in a smile. I love that she was raised here.

It's where she learned her tolerance of all people. Her acceptance of all ideas, no matter how backward they may seem. It's where she learned her patience. Her appreciation. For those different from her.

Like her parents.

Like me sometimes.

I think it's why I never felt judged by my bullshit decisions.

It's why she welcomed Blakely with open arms.

It's probably why she accepted Logan's bullshit for so long, too, but I think she learned from the experience.

What's acceptable. What isn't.

And I love her even more for it.

If only she felt appreciated and accepted for her differences, as well.

Tucking her hair behind her ear, she forces a smile and says, "Sorry, I took so long--"

Ash's mom cuts her off by pulling her into a hug. "We are *so* proud of you, Ashlyn."

Her dad joins in, wrapping his arms around both of them. "So. Damn. Proud, baby girl." He drops a kiss on the top of her head. "Now, let's get some lunch and catch up. Wherever you want to eat. Your mom and I can eat at the vegan place later. We'll go where you want to go. Our treat."

54

ASHLYN

"Okay. What did you do?" I ask as the Uber driver pulls out of the driveway.

Colt gives me the side-eye, confused. "What are you talking about?"

"I'm talking about the two strangers we stayed with last night."

"Your parents?" he clarifies, dumbfounded.

I hold myself back from smacking his arm as we head toward the airport. "Yeah. My parents. What did you say to them? After I came out of the bathroom when we first arrived, they were so sweet and attentive. And the fact they're flying out to see you play in the last game this season even though they *hate* flying? Like seriously. It's a big deal. They even remembered your name, and that's saying something, by the way. So, my question is, what did you do?" I demand.

He hooks his arm around my shoulders and pulls me into his side as the scenery whirs past the passenger window.

"Seriously. Tell me," I order.

"I told them I love their daughter," he offers, looking cool as a cucumber as I peek up at him, convinced he's being sarcastic or that I heard him wrong.

I must have.

But he isn't joking.

"You told them you love me?" I ask.

He shrugs, and pulls me closer. Like he didn't just rock my world with a few simple words. "Yeah. Then, I explained that their daughter might be a badass, but she's a badass who still needs parents."

"Colt--"

"You deserve to be happy. And to be treated fairly. I think they just needed the reminder."

He said that?

And lived to tell the tale?

If I was ever unsure about his feelings for me, they're officially debunked. Colt Thorne really is the sweetest, most thoughtful man I've ever met, and I don't even know how to handle it.

Blinking back tears, I kiss his cheek and whisper, "Why did you say those things?"

He looks down at me like he's confused I even have to ask. "Because I love you, Ashlyn."

There it is again. So matter of fact. So black and white. Like saying--and feeling-- those three short syllables are as easy as breathing. And with Colt, I guess they are.

In fact, loving Colt is the most natural thing in the world.

Biting back my watery grin, I murmur, "I love you, too."

I can feel his smile against my skin as he drops a quick kiss to my forehead, his muscles melting beside me. And I love it. How confident, yet vulnerable he is around me. Like he assumed I love him back but couldn't fully relax until he heard me say it out loud.

Silly, arrogant man.

A breath of laughter slips out of me before I rest my head

on his shoulder, and ask, "So...did you say anything else to my parents?"

He chuckles. "Nosy much, Ash?"

I smack his chest. "Come on, I wanna know!"

"All right, all right," he concedes. "Let me think." Mindlessly toying with a few strands of my hair, he adds, "I also told them that even though they know you can tackle anything on your own, you deserve to have your parents be there for you, so you don't *have* to tackle it on your own."

My heart swells.

This man knows me too well. He hit the nail on the head.

I *do* try to handle things by myself. I *do* try to take care of my own shit while usually carrying a few extra things while I'm at it for the people I love. I rarely ask for anything. Honestly, I probably wouldn't know what to do with someone's help if they gave it to me in the first place. Even when Colt showed up in the pouring rain when my car broke down, I didn't know how to handle it. He practically had to force me into his truck.

But support would be nice. And it's so hard doing it alone. Tackling projects, and school, and my future all by myself. It's exhausting. Or at least, it was until I found Colt. He's given me the support I crave without asking for anything in return.

Going to battle against my parents is a perfect example of exactly that. It's the most flattering, thoughtful thing anyone has ever done for me. Pretty sure I couldn't love him for it.

"How 'bout you?" I ask, touching his thigh. "Will you be here for me too?"

He tilts my head toward him, making sure he has my full attention before leaning in for another kiss. But he doesn't brush his lips against mine. Nope. The bastard enjoys teasing me too much to put me out of my misery. "For as long as you'll have me, Sunshine."

"Such a gentleman," I quip.

With a dry laugh, he tangles his fingers into my hair and drags me even closer, kissing me until I'm a panting mess in the back of a freaking Uber.

And even though I should probably be embarrassed, I'm not. Because it's Colt Thorne.

Colt.

Thorne.

The man who loves me and isn't afraid to stand up for me no matter what.

I kiss him harder, dragging my tongue against his before he pulls away, and growls against my lips. "Always."

55
ASHLYN

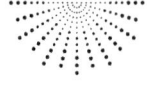

"Colt's gonna kill me," Blakely mutters as she tugs at the hem of her dress. It barely reaches her mid-thigh.

I grab her hand to keep her from fidgeting. "Stop. You look cute."

"I look like--"

"A gorgeous girl?" Mia offers. Apparently, while Colt and I were away, Mia and Kate gave Blakely a makeover and knocked it out of the park. "Besides. Colt's not the one you have to worry about. Theo's gonna shit his pants."

"Greaaaat." Blake drags out the word while eyeing the front of the Taylor House like it's straight out of a horror movie.

"Seriously. You look awesome," I tell her. "Why are you freaking out?"

"Because this"--she waves her hand at the house literally thumping with rap music--"is not where a girl like me usually hangs out. Especially when looking like this." She waves her hand around again, this time showcasing her gorgeous black dress hugging her like a second skin. "Or this." She picks up a wave of hair and flicks it over her shoulder. "Or this." Her finger points to her smokey eye shadow that makes her green eyes practically glow to prove her point.

"You're in a new place now. You get to start over. Be who you want to be. Look how you want to look. Attract who you want to…"--Mia winks--"*attract*."

Blake glares at Mia. "I don't want to attract anyone. I only want to fit in and have fun without getting yelled at by a certain--"

"What the hell are you wearing?" Theo barks from his porch and rushes toward us on the front lawn. With a beer bottle in one hand, he grabs Blake's arm with his other one. Not roughly, but with a possessiveness that causes Blakely's breath to hitch.

"She's wearing *my* dress," Mia interrupts, yanking Blakely from the opposite side like she's in some twisted game of tug-of-war. "Doesn't she look hot?"

His nostrils flare as he lets her go and clenches his hand at his side. "You really think Colt's gonna let you inside looking like this?"

"Pretty sure it's my decision, and even if it wasn't, you would *still* have no say in the matter," Blakely reminds him. "I'm not the little girl you can boss around anymore, Teddy Bear."

His jaw ticks as he towers over her, two seconds from having an aneurysm.

"I thought we discussed you calling me that," he growls.

With a syrupy sweet smile, she replies, "Must've slipped my mind."

"O. M. G.," a gorgeous brunette interrupts, almost tumbling into Theo. One of her heels is caught in the grass, and she's laughing like a hyena, clutching at his bicep like he's her own personal savior.

"Oh. Hi, Theo," she purrs when she recognizes him. "Good to see you again."

Blake mutters something under her breath, her cheeks flushing as she heads inside the house without a backward glance.

Mia and I share a look, both of us cringing.

Great timing, Theo.

Ignoring the girl hanging on his arm, Theo turns to us and orders, "Keep an eye on her. And next time, let her borrow a hoodie or something. Not a dress like *that*," he adds, grumbling over the rim of his bottle and throwing back the rest of what's inside like it's water.

We laugh and step over the threshold of the Taylor House, leaving Theo with his *friend* on the front lawn. It's getting warmer, so there are about as many people outside as there are inside. Colt, however, must still be inside, which means it's where I want to be too.

The lights are dimmed, and the music is thrumming, practically vibrating through our veins as Mia and I look around the main floor. I'm still not quite sure why Colt and I are here instead of hanging out at my place, but Mia wanted to introduce Blakely to the Taylor House, and I wanted to prove I'm not still hiding from Logan, so…here we are.

Whether it's a good idea or not is yet to be seen.

When I spot Colt across the room, my mouth tilts up with a smile. He's talking to Tukani, one of the defensemen on the hockey team. The fans call him Tukani Tsunami. The guy's from Hawaii, and has tribal tattoos wrapped around both his massive arms. How he wound up playing hockey, I have no idea, but he's nice. And I like him even more for entertaining Colt instead of one of LAU's puck bunnies.

Not that Colt would do that in the first place. He's nothing like Logan. But still. It's refreshing. Seeing my boyfriend at a party without a girl hanging on his arm. Hell, there isn't a girl within a five-foot radius of him. The sight makes me even more grateful that I found Colt. That he found *me*. It's so different from all the times I'd seen Logan at these parties. I used to sweep so much under the rug with him. Convincing myself that waving off women came with the territory of being a hockey player, and if I wanted to date one, I'd have to get used to it. It's the lie Logan led me to believe.

And I had no idea how wrong it really was. How many times Logan took advantage of my trust. Of my desire to be loved when he knew it was already lacking in my personal life. How many times I turned a blind eye.

He knew how hard it would be for me to let him go because I craved stability in my life. He knew I was desperate for someone to love me, and he took advantage. Don't get me wrong. I think he did love me in the beginning. At least for a little while. But seeing Colt surrounded by beautiful women while being blind to all of them? It's what I deserve.

And Colt helped me see it.

I know I shouldn't compare them, but I can't help it sometimes. They're so black and white. I guess the saying is true; you have to kiss a lot of frogs before you find your prince and boy, did I find mine.

His arms are folded, and the fabric of his red T-shirt is stretched across his chest and biceps, making my mouth water. He's pinching the neck of a beer bottle between his fingers, nodding at something his buddy's saying while looking like a freaking Greek god.

I could stare at him for days.

Watching him in his element.

Effortlessly sexy.

Effortlessly commanding the room.

Effortlessly breaking hearts around him without giving a shit about hurting their feelings.

Because he's all mine.

Mine.

When he catches me staring at him, his mouth tilts up in a smile, and he walks toward me, ending whatever conversation he'd been having.

With a quick peck to my cheek, he greets me. "Hey, Sunshine."

"Hey."

"You look beautiful." He leans closer, his breath fanning across my cheeks. "Love the dress, by the way."

"Oh, you noticed?" I quip.

With a low chuckle, he grabs my hip with his hand and drags me closer, kissing my forehead.

"Hello to you too," Mia interrupts from beside me.

Colt cringes and gives me a bit of breathing room, looking at Mia as if he just noticed she's here. "Hey. Sorry--"

"For the lack of hello? It's fine. I know I'm chopped liver compared to this girl." She hooks her thumb at me. I don't get a chance to argue how gorgeous she looks because she adds, "Don't worry, Ashlyn. I was kidding, and I know I'm a babe. Besides, I think it's cute how Colt has goo-goo eyes for you and *only* you."

"He does not," I start to say, but Colt cuts me off.

"I do." He presses a quick peck to my temple to prove his point, turns back to Mia, and comments, "You look nice tonight, Mia."

She snorts. "Gee. Thanks."

Realizing he isn't going to get anywhere by kissing her ass, he looks back at me and asks, "Are you ready to leave yet?"

With a laugh, I shake my head. "I just got here. Besides, it's your little sister's first college party. And since this is her first time with roommates, Mia and I have to show her how to have a good time."

He looks around the crowded house, keeping his hand pressed to my lower back like he can't get enough of me as he searches for Blake in the crowd. And I love it. The way he wants to keep me close. Within reach. It makes me melt a little. When he spots her in the kitchen, currently pouring vodka into a red cup, Colt scratches his temple and tilts his head toward her. "As long as you're the ones cleaning up her puke."

"Ew!" Mia and I return in unison. Mia adds, "But also, point taken. Now, if you two love birds will excuse me, I'm gonna go make sure our little Padawan takes things slow, so we won't have to clean up any puke tonight."

She slips between Colt and me, making her way toward the kitchen and out of sight when someone pushes Colt from behind. He almost bumps into me but catches himself on the railing behind my head with gritted teeth.

"Still can't believe I enjoyed these things before we met," he mutters under his breath while tossing a glare at the culprit, who's too drunk to notice.

I tug at the fabric stretched across Colt's chest to get his attention. "You can still enjoy them even though you have a girlfriend now."

"I don't need the alcohol or the music anymore, Sunshine. I don't need to escape. I only need you." He kisses my forehead. "How are you feeling?"

I glance around his broad shoulders, refusing to acknowledge who I'm looking for. "Good. It's kind of weird to be here, though."

"Why?"

"Because the last time I was at a party like this, Logan was still my boyfriend, and we haven't spoken since…"

"Since I told him you were mine?"

I laugh. "Since he broke up with me over a text, and I started dating his best friend? Yeah. *That.*"

His fingers dig into my hips as he pulls me closer. "I told you he was fine with it. He's the one who wanted you to come tonight to *prove* he was okay with it."

My teeth bite into my lower lip, and I scan the house again. "If you say so."

"Want me to get you a drink?"

I nod. "Yes, please. Anything to calm the nerves and rip this thing off like a Band-Aid would be great."

With another soft smile, he leans forward and kisses my temple. "Be right back."

"Perfect. I'm going to use the ladies' room. I'll meet you in a sec."

I weave through the crowd, find the hall leading to the bathroom, and gasp when I catch Logan feeling up a girl from one of my classes.

My eyes widen, and I choke back my laugh as I slip past them, mumbling, "Don't mind me."

The door closes with a quiet click, and I lock it behind me, surprised by how little it hurts to see Logan sucking face with his hand full of a boob not belonging to me.

And hallelujah for it.

I lean against the door and let out a breath of laughter.

Actually, it feels great. To see him moving on. To see he isn't hurting.

Maybe Colt's right. Maybe we can all move forward. Maybe I won't be the wedge between friends. Maybe he really will be happy for me. For us.

After going to the bathroom, I wash my hands, dry them on a towel, and open the door.

The hall's empty. But as I turn toward the main area, I find Logan with his back against the wall, one foot propped up on it, and his arms folded.

My heels dig into the ground.

"Hey, Ashlyn."

56
ASHLYN

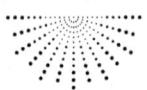

Logan steps up to me, his expression amused and laced with pity as the glow from the main area casts his front in shadows.

"Uh, hey," I greet him. "Where'd your little friend go?"

"I told her I'd meet her in a few minutes."

"Oh. Cool. So…how are you?" I ask, crossing my arms.

This feels weird. And *so* awkward. I don't know where to look. Where to stand. What to say. I don't feel threatened or anything, but something still feels off, and I can't quite put my finger on what.

"Fine." He tucks his hands into his pockets and steps closer. "Heard about you and Colt."

"Oh. Yeah." I gulp. "Colt mentioned he told you. Thanks for being so great about it."

He scoffs, revealing a tiny chink in his armor of indifference.

"Is there a problem?" I ask.

He scratches his jaw and shrugs one shoulder. "I think it's funny."

"What's funny?"

"How you honestly bought his bullshit."

His chuckle makes my nose wrinkle, but I take the bait anyway. "What bullshit?"

"About him actually liking you."

I roll my eyes.

Of course, he'd go there. Of course, he'd try to prey on my insecurities.

Freaking asshole.

"You know, Logan," I tsk, "I really wanted to believe Colt when he said you were fine with me and him seeing each other. It's a shame he was wrong. Now, if you'll excuse me."

I go to step past him, but he grabs my arm and stops me. Not roughly, or in a scary way. If anything, the move only proves how desperate he really is. I look up and meet his gaze, my own laced with pity.

"Let me clarify something for you," he murmurs. "I don't give a shit about him dating you. Honestly, I'm only looking out for you."

"Oh, really?" I laugh. "How so, exactly?"

"Because he's using you."

"You're full of shit, Logan." I tug my arm out of his grasp and take a step toward the left, but he steps in front of me, keeping me in place like we're in some sort of twisted tango.

"Can you move?" I snap, my amusement shifting to annoyance. I want to get out of here and find Colt. Maybe we can go back to my place and drown my frustration in some more Ben & Jerry's. I'm sure Mia left a pint in the freezer, didn't she?

"Gotta say, I'm a little surprised you'd cheat," he tells me. "Didn't think you had it in you."

"I'm not a cheater," I spit. "And neither is Colt."

"Colt's not a cheater, huh?" His chuckle is dark and throaty like he's gargled gravel or something as he leans closer and glares down at me. "So, he didn't tell you why he got kicked out of Dixie Tech?"

"I--" I shake my head. "Why does it even matter right now?"

"You said he isn't a cheater," he notes. "But he got caught screwing his professor's wife. I'd say that's cheating, don't you?"

With a huff, I stick a pin in that particular tidbit and argue, "Doesn't matter. I'm sure he has an explanation, and even if he didn't, it's in the past, which means I. Don't. Care. Now, if you'll excuse me." I lean to my right, but he mirrors my movement, using his massive body to prevent me from leaving. "Seriously, Logan. You're pissing me off."

"What else is new?" He scoffs.

"You know, I thought we could be amicable about this, but apparently, I was wrong."

"You always were delusional," he agrees.

Tongue in cheek, I tilt my head up and finally let loose all my pent-up frustration, all my pent-up disgust, and let it rise to the surface. "You wanna know something funny, Logan? I never really understood how toxic you were. I brushed aside all your little annoying idiosyncrasies because I was grateful I had someone to love me. What I never understood was you didn't love me. You never did. You played the part, wanting to have your cake and eat it too. You knew I could've had plenty of other guys, so you wanted to claim me for yourself, and because I was young and naive, I let you. But can I let you in a little secret, Logan?"

"What's that, babe?"

I smile and rise onto my tiptoes, dropping my voice to a mock whisper when part of me wants to scream the truth from the rooftops. "I was never really yours. I was simply numb and scared. But I'm not either of those things anymore." I laugh dryly, letting the truth sink in. I add, "I'm happier than I've ever been, more in love than I've ever been, and more spoiled and grateful than I've ever been. So, thank you. For treating me like shit. For cheating on me countless times. For showing me exactly what I *don't* need so Colt could swoop in and give me the opposite. You can keep your puck bunnies, by the way." I pat his shoulder to drive my point home. "Honestly, I should thank them for taking you off my hands. But let me be clear, Logan. You and I are over. Even if Colt and I weren't a thing, we would *still* be over. Now, let me out of this hallway so I can get back to my amazing boyfriend who loves me for me."

His jaw ticks, but he doesn't move a muscle as he glares down at me. And I know I've struck a chord. I know I've made my point very clear. And I know it's only pissed him off more.

"Nice little speech, babe," he tells me. "Did you rehearse it in front of the mirror before you came over?"

I roll my eyes and shake my head. "I'm leaving."

But as I go to slip past him, he steps in front of me again.

"He wants to get back at me, you know," he adds with a mock frown. It only fans my frustration.

Pinching the bridge of my nose, I mutter, "This isn't about you--"

"Yes, it is, Ash."

"For what, Logan?" I ask, exasperated. "What would he have against you? You guys are friends--"

"I slept with his girlfriend behind his back."

Wait. What?

The blood drains from my face as I register his comment.

I slept with his girlfriend behind his back.

Logan was sleeping with Colt's girlfriend? Brooke? As in, the same girlfriend that made him late for one of his hockey games in high school? And not just hockey game, but *the*

307

hockey game? The one before the accident? The accident that killed his dad?

My lips part on a silent gasp.

Did Colt know?

How could Logan do something like that? To his own best friend? It's despicable. If the guy wanted to make me feel like I've been sucker-punched, he officially succeeded.

My mind feels like it's short-circuiting as I stutter, "W-what are you talking about?"

"His girlfriend in high school. I slept with her behind his back, and now he's sleeping with you to get back at me."

"I--" I shake my head, convinced I'm hallucinating. "You're lying."

"I'm really not," he tsks. "He's using you, Ash. He doesn't like you. He doesn't want you. Just like your parents don't. He wants to flaunt you in my face to prove he won." Tongue in cheek, he looks over his shoulder toward the main area, practically bursting with our fellow students, and lets out a low chuckle. "Honestly? It's pathetic, Ash. I ended shit with you. Why does he even think I'd care?" He laughs a little harder. "Didn't think you'd fall for it, though. You really think someone like Colt Thorne would want you?" Another scoff. "Tell me. How long did you wait until you jumped into his bed?" He lifts his hand and shakes his head. "Actually. I don't even care enough to know. Run along, Ashlyn." He steps aside, finally giving me space to slip past him. "Glad I could shine some light on the situation for you."

But I keep my feet planted and stare at him. I want to yell. I want to scream. But I'm too stunned to do anything. Hell, I feel like I've been kicked in the stomach.

Breathe, I remind myself. *He wants to hurt you. Don't let him hurt you.*

"Nice catching up, Logan," I spit, nearly choking on the

lump in my throat, but I swallow it back. "I hope you catch an STD and your dick falls off."

With my head held high, I walk out of the hall and through the crowded main area, desperate for some fresh air. For a chance to clear my head. For a chance to understand.

Logan can't be serious, can he? And even if he is--which considering the messenger, could be a load of shit--so what?

So. Freaking. What?

I don't believe Logan.

Why should I?

He's nothing but a liar.

A sniveling asshole who hates losing.

And he knows he lost me to his best friend.

But Colt and I? We're solid.

He cares about me.

I *know* he does.

But I also know I need some freaking air after that shitty conversation, or I might pass out.

"Ash!" a voice calls from behind me, but I don't bother to turn around. I need air.

Some freaking air.

Then I'll be able to clear my head and make sense of what Logan told me.

It'll be fine.

Everything will be fine.

Because he's lying.

Logan has to be lying.

Doesn't he?

57
COLT

"Ash!" I yell, but she doesn't turn around. She continues stumbling toward the door like she's drunk off her ass, and a pack of wolves is chasing after her. Her shoulder bumps into a few people, turning herself into a human pinball as she makes her escape, and I set the drinks on the nearest table to chase after her.

"Ash!" I call again.

"You okay?" Theo asks as I rush past him and out onto the front lawn, but I don't answer.

Because I don't know.

Ash's hands are on her head, and her face is tilted up toward the sky as she breathes in deep. Like she's drowning. Like something happened.

"Ash." I grab her shoulders and cup the back of her head, forcing her to look at me as the slight wind ruffles her hair. "Ash, what happened?"

"Why'd you get kicked out of Dixie Tech?"

An ache builds in my throat, but I swallow it back. "Ash--"

"You said you weren't a cheater."

"I'm not," I argue, desperate to explain everything. To help her understand. To make her listen.

"And the professor's wife you were sleeping with?" she demands, licking her lips and trying to stay calm when I know she's seconds from losing her shit.

Squeezing my eyes shut, I rest my forehead against hers and breathe her in, desperate for forgiveness. "I didn't know she was my professor's wife. When I found out, I ended things, but the school still expelled me." I open my eyes and hold her gaze. "You know I wasn't lying when I said I'm not a cheater, Ash. You know my history."

"Yeah, with Brooke," she clarifies, her expression darkening. "Tell me. Who was she sleeping with again?"

I keep my hands on her face but lean back, my stomach knotting with dread. "Wait. What?"

"Who was Brooke sleeping with behind your back? You said she was cheating on you."

"I don't know," I answer. My attention darts around her face as I try to decipher what she's thinking, but I can't.

I don't fucking know.

I don't know what happened. I don't know why she's asking me this. I don't know where this came from or why she cares.

We were separated for five minutes. Five fucking minutes, and she's looking at me like I'm a stranger. Like I've disappointed her, and I have no idea how.

"Ash, talk to me," I beg.

She laughs, but there isn't any humor in it. "You don't know who Brooke slept with while you were together?"

"No, I don't know," I reiterate.

She searches my eyes, desperate for the truth. When she finds it, the hardness in her gaze softens, and a tear slips down her cheek. Like she isn't angry anymore. She's heartbroken. For me.

"Ash--"

"You really don't know?" she whispers.

"She never told me, and I never cared to ask. I was too pissed. I'd just lost my dad--"

"It was Logan." She sniffs and wipes at her tear-stained cheeks. "He was sleeping with Brooke. He said it's the only reason you're with me. Why you wanted me. Because you wanted to get back at him for what he did to you."

Shit.

I'd always wondered who had the balls to stab me in the back. Never would've expected it to be my best friend. Not that it matters anymore. Or at least, it wouldn't have if Logan hadn't wielded his betrayal like a knife so he could hurt Ash with it.

My blood boils as I lean down and press my forehead to hers again, attempting to reel in my rage, but it's a losing battle. "Listen to me, Ash. And I mean, really listen. I didn't know. I didn't know Logan stabbed me in the back. And I sure as shit didn't start dating you to get back at him. I started dating you because I felt a connection with you. Something I've never felt with anyone else in my entire life. And I've kept dating you because I care about you. Because I love you. Because you light up my whole world, Sunshine. Do you understand?"

More tears slide down her cheeks, but she nods.

"You promise? You promise you know I'm not using you?"

She nods again and chokes out, "I-I believe you."

"Okay." I breathe in deep, but the oxygen does shit to give me clarity. Right now, all I see is red. Pressing a rough kiss to Ash's lips, I say, "Now, I'm gonna go inside. And I'm gonna have a chat with Logan. But I need you to know it has nothing to do with Brooke. Do you understand me?"

"Don't go in there," she begs, reaching for me, but I stay out of her grasp.

"I'll be back in a minute."

She wraps her arms around my waist and clings to me with all her strength. "No. No, don't go."

"He isn't allowed to make you feel anything less than perfect, Ash. He isn't allowed to twist our past, and hurt you with it. I have to--"

"Colt--"

"Everything all right?" Theo asks, approaching us warily. But he isn't the only one who looks on edge. Everyone in the front yard is staring at us, their drinks forgotten as they watch the drama unfold right in front of them.

And it's all Logan's fault.

I pass Ash to Theo, and he takes her without hesitation as a sob slips out of her.

"Colt! Don't!"

"Keep her here," I order Theo.

"Colt!" Ash's voice cracks, but I ignore her and take the stairs two at a time. Reaching the front porch, I step into the house and scan the main floor. It's so loud I can barely think straight, let alone register the music as it pulses through the house. My rage is thrumming through my veins and in my eardrums.

Where is he?

58
COLT

After the shitshow Logan put Ash through, I'm ready to rip his head off. But I need to find him first. There are so many people. So many students who are about to see shit go down. Shit that *should've* gone down a long time ago. But I don't care. I've never cared about saving face in front of strangers. The only person who matters to me was manipulated--*used*--by one of my best friends.

And it's all my fault.

He lied to me.

He said we were good.

Said he was okay with me dating Ash.

Instead, he used our friendship to get close to her again, so he could make her feel like shit. And I can't believe I fell for it. I'm sick of letting him off the hook--letting him maintain his golden boy persona--and I refuse to let it continue. Not for another second.

When I spot Logan in the crowd, my hands clench into fists.

He's talking with Depp, cackling as I hear the words *slut*

and *pathetic* slip out of his mouth. His gaze meets mine, and he arches his brow.

Shoving through the crowd, I grab the collar of his T-shirt and cock my arm back, hitting him square in the jaw without waiting a single fucking second. His head swings to the side, followed by a spray of blood from his mouth and a low, guttural curse.

I'm surprised I caught him off guard. He knew I was coming. Knew I'd demand retribution. He must not have expected me to be as pissed off as I am.

This isn't some hockey tussle like when we're on the ice. This is more. This is about Ash and how he hurt her. How he *wanted* to hurt her. How he convinced me to invite her to the party tonight under the guise of everything being good between us so he could cause her pain.

My hand pulls into another fist, another wave of disgust rolling through me. Logan tries to scramble away from me, guarding his face with his hands, but I don't let his shirt go as I throw a second punch. It lands along the bridge of his nose, easing the tightness in my chest, though the relief only lasts a second. I let him go, and Logan crumples to the ground.

With a curse, Depp jumps back, his hands in the air, unsure whether or not he should intervene. I turn to him and growl, "Did he call Ash a slut?"

"Dude, I don't want anything--"

When Logan realizes everyone is watching us, he stands up and wipes the blood from his mouth with the back of his hand, his expression twisted and angry. "Calling it like it is, Colt."

"Fuck you, Logan," I spit, my hands fisting at my sides as I fight the urge to deck him another time. "Fuck. You." I turn around, ready to storm away but stop myself and face him again. I can't help it. I need an answer. An explanation.

"Why?" I demand. "Why would you tell me we were good and go behind my back so you could hurt her?"

He glares back at me, his lips flat as he grinds his teeth. "You can't be mad I called you out, Colt."

I step closer, my anger pushing me forward. "I don't give a shit about Brooke, all right? Didn't even know what you did until you decided to throw it in Ash's face. My problem is that you think you can make her question whether or not I love her--whether or not she's my world--it's bullshit!"

"You crossed that line first--"

"Bullshit!" I repeat, my upper lip curling as I tower over him. "You lost her because you refused to treat her the way she deserves. That's on you. Not me. And now that she's mine, there is nothing that will take her away from me. *Nothing*. Do you understand me? And if you don't keep your bruised ego out of our relationship, I'll ruin your pretty little face beyond repair. We clear?"

"We're through." He spits the blood which had collected in his mouth in my face, and I wipe it off with my hand, too pissed to hit him again when I know he's goading me.

He isn't even worth the bruised knuckles on my right hand.

"Fine by me," I return and head out the door without a backward glance.

Everyone's eyes are on me as I storm through the crowd, but the only ones who matter are shining back at me, full of hurt at the door.

"I told you to keep her outside," I seethe at Theo standing beside her.

"Heard everyone go quiet in here. Had to see what was going on." His attention shifts to someone behind me--probably Logan--and back to me. "You all right?"

"We're gonna get outta here." I grab Ash's arm, ready to

get the hell out of this place. She follows without a word, her sniffling the only clue as to how much she's hurting.

And those tears? They make me want to hit Logan all over again.

"What happened?" Mia demands as she races down the stairs from the second floor as the rest of the crowd stays quiet, anxious to see what happens next.

"I'm sure Theo will catch you up," I tell her, ignoring everyone else around us. "I'm taking Ash home. Can you drive Blake?"

Theo answers for her. "We'll take care of her."

"Good."

I guide Ash to my truck, praying she gives me the chance to make this okay.

Because I need us to be okay.

I need it more than anything.

59
ASHLYN

"I need you to tell me we're okay," Colt growls from behind the steering wheel.

Everything happened so fast. I'm still reeling. I can't believe Logan said those things to me. I can't believe Colt punched him for it. I can't believe I'm sitting in the passenger seat of his truck, and we're flying down the road while the angry clouds in the sky look ready to burst.

"Talk to me," he begs. I glance at his hands and find them throttling the steering wheel as little rain droplets start hitting the windshield.

Split-splat.

Split-splat.

He flicks on the wipers, and looks at me again, his expression painted with fear, but I'm too overwhelmed to register it.

It's weird. Being here again. On this same road. So much has changed in such a short period of time. But it's funny. How easily a little thing like rain against a windshield can imprint on your memory, reminding me of the last time we were here.

Me in the passenger seat of his truck. The rain pouring down. The need in the pit of my stomach. The frustration oozing from the driver's side.

I remember all of it.

And it's eerily similar to tonight.

"Ash," Colt prods, glancing my way before turning his attention back to the road.

"Pull over," I whisper. My voice is barely loud enough to be heard over the pitter-patter of rain, but somehow he hears me.

"Ash--"

"Pull over, Colt."

The tires crunch on the gravel on the side of the road as Colt follows my request and shoves his truck into park, his head hanging in defeat. As the heavy, dark clouds release their moisture, the rain cuts through the headlights shining in front of us, causing slashes along the road. It's mesmerizing. Hypnotic. Cathartic, almost. I soak it up as the adrenaline from tonight seeps out of me.

I'm not sure how long we sit like this. In silence. The only sound coming from the rain, and the occasional lightning strike in the distance. But I need it. A moment to register what just transpired. An opportunity to acknowledge that Colt and Logan's relationship will never be the same. A minute to grasp the fact that Colt put everything on the line. For me.

"Don't hate me, Ash," he whispers.

The pain in his voice slices through my memory of what happened tonight, and I tear my gaze from the storm outside. He looks so distraught. So torn up. His right hand is bruised and bloody, digging into his thigh. Like he wants to reach for me, but is holding himself back.

Why is he holding himself back?

I keep my touch gentle as I grab his hand and examine his

busted knuckles in the glow of the dashboard, fighting the numbness from spreading any further. "You shouldn't have hit him. He wasn't worth it."

"He shouldn't have made you question my feelings for you."

I bring his knuckles to my lips, careful not to touch the open sores, only the bruised portion. "He didn't make me question your feelings for me."

Pained, Colt looks over at me. "Don't lie."

"I'm not lying." I kiss his hand again. "I know you love me, Colt Thorne."

His expression pinches with anguish, but he doesn't say a word.

"If you didn't, you would've never picked me up in the rain before walking home in it," I whisper. "You would've never stolen my orange juice or refused to take back your T-shirt when I tried to give it to you. You would've never taught me how to ice skate or taken me to Sunday brunch or to visit my parents. You've made me feel more loved in the short time we've been together than Logan was able to do in years. Hell, even more than my parents were able to do in my entire life." The tears flow freely from my eyes as I lick my lips and peek up at him. "Some stupid words said by a stupid boy aren't going to erase those moments, Colt. No one--not Logan or anyone else--can touch what we have. Only you and me. And I really hope you know how much I love you too--"

He kisses me hard and rough, and with so much passion, it only makes the tears fall faster. Because I can feel it. His love. In a simple kiss. A simple brush of his hand against my skin. I can feel it so deeply. Like it envelops me in warmth. He's a fool to think I'd give that up. For anything, let alone my asshole ex.

After a few more seconds, Colt pulls away and presses his

forehead to mine. "Thank you. For seeing what I wanted you to see. What I needed you to see. Past the bullshit. The lies."

"I see you," I clarify with a watery smile. "I love you, Colt. And I know you might think you're the villain, but I don't think you could be more wrong."

"Love you, too, Ash. More than anything."

He grabs my hips and drags me across the car, lifting me up until my knees are straddling his waist. With flashes of lightning and claps of thunder, we make love in his truck. In the middle of a rainstorm. And I love it too.

More than anything.

EPILOGUE

ASHLYN

"Mom. Dad," I greet them, refusing to let any awkwardness settle over us as I stand up and motion to Colt's family. "This is Becca Thorne, Colt's mom, and his little sister, Blakely. Blake and Becca, this is Wade and Angelica, my parents."

"Nice to meet you," my parents reply, their attention shifting from the red and black face paint on Becca and Blakely's faces to the ice rink where the LAU Hawks are currently playing.

I still can't believe Colt convinced them to fly down for his first game and the last of the season.

After the blow up with Logan, and my little make-up session with Colt in his truck, Colt drove me home and spent the night at my house. The next morning, he received a text from Theo, informing us that Logan had been kicked out of the Taylor house. By the time Monday rolled around, Logan had moved out, and wasn't welcome unless he got his head out of his ass. Theo's words, not mine.

I'm not going to lie, it took a few weeks before I finally felt comfortable coming back to the Taylor House. It's still a little bit of a whorehouse on the weekends, which is when Colt and I hang out at my place, but during the week, it's almost homey. And it's been nice. To see Colt's real friends rally around him instead of letting Logan get away with his awful behavior any longer.

Shorty moved out too. In fact, he lives with Logan and Graves. I can only imagine the shitstorm taking place in their house, but thankfully, I don't have to care. Because it isn't any of my business anymore.

Halle-freaking-lujah.

As the opposing team rushes to our goal, the audience starts chanting, "De-fense! De-fense!" My mom slides off her tie-dyed shawl and folds it over her arm as she and my dad wiggle past the rest of us to get to their seats.

We're halfway through the first period, and the score is still zero to zero, when Depp steals the puck--which Colt informed me is also called a biscuit--from the opposing team and passes it across the ice toward Logan, who's the right wing. Logan shoots the puck toward the net, but the goalie blocks it with his leg when Colt swoops in like a freaking ninja and catches the rebound.

"Go, Colt! You got this!" I scream, my veins flooding with adrenaline.

Colt takes the puck around the net, chips it off the board, around the defenseman, and toward Theo, who's ready and waiting at the center of the rink. The opposing defenseman scrambles to get into position, putting himself between Theo and their goalie, but he doesn't make it in time as Theo slaps the puck into the top right corner of their net.

Cupping her mouth, Blakely screams Theo's name, and my parents join in as the red light behind the goal lights up, confirming a point for our team.

And I love it. The energy. The cold air. The cowbells

clanging in the arena. The posters with Colt's number painted in LAU's school colors dotting the crowd.

I love it all.

And when the game ends two periods later, and we meet Colt outside after his little press conference with a few journalists, I love his smile. The one reserved for me. Along with the panty-melting kiss he gifts me with before remembering our families are here to witness it.

With his arm still firmly around my waist, he turns to the rest of the family. "Hey, guys. Sorry about the wait."

"Don't be," Becca replies. "How'd the interviews go?"

"Good. Surprised everyone's making such a big deal about me being back on the ice."

"Surprised?" Blake quips. "Really? They've been knocking down your door for years, and after a game like today? They've gotta be chomping at the bit to welcome the Prodigal Son back to the ice."

I pinch his side, and he squirms away a few inches and looks down at me. "Hey. What was that for?"

"Nothing. You're cute when you blush."

He rolls his eyes but pulls me tighter against him, probably still reeling from the whirlwind his hockey career has already become.

"Good game, Colt," my dad interjects, offering his hand to Colt.

Colt shakes it with his hand not pinning me to his side, unable to remove his boyish grin even if he wanted to. "Thanks. And thanks for coming. It means a lot."

"Wouldn't have missed it," my mom returns. "Are all the games usually this high-scoring? Nine points. It's a lot, isn't it?"

"Nah," Blakely chimes in, her hands in the pockets of her jacket. "I mean, yeah, I guess it's pretty high for a normal hockey team, but with Colt playing with Theo again? LAU's gonna be unstoppable."

Still shy, Colt squeezes the back of his neck and looks down at me again. "Only if I have my Sunshine in the arena."

"And your mom and sister," I add.

"And your dad who's watching from heaven," Becca adds. "He'd be proud of you, Colt."

Colt's gaze flicks up toward the dark sky as he pulls his mom into a hug and my parents flank my sides, wrapping me in one of their own.

"Love you, Ashlyn," my dad murmurs.

"Love you too."

"Colt's a good egg," my mom adds. "We're really happy for you."

With a smile, I peek through their bodies huddled around me and meet Colt's gaze with my own. "I'm really happy too."

And I really, truly am.

The End

Curious about Blakely and Theo?
Read their story now in
Don't Let Me Go

Chapter One
Blakely

"COLT'S GONNA KILL ME," I MUTTER AS I TUG AT THE HEM OF Mia's tight, black dress. It barely reaches my ass, but she insisted I wear the damn thing before curling my hair and doing my makeup. Pretty sure I'm her own personal Barbie. Not that I'm complaining. Growing up with three older brothers didn't exactly encourage femininity. I was just...one of the guys.

Until I moved in with my new roommates..

Ashlyn grabs my hand, stalling my fidgeting. "Stop. You look cute."

She's dating my brother, Colt. She's also the mastermind behind my new living arrangement. When she offered to let me move in with her, Mia, and Kate, I felt like I'd won the lottery. She's also one of the reasons I'm standing in front of this house currently thumping with music. Colt lives here with his best friend, Theo.

Apparently, the girls aren't only fanning my femininity, they're also showing me the ropes of college life, including but not limited to parties with hot guys.

I smooth out the front of the dress again, another wave of indecision pulsing through me. "I look like––"

"A gorgeous girl?" Mia offers.

I puff out my cheeks, and let out a sigh. Maybe I should've stayed home with Kate. She's the third roommate. She's also the anti-partier of the group. Part of me doesn't blame her. The other part? I look up at the massive house that reminds me of the movie, *Home Alone*, complete with red brick, rows of windows, and music thumping through the open front door.

Well, I guess I can see the appeal.

"Besides. Colt's not the one you have to worry about," Mia adds, stealing my attention from the daunting house in front of me. "Theo's gonna shit his pants."

Theo.

Also known as Theodore Taylor.

He might be my brother's best friend, but he's my arch-nemesis.

Kind of.

His name alone causes a lump to lodge in my throat, but I choke it back.

"Greaaaat." I drag out the word while eyeing the front of the Taylor House like it's straight out of a horror movie.

"Seriously. You look awesome," Ash tells me. "Why are you freaking out?"

"Because this"--I wave my hand at the house literally thumping with rap music--"is not where a girl like me usually hangs out. Especially when looking like this." I wave my hand around again, this time showcasing the dress that feels like it's practically painted on me. "Or this." I pick up a wave of red hair and flick it over my shoulder. "Or this." I motion to the smokey eye shadow Mia painted on my face before we left our townhouse.

To say I'm a tomboy would be an understatement. But I think it's par for the course when you're raised with three older brothers and have a penchant for sports.

"You're in a new place now," Mia reminds me. "You get to start over. Be who you want to be. Look how you want to look. Attract who you want to…"--she winks--"*attract*."

I glare back at her. "I don't want to attract anyone. I just want to fit in and have fun without getting yelled at by a certain--"

"What the hell are you wearing?" Theo barks, rushing toward us on the front lawn from his porch with a beer in one hand before grabbing my arm with his other one. Not roughly, but with a possessiveness that makes my breath hitch.

It's annoying.

"She's wearing *my* dress," Mia interrupts, yanking me from the opposite side like I'm in some twisted game of tug-o-war, though I appreciate her protectiveness. I'll take anything to distract me from drowning in my feelings for a guy who will never feel the same.

"Doesn't she look hot?" she adds, scanning me up and down.

Theo's nostrils flare. He lets go, clenches his hand at his side, and glares at me. "You really think Colt's gonna let you inside looking like this?"

"Pretty sure it's my decision," I remind him. "And even if it wasn't, you would *still* have no say in the matter. I'm not the little girl you can boss around anymore, Teddy Bear."

I say the nickname through clenched teeth, well aware of just how many buttons I'm pushing right now. But I refuse to back down. Not with anyone, let alone Theodore Taylor, asshole extraordinaire.

His jaw ticks as he towers over me, two seconds from having an aneurysm.

Good.

"I thought we discussed you calling me that," he growls.

With a syrupy sweet smile, I answer, "Must've slipped my mind."

"O. M. G," a gorgeous brunette interrupts as she stumbles into Theo. I flinch beside him. One of her heels is caught in the grass, and she's laughing like a hyena, clutching at his bicep like he's her own personal savior.

My hackles rise, and it takes everything inside of me to keep from sneering at her.

"Oh. Hi, Theo," she purrs when she recognizes him. "Good to see you again." Her hand brushes against his exposed forearm, a coy smile curling at the edge of her dark red lips.

My cheeks feel like they're on fire as I mutter under my breath, "Of course, she knows him."

Without another word, I march into the Taylor House with my head held high, trying to ignore the frustration boiling in my veins. But I can't help it. Theodore Taylor seems to have that effect on me.

He *always* has.

I'm too pissed off to appreciate the energy pulsing through the main floor of the Taylor House as I slip inside and dart straight toward the kitchen where I assume the booze is located.

After all, attending my first college party should have at least a few perks, right? One of which is free alcohol. Since I'm only nineteen and can't purchase the stuff myself, I plan on taking full advantage. Hell, I'm gonna need it after my little run-in with Theo.

And why does he care what I'm wearing anyway?

I twist the cap off the clear liquor bottle, slam it against the surface, and reach for the stack of red Solo cups in the center of the table. After grabbing the top one from the stack and inspecting it for cleanliness, I scoop some ice into it from a large, plastic bowl, then add a generous splash of liquor followed by some orange Crush soda.

Which I regret instantly.

Orange Crush will always remind me of him.

Theo.

Teddy.

The boy next door who happened to be my hero.

Once upon a time, anyway.

With a frown, I shove the memory of warm summers and drama-free childhoods away and shoot the entire drink back, keeping my throat open so it slides down without protest before almost choking on an ice cube.

"Whoa there," Mia interrupts. She sidles up next to me and pats my back. The girl looks like a badass. Someone who's a little on the intimidating side but has a heart of gold. She has tattoos on her left arm, piercings lining the shell of her ear, and a past rough enough to make even the most numb, heartless bastard weep. Not that she's opened up to me about it, but I've picked up a piece or two. Something about her father being a drug addict who was murdered a few years ago, though I haven't asked for details. Not yet, anyway.

She's also insanely good at reading people, and I hate knowing it's exactly what she's doing to me at this very moment.

With a quick side-eye toward her, I grumble, "Don't judge."

"No judgment," she clarifies as a few hockey players join us in the kitchen and start reaching around our bodies to make their own drinks. Keeping her voice low, she adds, "Wanna talk about it?"

"Nothing to talk about."

"Are you sure?" She watches as I splash some more vodka into my cup and top it off with Sprite, while glaring at the Crush soda as if it offended me.

I chug this drink down, too, clearing my throat to relieve the burn.

Okay, that one was a little stronger than the last.

Mia frowns. "Blake––"

"I'm fine," I rush out.

With a sigh, she touches my shoulder. The same shoulder left bare thanks to her dress I'm wearing. The dress that somehow caught a certain someone's attention as soon as we walked up to the infamous Taylor House belonging to the devil himself.

I shrug out of her grasp and pour another drink, making a mental note to pace myself after this. Heaven forbid I get shitfaced in my brother's best friend's house.

Well, technically, I guess it's Colt's house, too, since he lives here. But he doesn't have quite the same stick up his ass a certain someone else seems to have, so I'm not sure if he counts.

So. Fucking. Annoying.

Once the players have their drinks, they disperse, giving us another ounce of privacy.

"Seriously, Blake. You sure you're okay? Do you want me to get you some water or something?"

"Look around, Mia. It's a party. A *college* party. And what does one normally do at college parties?" I tip my cup in her direction, then lift it to my lips. "Drink, of course."

"Drinking at a party is fine as long as it's to have fun and not to erase a certain someone from your mind."

My lips purse, and I take another small-*ish* sip. So sue me. "Who said I'm trying to erase a certain someone from my mind?" I lift my hand and stop her from answering. "You know what? Don't answer that. Because it doesn't even matter. I'm not going to play the game anymore," I decide, more to myself than anyone else. "It's like you said. This is the perfect time to turn over a new leaf. Be who I want to be, attract who I want to attract, and I'm not going to play his game again. I'm done."

"So, what are you going to do?" she asks.

"I'm going to…" I bite my lower lip as my gaze catches on a group of people cheering in the backyard. A pair of French doors are propped open in the kitchen, probably to let in the fresh air. They lead to the back of the property where a folding table is set up. It's littered with red Solo cups, and there's a concrete pad beneath it. My smile widens when a Ping-Pong ball bounces off the surface and into the grass. "I'm gonna play a game of Beer Pong. Wanna join?"

She frowns. "Blake, you sure that's a good idea?"

I'm not sure if it's the copious amount of alcohol streaming through my system or my newfound desire to move on with my life and make a new name for myself. But at this point, I don't really care. Besides, if there's anything I'm good at, it's being one of the guys. It's all Theo ever saw me as, anyway. And the guys outside? It looks like they're having fun. I'm in desperate need of something fun.

"Seems like an excellent idea to me," I announce, keeping my head held high. "You wanna come?"

With another sigh, she looks out the open doors leading to the backyard and turns to me. "I'm gonna go use the ladies' room first. I'll meet you out there." She points her finger at me. "Don't get bombed."

"Who said I'm gonna get bombed?"

Her gaze narrows as if she isn't convinced. "I'm serious. I really don't want to clean up puke tonight."

I laugh and head toward the exit as I call over my shoulder, "I'll be fine! See you in a few."

I walk over to the Beer Pong setup a few feet away, the cool wind kissing my cheeks and bringing an ounce of clarity with it. There's a small crowd––most of them are guys––and they're laughing as a Ping-Pong ball plops into a cup. The person closest to the cup groans before downing the warm beer inside. Once he's finished, he raises his hands in surrender, slightly stumbling to the left. "All right, man." He laughs and tosses the cup onto the grass. "You win."

"Any more takers?" his opponent calls, searching the crowd huddled around the Ping-Pong table. Apparently, I'm not the only one who finds the game interesting.

Stepping forward, I announce, "I'll play."

All eyes turn to me.

Most of the guys are hockey players. There's something about the way athletes carry themselves. Confidence bordering on arrogance. An aura screaming they're on top of the world, even when they're drunk off their asses. They also like to stay together. Like a pack of wolves or something. It's rare to find one on their own out in the wild. And tonight isn't any different.

They each take their turns scanning me up and down,

probably wondering who the hell I am since they've never seen me before. Most of their mouths turn up into smirks as one of them---the previous winner---motions to the now-empty space across from him.

"Be my guest."

The guy's cute. Or at least I think he is. There's only one of him so far, so I don't think my beer goggles are skewing his features, but the night's still young. Dark, curly hair cropped short to his head. Dark skin. Dark eyes. *Kind* eyes. And his smile? Hello, butterflies. His straight, white teeth are freaking perfect and only add to his chiseled jaw and handsome features. He's balancing himself on a set of crutches. His boyish grin ish showcased as he laughs at something one of the other players is saying, though I don't hear what's said as I close the distance between us.

"Hi," I greet him, offering my hand. "I should probably introduce myself before I beat your ass."

He grins, looking like the perfect candidate to distract me from a certain someone I want to get off my mind. A pinch of guilt spreads in my chest as I check out the stranger, but I shove it away. I don't need to be loyal to Theo. I don't owe him anything except maybe a dead leg for all the shit he's put me through.

Besides, I'm here to turn over a new leaf. That means I should *not* be pining over someone who looks at me like I'm a little kid, thank you very much. And who better to distract me than the man in front of me?

The stranger chuckles and takes my offered hand. "Hey. I'm Burrows. Shawn," he clarifies. "But everyone calls me Burrows."

"Blakely," I return. "Most people call me Blake. Nice to meet you."

His eyes are curious as they slide down my body. Not in a

way that leaves me feeling skeevy or anything. Only…curious.

"You too," he replies. "You ready to play?"

"Yup." I grab the Ping-Pong ball from Burrows' grasp and toss it a few inches into the air. But as it comes back down, it misses my hand entirely and bounces off the ground, pulling a chuckle from the guy beside me.

"Are you usually this uncoordinated or have you already had a few drinks tonight?" Burrows asks.

My lips pull into a thin line. "No comment."

His chuckle is warm and inviting as he grabs another Ping-Pong ball from the table, tosses it into the air--successfully--and catches it again. "Do you know the rules?"

"Yup." *Okay, I most definitely don't, but it can't be that hard, can it?* "I bounce the ball, and if it falls into a cup, you have to drink it, right?"

"Yup. That about sums it up." He motions to the table. "But we're gonna play on the same side of the table."

"Why?"

"'Cause I'm afraid you might fall over after a round or two. Gotta keep you within arm's length so I can catch you in case you pass out."

I laugh. "You're that confident you're gonna win?"

He turns to me again, the same boyish grin turning my insides into melted butter as his eyes crinkle in the corners. "Yeah, Blake. I'm *that* confident."

"Care to make it interesting?" I ask. I can't help it. Even when the ground is spinning, I'm a competitive person, and he just threw down the gauntlet.

Burrows leans closer, balancing on his good leg while towering over me. "Maybe. What're the stakes?"

"If I win--"

"Blake!" Colt calls from the open French doors. My neck snaps in his direction, and I paste on a smile. "Yes?"

"You good out here?"

My grin widens. "Yup!"

He points his finger at Burrows. "She's my little sister, man. Keep that in mind, all right?"

Burrows dips his chin. "Yeah, Colt. I got you."

With a slow nod, Colt turns back to me and adds, "Don't puke," before disappearing into the house.

A bout of silence rolls over us while Burrows realizes my not-so-well-hidden secret. His curious gaze makes me twitchy as he looks at me again, this time with a new wave of curiosity. I keep my head held high and quirk my brow, as if to say, *Is there a problem?*

I shouldn't be surprised. I've grown up in Colt's shadow for as long as I can remember. Between him and my two other brothers, Knox and Garrett, people have always looked at me this way. Like they're curious what the youngest Thorne can bring to the table or if her vagina makes her weaker and less significant.

Fun fact. It doesn't.

Being taken seriously or looked at like I'm my own person, however, has definitely been a challenge. But I don't see it changing anytime soon, especially not with the guy in front of me.

"So, you're Colt's little sister?" Burrows asks, continuing his examination of me with his head cocked to one side. He's probably searching for any resemblance between Colt and me, though I doubt he'll find it. I've got red hair, freckles over every inch of skin, and am basically a walking stick, while Colt has dark hair, olive-ish skin, and muscles. The only things we have in common are our potty mouths and obsession with sports.

That same sugary-sweet smile spreads across my face as I fake curtsy and say, "The one and only. Now where were we?

Oh, yes. I believe we were discussing the terms for our bet. When I win, you can buy me dinner."

"When?" he challenges, stepping closer to me.

I tilt my head up but don't back away from him. "Did I stutter?"

He snorts. "All right, I'll take the bait. And if I win?"

I shrug one shoulder. "What do you want?"

His mouth quirks up. "A date with you."

"So I...still get dinner?"

"Apparently."

My eyes light up. "Deal."

"Deal," he agrees, handing me another Ping-Pong ball. "First to five?"

"Five?" I ask. I realize how stupid I must sound right now, but I'm also drunk off my ass, thanks to the Crush and Vodka, so it's not exactly my fault.

"First to get five balls in the cup wins," he explains.

"Oh. Deal."

He nods. "Ladies first."

I blink slowly, attempting to concentrate and toss the small, white Ping-Pong ball onto the table. It bounces once but misses the cups by a long shot and lands on the ground, pulling a dark chuckle from the man beside me. Following suit, he grabs a second ball and bounces it onto the table. With a wet plop, it lands in a cup, and the crowd around us cheers.

"Drink up, Blake," he urges, his mouth tilted up in a triumphant smirk.

I laugh and drink the warm beer, my nose wrinkling as it spreads across my tongue.

Once I've gagged it down, I grab the still-wet ball from my cup and bounce it off the table toward my targets.

It misses. Again.

"This is gonna be a quick game," Burrows jokes, landing another ball into the row of cups across from us.

I groan and swallow the stale beer back. "How are you so good at this?"

"'Cause I start the game sober. Leaves me a little more wiggle room than my opponents," he informs me and waves his hand toward the table. "Your turn."

My vision is blurry at best, and my tongue feels swollen in my mouth as I take the ball from Burrows' fingers and attempt to throw it at the table. But I swear the ground is moving beneath my feet. As the Ping-Pong ball slips from my fingers, I lose my balance and stumble into Burrows' rock hard chest.

Oops.

His hand slides around my waist, keeping me from face-planting on the concrete when a low voice barks, "Blake!"

I flinch and turn toward the familiar voice, but the backyard keeps spinning.

Aaaand it's official. I've had too much to drink.

A pair of hands wrench me away from Burrows, and before I can even register what's happening, I'm plastered against a solid chest. It's warmer than Burrows'. More familiar, though I'd never admit it out loud. It takes everything inside of me to keep from snuggling against it, but I keep my spine straight and my muscles from melting into Theo's grasp.

"What the hell are you doing, man?" he growls, the sound vibrating from his chest and against my palms firmly planted against his pecs.

"Calm down," Burrows replies. "We're just playing a game--"

"This is Colt's little sister!"

"Yeah. I know." Burrows' tone is calm and level-headed,

unlike the man who's holding me hostage. "He saw us playing and was fine with it."

"Did he know you were gonna get her wasted too?"

"I wasn't——"

Smacking Theo's chest, I wiggle out of his arms and nearly fall on my ass. His grip tightens around my bicep, keeping me upright, though I refuse to thank him for it.

"He wasn't doing anything, you big neanderthal," I argue. "We were just playing——"

"Yeah, well, you're done."

"Who do you think you are?" I demand. Or at least, it's what I'm trying to demand. My tongue isn't exactly working at top speed. Nope. Instead, my speech is slurred, and I'm pretty sure I sound like an idiot. But it isn't my fault. It's Theo's. He shouldn't have pissed me off as soon as I walked up to his house. He also shouldn't be smelling this good. What is that? Cologne? Or is it his own natural scent? If it is, it isn't fair. That's for sure.

"Look. I've already had enough shit go down for one night," Theo growls, glaring down at me before he shakes his head. "I don't need to deal with you too."

"Then don't," I argue. "I'm fine."

Without bothering to tear his gaze from mine, Theo yells, "Everyone! Out!"

I flinch at the sharpness in his tone. He isn't usually an angry guy. Most of the time, he's laid back and——dare I say it——almost jovial. Like Santa Claus. Except sexier and without the massive belly.

Well. Unless I'm around. Then, he's the Grinch with a side of Jack the Ripper. And with the way he's looking at me right now? I might as well dig my own grave next to the tree in the backyard, 'cause I'm not walking out of here tonight.

"Now!" Theo snaps.

Welp. Apparently, the party's over.

Chapter Two
Blakely

A COLLECTIVE GROAN ROLLS THROUGH THE BACKYARD AS people start heading inside and toward the front door, repeating Theo's order to those who hadn't heard him yet. I'm surprised no one protests though.

Nope. Just me.

Smacking at Theo's chest--again--I spit, "Who said you get to end the party? They were having fun. *I* was having fun!"

"Yeah, I can see," he grumbles. "Can you walk or do I need to carry you?"

I blink slowly as I register his question. My mind feels like it's stuck in quicksand, making every thought, every decision feel like it's happening in slow motion. Like I can't catch up. Like I'm always a beat or two behind.

Impatient, Theo bends down and grabs the back of my thighs before hauling me over his shoulder like I'm a sack of potatoes. It isn't sweet or romantic. It's tainted with annoyance. Obligation. Like he'd rather be anywhere else than holding me against him. And it pisses me off.

"You should let me down," I slur, hating how good he smells. Seriously. It's delicious. Like aftershave and sweat. But not gross sweat. Good sweat. I didn't know there was good sweat until this moment. But it's official. There's such a thing as good sweat. Clean sweat. And I want to wrap myself up in it. Not to mention the view. Hello, tushy, tush. I kind of want to pinch it, bite it, and smack it all at once. Maybe if I do he'll even put me down.

Now that's what I call a win-win.

"Well this is just great," a familiar feminine voice

announces as Theo steps inside the Taylor House. "I swear I only left her for five minutes. But then Colt punched Logan and--"

"I get it," Theo replies as I turn my head toward the voice and find a very upside down roommate staring back at me.

"Mia! My Mama Mia!" I snort. "Get it? Mama Mia? That movie's great--"

"She's totally gonna puke in Ash's car," Mia mutters. She turns on her heel toward the front door. "Come on--"

"I need to pee," I announce.

Pinching the bridge of her nose, the keys dangling from her other hand, Mia sighs while Theo takes a sharp turn toward the bathroom on the main floor.

My legs feel like overcooked noodles as he sets me down on the gray tile. I grab his arm to keep from falling over, my vertigo practically assaulting me. Seriously. It's official. This is the most drunk I've ever been, and I'm gonna be miserable tomorrow.

Nice move, Blake.

"Can you pee on your own?" Theo grumbles. I swear, the bastard isn't even trying to hide his annoyance.

Rude.

Although, it is an excellent question.

Can I pee on my own right now?

I gulp, my stomach knotting as the alcohol settles inside of me, then nod at him.

Unconvinced, he stays close to me and cocks his head to one side. "You sure?"

"Yup," I lie, giving him a thumbs up with my hand that isn't digging into his arm to keep me upright.

Gaze narrowing, he grabs my wrist, removes my death grip on his bicep, but makes sure I have my balance somewhat steady before he lets me go and steps away from me. "I'll be outside."

The door closes behind him with a quiet click.

I don't know how long I'm in the bathroom, but I do know it's spinning. Round and round, like I'm on a carousel, when I'm most definitely sitting on the toilet with my thong around my ankles and my dress pooled around my waist.

Classy, I know.

I shouldn't have had the last drink.

Damn you, Burrows. You're too good at Beer Pong.

"Bad idea, Blake," I scold myself, resting my head in my hands with my elbows perched on my knees as I close my eyes.

A soft knock echoes from the door, and my head lolls to the side.

"Who is it?" I say in a sing-song voice.

"Blake," a familiar low voice barks.

"Who is it?" I repeat a little louder this time while dropping the song.

"Unlock the door, Blake. Now."

I locked the door?

Not gonna lie, I don't even remember closing it.

Too. Much. Alcohol.

With a frown, I push myself onto my feet and pull up my underwear before stumbling to the sink. The water feels good against my hands as I wash them. The towel feels gross though. Like it hasn't been washed recently.

Or maybe it's because there were so many people at the party.

I guess it makes sense.

The loud, jarring knock vibrates against the door again, and I jump in surprise.

"Now, Blake," the low voice warns.

So bossy.

I roll my eyes and unlock the door. The handle twists on

its own before the door is shoved open to reveal a very pissed off Theo.

"What's your problem?" I slur.

"Mia and I have been trying to get you to open this door for five minutes."

My brows furrow. "What?"

"We thought you'd passed out––"

"Blake!" Mia calls, squeezing past Teddy's massive body through the doorframe and pulls me into a hug.

"I'm sorry. Why are you hugging me?" I ask against her blonde hair. She smells good too. Like shampoo. I grin and take a giant whiff. "Girl. Why do you smell so good? You should let me borrow your shampoo next time along with this kickass dress."

With a laugh, she pulls away from me. "Deal. But for now, let's get you home, okay?"

"Cool." I sway on my feet, and my stomach churns. "First, I gotta puke."

The tile is cold against my knees as I collapse in front of the toilet and vomit like there's no tomorrow. My chest heaves. My stomach twists. My throat burns. And my eyes water.

It freaking sucks.

I hate throwing up. The lack of control. The bitter, acidic taste. It's seriously the worst.

Hands are in my hair, holding it away from my face as I hurl my guts out until there's nothing left in my stomach but the realization I just vomited in front of an audience.

Fan-freaking-tastic.

I want to go home.

I want to go to sleep.

I want to erase this entire night.

Especially those last couple drinks.

Man, I'm so embarrassed.

How can this be happening right now?

I rest my head against the hand cupping my temple while the other one keeps a firm grasp on my messy hair. It feels nice. The hand. It's warm. Calloused. Gentle.

"You good?" a low voice murmurs.

Theo.

Yup. Theo just saw me puke.

And act like an idiot at my first college party.

No, not an idiot.

A child.

He saw me act like a child.

The same thing I've been trying to change for years.

Dammit!

I rub beneath my nose with the back of my hand as Theo helps me to my feet in silence. The room is still spinning but not quite as badly as before, so at least there's that.

He doesn't let me go as he leads me to the sink to clean up. And boy, do I need it. When I catch a glimpse of myself in the mirror, a lump clogs my throat.

My dark, smokey makeup is smudged, making me look like a racoon instead of the sexy goddess I'd been channeling. Not to mention my naturally curly, red hair. It's sticking up in every direction like I just rolled out of bed. I don't look sexy anymore. I don't look put together.

I look like a freaking train wreck.

Like Merida from Brave. Except without the Disney Princess filter. Just pale, and pasty, and…a mess.

I want to go home.

My attention shifts from my own reflection to Theo's as embarrassment floods my cheeks, turning them red. Then again, maybe it's from the vomiting. He's standing behind me, his brows pulled low and angry. And it hurts. To see him mad at me. To see him disappointed.

"I don't want a lecture," I whisper. My voice echoes in the

otherwise silent bathroom, and the quiet that follows is almost eerie. Like he doesn't know what to say or how to express how much of a screw-up I am.

Fun fact, Theo. I already know.

With a soft curse under his breath, he leans down and grabs something from beneath the sink.

Mouthwash.

I take the bottle from his grasp and swish it around, the minty flavor a welcome change from the taste of acid and alcohol.

After a solid thirty seconds of swishing, I spit it in the sink and twist the cap back onto the bottle, setting it onto the counter while Theo simply…watches me.

Avoiding his gaze, I tuck my hair behind my ear, and murmur, "I should probably get home."

"I told Mia to leave."

I crane my neck toward him and look over my shoulder, meeting his gaze with my own as he stands behind me. "What?"

"She shouldn't have to clean up your puke."

Ouch.

His sharp words shouldn't hurt, but they do. I'm not surprised. Everything hurts when it comes to Theo. My heart. My pride. My confidence.

Why would tonight be any different?

But I refuse to let him see it. How much it hurts to be around him.

I turn and face him fully, crossing my arms over my chest. "She won't need to clean up my puke. I already got everything out——"

He scoffs. "For now. Who's to say you won't throw up again? It's not her job——"

"So what? It's yours?" I challenge.

With another scoff, he takes off his beat up baseball hat

and scrubs his hand over his face like he doesn't know what to say before he mutters, "Apparently."

I step to the side, leaving some space between us. Some much needed space. "I'm not a little girl--"

"Then stop acting like one," he growls, closing the space between us, covering his wavy hair with his hat again. It shields the bathroom light from hitting his eyes, making them darker and more intense than usual. They're almost animalistic, lacking any humanity or softness at all. Only bitterness. And it's all directed at me.

I shake off the realization, and argue, "You shouldn't have embarrassed me when I was playing Beer Pong."

"You shouldn't have been playing in the first place."

"Why? Because I don't belong here?" The question slips out of me before I can stop it, laced with vulnerability and a sharp accusation I've been too scared to voice aloud until this moment. But now that it's out in the open, I want to know if I'm right. If it was a mistake to come here. If he'll always look at me like I'm a burden--like I'm a little kid--or if he'll ever see me as the adult I want him to see. I've been asking myself if it was a mistake to come to LAU since the moment he moved me in with Ash and the girls. And apparently, buzzed Blake wants to know too.

Theo pulls back, confused. "You don't belong where? At LAU?"

"Why stop there?" I demand, my frustration finally boiling over. "Not just LAU, but the Taylor House too. You don't want me here at all," I tell him. "Am I right?"

"It's not my fault any of those guys would love to chew you up and spit you back out."

"Burrows is nice--"

"He's a hockey player, Blake. None of us are nice. Not to girls like you."

"What's that supposed to mean?" I demand, reaching onto my tiptoes to close a bit more of the distance between us.

"It means you're too innocent to be here."

"Who says I'm innocent?"

His gaze slides down my body, and for the first time ever, there's a glint of heat in it. Not much. Hell, it's barely a spark. But it's still there. Still tempting me. Still testing me. My resolve. My self-preservation. My restraint.

I lift my chin and meet his gaze with my own. "Maybe I'm not so innocent anymore." I let out a shuddered breath, our lips so close I can practically taste him. "You haven't seen me for over a year, Teddy. You don't know where I've been. Who I've kissed. Who I've fucked."

His upper lip curls. "If Colt heard you say that--"

"Colt isn't here," I remind him with a dry laugh. "It's just me and you. And I'm tired. Tired of this…responsibility you've decided to put on yourself. To be my surrogate brother when all I ever wanted was a friend. You've decided it's your responsibility to boss me around. To make sure no one touches me when guess what, Teddy? No one asked you to take on those responsibilities. And here's the real doozy, my friend. I *want* to be touched. I *want* to be kissed, to be fucked--"

He slams his mouth against mine, and I gasp as he shoves his tongue between my lips. It isn't soft or sweet. It isn't innocent. It's freaking dirty. And selfish. Like I'm being used. Like he's proving exactly what it's like to wind up with a hockey player instead of some sweet and caring gentleman that he thinks I want.

But I like it.

The way he takes what he wants without giving a shit about me or how I feel. It's like he's trying to prove a point, though he's far from successful. Because I like this. I don't want to be treated like a child, like a breakable doll.

Fucking break me, Theo, I want to beg. But I don't. I just let him kiss me. Let him take what he wants. Let him try to prove this isn't what I crave, when it's the opposite.

I've craved him for years.

And now…here he is.

Kissing me.

Read their story now in
Don't Let Me Go

ALSO BY KELSIE RAE

Kelsie Rae tries to keep her books formatted with an updated list of her releases, but every once in a while she falls behind.

If you'd like to check out a complete list of her up-to-date published books, visit her website at www.authorkelsierae.com/books

Or you can join her newsletter to hear about her latest releases, get exclusive content, and participate in fun giveaways.

Interested in reading more by Kelsie Rae?

Don't Let Me Series

(Steamy Contemporary Romance Standalone Series)

Don't Let Me Fall

Don't Let Me Go - Blakely and Theo's Story

Don't Let Me Break - Kate and Macklin's Story

Don't Let Me Down - Mia and Henry's Story

Wrecked Roommates Series

(Steamy Contemporary Romance Standalone Series)

Model Behavior

Forbidden Lyrics

Messy Strokes

Risky Business

Broken Instrument

Signature Sweethearts Series

(Sweet Contemporary Romance Standalone Series)

Taking the Chance

Taking the Backseat - Download now for FREE

Taking the Job

Taking the Leap

Get Baked Sweethearts Series

(Sweet Contemporary Romance Standalone Series)

Off Limits

Stand Off

Hands Off

Hired Hottie (A *Steamy* Get Baked Sweethearts Spin-Off)

Swenson Sweethearts Series

(Sweet Contemporary Romance Standalone Series)

Finding You

Fooling You

Hating You

Cruising with You (A *Steamy* Swenson Sweethearts Novella)

Crush (A *Steamy* Swenson Sweethearts Spin-Off)

Advantage Play Series

(Steamy Romantic Suspense/Mafia Series)

Wild Card

Little Bird

Bitter Queen

Black Jack

Royal Flush - Download now for FREE

Stand Alones

Fifty-Fifty

Sign up for Kelsie's newsletter to receive exclusive content, including the first two chapters of every new book two weeks before its release date!

Dear Reader,

I want to thank you guys from the bottom of my heart for taking a chance on Don't Let Me Fall, and for giving me the opportunity to share this story with you. I couldn't do this without you!

I would also be very grateful if you could take the time to leave a review. It's amazing how such a little thing like a review can be such a huge help to an author!

Thank you so much!!!

-Kelsie

ABOUT THE AUTHOR

Kelsie is a sucker for a love story with all the feels. When she's not chasing words for her next book, you will probably find her reading or, more likely, hanging out with her husband and playing with her three kiddos who love to drive her crazy.

She adores photography, baking, her two pups, and her cat who thinks she's a dog. Now that she's actively pursuing her writing dreams, she's set her sights on someday finding the self-discipline to not binge-watch an entire series on Netflix in one sitting.

If you'd like to connect with Kelsie, follow her on Facebook, sign up for her newsletter, or join Kelsie Rae's Reader Group to stay up to date on new releases, exclusive content, giveaways, and her crazy publishing journey.

Printed in Great Britain
by Amazon